PRAISE FOR ALEX BLEDSOE

"Imagine a book somewhere between *American Gods* and Faulkner. Absolutely worth your time."—Patrick Rothfuss on *The Hum and the Shiver*

"Beautifully written, surprisingly moving and unexpected in the best of ways."—Seanan McGuire on *Wisp of a Thing*

"The bone-deep mystery, the setting, the music, and the harsh beauty of its characters; it gives a new meaning to well played."—Rachel Caine on *Wisp of a Thing*

"The real deal when it comes to North American fantasy."—Charles de Lint on *Long Black Curl*

"*The Sword-Edged Blonde* is a new twist on an old theme and a genuinely fun read." —David Drake

★ "Try suggesting this to fans of Jim Butcher's Dresden Files." —*Booklist,* starred review, on *Dark Jenny*

★ "Captures the allure and the sometimes-sinister beauty of the Appalachian backwoods, filled with myths, haunted by ghosts, and touched, always, by death."—*Library Journal,* starred review, on *Wisp of a Thing*

★ "This beautifully handled drama of Appalachian music and magic once again comes complete with fascinating characters, a persuasive setting and intriguing complications. Bledsoe's on a roll."—*Kirkus Reviews,* starred review, on *Wisp of a Thing*

DANDELION

DANDELION

ALEX BLEDSOE

Charlotte, NC

FALSTAFF
BOOKS
WWW.FALSTAFFBOOKS.COM

To the C.G. class of 2019:
Michael, Lynne, and Caitlin Thomas
Kelly and Laura McCullough
Martha Wells
Caroline M. Yoachim
Bonnie Jo Stufflebeam
Aliza Greenblatt
Tracy Townsend

Brenda Holscombe wondered how they could afford to keep the TLC-Mart so *cold.*

She only ran her air conditioner part of the time to take the edge off the worst of the Mississippi summer heat; even then, her electric bill was astronomical. But the TLC-Mart, even during the height of July and August, was always cold enough to keep meat fresh. Her mother liked to joke that when she shopped there, she didn't age.

At twenty, Brenda was already a divorcee and a single mother. All she'd been taught was eternal had turned out to be transitory, and the bedrock of everything—her belief in the Pentecostal Church—was on shaky ground. She kept that to herself, of course, as no one, certainly not her family or her church friends, could be trusted with it. To admit doubt was to admit apostasy.

You always find Tender Loving Care
And the best prices anywhere
at TLC-Mart!

The jingle preceded every in-store announcement, and Brenda paused to see if the Surprise Special Deal was something she could use. But she had no need for 12-gauge shotgun shells, at least not since Donnie moved out; he'd taken all his guns with him.

"Mama?" Brenda's five-year-old daughter Jurnee said from her seat in the shopping cart.

"What, honey?"

"I want a stuffy!" They'd just passed a six-foot-high cage enclosing an immense pile of stuffed animals.

"No, honey, we can't afford it this week."

Jurnee slapped the metal cart frame. "I want a stuffy!" she repeated more insistently.

"*No*, Jurnee. Now, behave."

Brenda didn't see her daughter's face scrunch up in a hateful scowl all wrong for such a small child. She didn't see the way her little fists clenched, not in petulance, but as if they were about to beat someone to a pulp.

But she sure heard it when her beautiful baby girl snarled, "Listen, you motherfucking bitch, I said I want a goddamn stuffy, so don't give me any bullshit about it!"

The words didn't register at first, they were so out of character. But when they did, Brenda froze, and coupons fell in a slow-motion shower from her hand. "Jurnee!" she gasped.

Other shoppers nearby had overheard and stopped to stare.

Jurnee leaned forward as much as the little red safety belt allowed. "Don't fuck with me, Mama! I'm the only one who loves you, and you're on thin ice with me!"

In the silence, the store's jingle rang out again.

You always find Tender Loving Care
And the best prices anywhere
at TLC-Mart!

BROTHER CULLIGAN, Brenda's minister, listened seriously as she described the changes in her daughter's behavior over the past week.

Not just the cursing and tantrums, but the adult-sounding snideness and the sexual innuendo far too mature for a girl about to start kindergarten. There was something wrong, something *evil* about it all, and Brenda was at her wit's end.

The pastor's office was small and stuffy, despite the box fan that tried to move the air around. By the time she finished, tears and sweat ran down Brenda's skin in equal rivulets.

Brother Culligan nodded. He was not yet thirty, shaved bald, and with a tattoo of a cross on the back of his head. He dropped out of high school at sixteen to follow the Lord's calling and had read no book but the Bible in the decade since. He distrusted psychiatry, traditional medicine, and public education. So, when Brenda said, "And Brother Culligan, I'm afraid she's possessed by the devil," Culligan could only nod in agreement.

He took Brenda's hands in his own. "Let's pray together," he said, and led her in a moment of prayer. It comforted her to the point that she settled into a sniffly liminal state between hysterics and rationality.

When they were done, he said, "I know just the person to help us."

JURNEE WORE a demure dress and well-worn *Frozen* tennis shoes, Anna on one foot and Elsa on the other. Red nylon ropes bound her to the chair; the man in charge insisted they were necessary, even for such a little girl. The other tables and chairs had been pushed back against the walls to leave the child alone in the open center of the room. She idly kicked her feet as much as her bonds allowed, to all appearances unconcerned with what was happening around her.

No air conditioners battled the Mississippi humidity in the little church's fellowship hall. Located on the outskirts of Corinth, the nondenominational charismatic congregation consisted of two dozen families, most with more children than they could possibly supervise, all dependent on the government services they publicly denounced as the work of the devil disguised as Socialism. Brother Culligan stood

3

patiently beside Brenda, murmuring prayers and stroking his Bible like a Bond villain petting a cat.

Brenda held her own Bible against her chest, her eyes red from crying, her skin gleaming with sweat. She caught Culligan's eye and asked softly, "Is he all right in there?"

"Like it says in Ephesians, he's putting on the armor of God so that he can take a stand against the devil's schemes."

Brenda nodded. If it came from the Bible, it had to be true. "And you swear he'll be able to help her?"

"Brenda, I've seen him at work. The Lord flows through him, and the devil runs from him. If there's a man alive who can help your daughter, it's him."

As if on cue, the door to the men's room opened, and out strode the Reverend Deacon Elder. He was a tall, handsome man in a snake-skin suit jacket that shimmered when he moved. Elderly women always gushed that he reminded them of Rock Hudson. Not quite forty, he towered over everyone and radiated the kind of confidence Brenda, at least, needed so desperately.

"Miz Holscomb," he said to her, his voice a low, comforting rumble. "I'm about ready to begin."

Brenda sniffled. "Please save my baby, Reverend."

"Now, Mrs. Holscomb," Elder said with a patient smile. "As I explained during our consultation earlier, you have to be strong for her sake. Don't let her see you be afraid."

At the word *consultation*, Brenda blushed. When Elder came by her house to speak to her privately earlier that day, she'd been unprepared for his sheer masculinity and had given in to his gentle entreaties that the Lord meant for them to be together, to give him strength for the great battle to come. And he'd been gentle and patient with her, totally unlike her brutal alleycat of an ex-husband. Afterward, he'd told her, "Now I feel prepared to battle the infestation that's taken hold of your daughter."

In addition to Elder, Brenda, and Culligan, three large, mullet-sporting, thick-bellied men in dress shirts were there to help if needed. Two of them watched skeptically, doubting the little girl could be any sort of danger; the third had witnessed a deliverance before and knew that three men might not be enough to control her if things went awry.

"May the Lord bless you for coming, Reverend," Culligan said as he shook Elder's hand. "We've prayed deliverance over her for two weeks now, waiting for you, to no avail. The demon just laughs at us."

"That's all right," Elder said. "The devil is a liar and a cheat, so your good hearts just couldn't stand up to him. He has to be met by someone who knows his wily ways." He turned to Jurnee, still blithely tied to the chair. "The devil and I are in this room tonight, and only one of us is walking out under his own power."

He knelt before Jurnee, closed his eyes, and leaned forward as if he might kiss her on the cheek. Instead, he inhaled deeply. Then his brow knit in revulsion.

"Oh, you monstrous presence," he whispered. "I assure you, good people, what lurks in this girl is unholy. The smell of brimstone is upon her."

"Oh, please, Jesus, save my little girl," Brenda said, tears filling her eyes.

Elder held his own battered personal Bible in both hands. "Jurnee Holscomb, I know what afflicts you. I understand there's something inside you that's turning you against your mama and God. Come forth, you vile contemption, and tell me your name."

Elder's voice rose during the speech so that by the end, he was bellowing in the girl's face.

Then, in a voice that sounded like an old woman, Jurnee said, "Jesus I know, and Paul I know; but who are you?"

Brenda screamed, making them all jump, and flung herself on the floor in despair. "Oh, Lord, my baby! My baby!" Two of the big men helped her into a folding chair. "She's got the devil in her!"

"That's not the devil," Elder said knowingly. "That's a demon, all right, but he's just a vassal. An errand boy. He isn't strong enough to indwell in a full-grown person; he has to take a little child. Isn't that right, demon? Now tell me your name."

"You think to send me from this child?" the girl said in the horrible voice and leaned forward; the ropes creaked as they stretched taut. "You, you fraud? You adulterer? You liar, cheat, *fornicator?*"

Elder wasn't fazed. "The Lord knows my sins and forgives me. Now tell me your name, you vomitous weasel."

"You want a name? I'll give you a name. Grove Prosser."

The name meant nothing to the others, but Elder turned bone white. It took a moment for his voice to return. "Grove Prosser defeated your kind more than once, you pit-spawn. Tell me *your* name."

"Hey, I can see my breath," one of the bulky men said, his voice high in growing fear. The room had grown noticeably colder.

"Tell me your name!" Elder roared and pressed his Bible against the top of the girl's head, bending her neck and making her grimace in pain.

"Deacon?" the girl said, but not in the demonic voice; this one was male, weak, and sounded like it came through great effort. "Deacon, listen to me, please."

Elder didn't reply, but he recognized the voice at once. "Stop this mockery," he ordered.

"I need your help," the voice said. "He's still there, still attached to the girl."

Over the eerie voice, Elder began shakily, "Our Father who art in heaven, hallowed be thy name." He put his Bible against the girl's cheek. The others joined in the familiar prayer.

Jurnee Holscomb, though, spoke louder in Grove Prosser's voice. "He's just the vanguard, Deacon! Dandelion is coming! Dandelion! *Dandelion!*" The last was a high-pitched girlish shriek, the girl's own natural voice. Then she fell silent, her expression neutral.

The others continued the prayer, and one of the men began to babble in tongues. But Elder's voice trailed off, and he stared at the girl, overwhelmed by what she'd just revealed.

In the midst of this cacophony, the girl's father and two sheriff's deputies burst in.

THE OLD OFFICER rattled his nightstick against the bars of the holding cell. "Hey, you. Snakeskin. Time to see the judge."

Deacon Elder rolled off the lower bunk and got to his feet. He'd been alone in the cell all night and was sticky with sweat and uncomfortable sleep. When they'd locked him up, one officer had said smugly, "Air conditioner's out, Jimmy Swaggart, and there ain't no fan. Tough titty, ain't it?"

Elder draped his jacket over his arm and waited for the cell door to open. "This way," the old policeman said. In a real city, he'd be long retired, but Corinth, Mississippi had to take what it could get.

They passed the other cells, all empty. The smell of accumulated body odor, urine, and mold overpowered the still air. Elder's loafers whispered across the faded tile in counterpoint to the officer's hard-soled clacks. A lone roach ran frantically along one baseboard, looking for an escape route.

"They treating you all right here?" Elder asked.

"Oh, they let me stick around and pretend to be useful. Not many places care about us old folks these days. Unless I want to be a greeter at the TLC-Mart." He shook his head. "This was a nice little town until that place came along."

"Ain't that the truth," Elder agreed.

"People around here can't get enough of it. You can watch 'em on Sunday after church, rushing straight out to feed the beast that's killin' 'em. Used to be you'd have lunches, family gatherings, and such. Now they just go to the TLC-Mart and walk around like zombies."

"Maybe they'll catch on one of these days."

"Naw. They'll just watch their town shrivel up like my old pecker and then wonder what the hell happened to it." He snorted. "Just like I do about my pecker."

When they reached a wooden door marked COURTROOM, Elder asked, "Who's the judge?"

"Only one judge in Corinth, son. Judge J. Jackson Stewart."

"What's he like?"

"He don't like nothing. Especially when the AC's out."

Elder straightened his shirt, pulled on his jacket, and followed the officer into the courtroom, which was as hot and humid as the Mississippi morning outside. Old-fashioned fans turned slowly on the ceiling, stirring the air but doing nothing to cool it. Flies and bees buzzed in and out through the tall open windows, finding every candy wrapper and spilled drop of Coke in the ill-kept room.

Judge Stewart, one of those part-time small-town justices who usually handled things like parking tickets and stray dogs, took a sip of ice water; the cubes had already shrunken to marble size. He looked down from the bench, *hmphed*, and said, "Tell the clerk your name."

"Deacon Elder."

The clerk, an older woman whose face was pinched in permanent disapproval, said, "Is that your name or your job title?"

Elder gave her his smoothest smile and said in a soft drawl, "It's my name, ma'am. My job title is Reverend. The Reverend Deacon Elder."

"Well, *Reverend*," Stewart said, "it appears you're charged with custodial interference and harming the welfare of a child. What do you have to say?"

"I take exception to that, your honor. I had no idea custody was an issue, and I would never intentionally harm a child."

"The father seems to think that's what you're doing."

Elder looked around. "Is he here?"

"He's over in family court, trying to get custody. You're my problem. Just what were you trying to do to that poor girl?"

"Free her from the devil's influence and the presence of an indwelling demon, your honor."

Stewart looked at him for a long moment before saying, "Son, are you drunk?"

"No, sir. I'm like a policeman; I never drink on the job."

"You want to tell your smart-ass jokes for six weeks in the county jail?" the judge asked impatiently. "'Cause that's what contempt of court'll get you in my courtroom."

"No, sir. I do not want to do that. And I meant no contempt. I was telling the honest truth. I was invited to pray deliverance over a young girl. Her minister did the inviting, and her mother was present as well. I had no idea that it was against the wishes of her father."

"And just how do you tell if there's a demon in somebody?"

"I've been blessed with the ability of discernment, your honor."

"That a fact," the judge said, clearly not buying it. "Tell me, anybody here got any demons in 'em?"

Elder almost smiled. "Sir, you're making sport of me and my work."

"And you're taking advantage of the good people of this town. How much did you charge for your little performance?"

"I never charge anything, your honor. At most, I might get my gas paid for." *And a substantial love offering,* he thought bitterly, *which I hadn't gotten before those damn cops showed up.* Sure, he'd received a preview the previous evening, but he'd really been looking forward to seeing what gratitude might inspire in the surprisingly wanton Brenda Holscombe.

"*Hmph,*" the judge said again. Elder wondered how the court reporter wrote down that particular sound. "What's that on your hand?"

Elder held up his right hand. "A tattoo, your honor."

"Approach the bench, so I can see. Put 'em up here."

Elder made fists and put them on the edge of the bench. Across the knuckles of his right hand was tattooed the word LOVE. The left hand bore the word FEAR.

"Where'd you get them?" Stewart asked.

"A tattoo place in Gulf Shores. I got 'em done right after I dedicated myself to the Lord."

"Preacher fella in a movie had LOVE and HATE tattooed on his hands."

Elder knew the film: *The Night of the Hunter,* with Robert Mitchum as a demented false prophet. "I got no time for hate, your honor. Christ said, 'Let us love one another, for love is from God.' Don't say nothing about hate."

"Then why you got 'Fear' on there?"

"Because 'Hate' isn't the opposite of 'Love.' 'Fear' is."

"So, you don't hate anyone?"

"Hate doesn't come from the Lord. Hate comes from some other place entirely."

"So, you believe in the devil, then."

"Your honor, I believe in the devil just as surely as I believe in Mississippi."

The judge took another drink of ice water, swiped at the sweat bee buzzing around his face, and said, "Well, *Reverend,* I'm going to give you the benefit of the doubt on this one. Sounds like you didn't know what you were walking into, and since no money changed hands, I can't charge you with fraud. But let me ask you one thing."

He motioned Elder closer to the bench and asked, "If I let you go, how soon can I expect you back here again?"

"Never."

"Not even if the Good Lord tells you to?"

"The Lord doesn't send a man where he can't do any good."

"You sound pretty sure of that."

Elder's reply was as sincere as anything he'd ever said. "I truly don't believe that there's a thing I can do for the people of Corinth, Mississippi."

A POLICE CAR dropped Elder off back at the church. His old Chevrolet Nova, a 1969 classic with a "three on the tree" gearshift and an Alabama license plate that read ELDER 1, remained where he'd parked it, now all alone in the parking lot. No one appeared from the building to question him.

His car started on the first crank, and he turned the air conditioner on high. As he waited for it to cool off, he thought about the past few hours, specifically about the girl speaking in Grove Prosser's voice. There was *no way* that little girl could know about Grove Prosser. Just no way.

Dandelion. What did that mean?

Elder was no hero and certainly no saint. But he was a loyal friend, and genuinely committed to fighting the influence of the demonic in the world. Whatever his flaws, whatever weaknesses in his character, Grove Prosser knew that Elder would not walk away from someone who needed his help.

He could do nothing more for Jurnee Holscomb at the moment. But perhaps he could help the victim Grove had risked damnation to tell him about.

He pulled out onto highway 45 and headed north into Tennessee, toward the town of Somerton, where Grove Prosser had died the previous summer.

2

L inda Scote, sixteen years old, flushed the toilet and emerged
from the restroom stall in the Somerton TLC-Mart. The
women's bathroom was reasonably clean, but she still put
toilet paper strips over the seat so her skin never came in contact with
it. That was just sensible.

The restroom had been refurbished six months earlier after a
backpack with a portable meth lab had contaminated it. The kid they
arrested had once asked Linda out, and she now kind of wished she'd
accepted. She liked danger and dangerous guys.

She washed her hands and checked herself in the mirror. Although
the fixtures were all relatively new, that hadn't kept vandals from
marking them. Someone had scratched a Nazi swastika in the
mirror's metal frame, and Linda found herself staring at it. She knew
its meaning and connotations, of course, but for the first time, she saw
it as something beautiful, like a delicate flower with petals twisted by
a spiral wind.

An unbidden idea sprang into her mind and quickly swelled to an
irresistible compulsion. She headed to the toy department.

"IT'S CALLED A *WEEJIE* BOARD," Linda said as she put the box on her bedroom floor and tore off the plastic. It was finally fully dark outside, and she'd been waiting for this all evening. She'd locked her bedroom door, closed the blinds and drapes, and stuffed a towel under the edge of the door in case Susie brought a joint.

Still, she knew they should be undisturbed. Her father was in the basement watching porn and playing with his gun collection, and her mother was wine-drunk and asleep on the couch in front of one of the *Real Housewives* shows.

Linda's friends knew about her parents, who otherwise presented entirely respectable fronts to the world. They said nothing, however; their own parents were just as weird, self-involved, and hypocritical about their daughters. The main difference was Susie and Bethany were still scared of their parents. Linda never had been.

"How can it be 'Weejie' when it starts with an 'O'?" Susie asked. She was the oldest of the trio by six months, thus would turn seventeen first and, by the arbitrary standards of her parents, be able to start actually dating. She had perfect blond hair and high cheekbones, but her chin was small and made her look weak. She wore an old sleep shirt with a faded image of Edward Cullen. "Shouldn't it be, 'O-Weejie?'"

"That's 'cause it's Spanish," Bethany said. The three girls had known each other since kindergarten, and Bethany gave the other two a common target for their teasing and tormenting. Bethany, for her part, no longer even registered the abuse. She had long legs and a face still ringed by baby fat, and a lot of the other girls' taunting was driven by their unconscious certainty that, when she finally matured, Bethany would be the real beauty of the trio. She wore flannel pajamas despite the summer heat, and slippers covered her unpainted toes.

"It's not Spanish, it's French," Linda said, pronouncing the word *Fraynch*. She wore a genuine nightgown, ordered from Victoria's Secret as a present for her sixteenth birthday. "Them French people, they're always doing stuff like this."

"Like what?" Bethany asked.

"Like dealing with the devil," Susie said, drawing up her knees. "This ain't right, Linda. I don't want to do this."

"Oh, shut up, you big baby," Linda said. "It's just a damn board game. I bought it at the TLC-Mart. Look, it says right here on it, 'Parker Brothers.' They're the same ones who make 'Battleship.' I reckon you think 'Battleship' is all about dealing with the devil, too, right? Besides, ain't no devil gonna be interested in two dumbasses like you two." She opened the box and took out the board and planchette.

"You curse a lot," Bethany said. "Just like your daddy."

"Fuck you," Linda said.

"My daddy says your daddy is a son of a bitch," Bethany said.

"Yeah, well, your daddy smokes crack, and everybody knows it," Linda shot back.

"Can we not do this?" Susie asked, her voice low and serious. "The whole Weejie thing, I mean. Can't we just watch TV or look up videos or post pictures or something?"

"Or sit in different corners and text each other?" Linda said snottily. "Look, you want to do that, you can just have this sleepover without me."

"It's your house," Susie said.

"Right. So, you two can just haul your fat asses out the back door."

Bethany sighed. "All right, we'll play your stupid game."

There was a knock at the door. The girls sighed in unison. "What?" Linda said in a voice like nails on a chalkboard.

The door opened partway before sticking on the rolled-up towel. Her uncle Travis wormed his head through the opening and grinned lasciviously, the way he always did around any girls who were past puberty. "What up, dawgs?"

"We're talking about our periods," Linda said coldly.

"Oh, man, I better armor up," he said, putting up his hands to block his face. He laughed like he was in on the joke. Travis Scote was her father's youngest brother, and he still lived with their mother across town. Travis was nearly thirty, long and lean, with an impenetrable sense of self-worth and entitlement that translated into both arrogance and laziness.

Linda simultaneously glared and narrowed her eyes. Travis had a key to their house and tended to show up at odd hours, drunk or high. "Daddy's down in the basement, playing with his toys. Why don't you go find him?"

"Maybe I came to see you pretty ladies," Travis said, leering at Linda the same way he did her mother, the same way he did every girl. She knew the nightgown made her look much older than sixteen, and usually, she reveled in it. But now, she felt conspicuous and icky.

Bethany giggled, then blushed. "You're too old for us, silly."

"Well," Travis said, "you know what they say—"

Linda had had enough. "So help me God, Uncle Travis, if you say that stupid 'old enough to bleed' line again, I'll kick you in the balls so hard Grandaddy will feel it. And he's dead, so you can imagine how hard that'll be."

"Whoa, you bitches really *are* on your periods, ain't you?" he said and backed out the door. "Excuse the fuck out of me."

Linda closed the door with her foot after her uncle withdrew. "I hate him."

"He's cute," Bethany said.

"He's got herpes," Linda said. "But you go suck his dick if you want to."

"Can we just play with the damn Weejie board?" Susie said.

"I thought you were scared of the devil?" Linda taunted.

"Can't be much worse than that uncle of yours," she said without meeting Linda's eyes. There was real fear in her voice and a secret that she desperately wanted to share with someone, *anyone*. But Linda, she knew, had no interest in being a shoulder to cry on.

Linda held up the planchette. "All right, here's how the Weejie works. We all sit around the board and put our fingers real lightly on this thing. Then we ask a question, and it answers by moving around."

"You mean we push it around?" Bethany asked.

"No, dumbass, the *spirits* move it. You'll see. Susie, you get a pencil and paper and write what it says, in case it needs to spell something."

"I still don't feel right about this," Susie said.

"All right, then, that'll be our first question," Linda said. "Come on."

They sat on the floor, the board in the center, and each leaned forward to rest their fingers on the planchette.

Linda said archly, "Oh, spirit world, is anyone there?"

"Knock once for yes, twice for no," Bethany added.

"That's the dumbest thing I've ever heard, Beth," Linda said. "How do you answer that question, 'no'? That's like asking someone if they're awake."

"Sorry," Bethany said, looking down.

For a moment, there was nothing. Then the planchette slid across the board until the word YES was visible through the little round plastic window.

"There," Linda said smugly.

"You did that," Bethany said.

"I did not," Linda insisted. "The spirits did."

"You mean the devil," Susie said.

"Oh, spirit, are you the devil?" Linda asked snidely.

The planchette slid over to, NO.

"So, who is it?" Bethany asked in a whisper.

Linda said, "Oh, spirit world, please tell us, who has contacted us?"

This time the planchette roamed around the board before moving to the alphabet and beginning to spell something.

"Get ready, Susie," Linda said. "J-E-S-S-E-G-A-R-O-N."

"Jessegaron," Susie said as she finished writing. "What language is that?"

Linda snatched the paper from her and studied it. "That first part could be a name. Jesse."

"But what's a 'Garon?'" Bethany asked, pronouncing it "GAY-ron."

Suddenly Susie gasped and covered her mouth with her hands. Her eyes were huge. "Oh, my God," she said through her fingers.

"What?" Linda said, annoyed. "I swear, if you start talking about the devil again—"

"No! I know who that is! Jesse Garon!"

"All right, who?" Linda demanded.

"*Jesse Garon Presley!*" When her friends looked blank, she said, "Elvis's twin brother!"

"Elvis didn't have a twin," Bethany said.

"No, Jesse Garon died at birth," Susie said, so excited she could barely sit still. "My grand-mama told me all about it. She met Elvis once!"

"Oh, my God," Bethany whispered.

"All right, all right," Linda said, "just keep your panties out of your wad. Let's ask him if that's who he is."

The girls, torn between excitement and fear, put their fingers back on the planchette. Susie's shook so much that the plastic rattled against the board until Linda's glare calmed her down. Linda said, "Is this the spirit of Jesse Garon Presley, twin brother of Elvis?"

The planchette rattled on its own, then slid quickly to the word, YES.

"Well, fuck me," Linda said softly.

TRAVIS SCOTE HAD FORGOTTEN ENTIRELY about the girls by the time he got to the basement. His older brother Blanton had turned the space into his man cave, with a huge Confederate flag on one wall, a picture of crucified Jesus on the opposite, and between the two hung various centerfolds faded by age and fluorescent lighting.

He had the big gun safe open and was busy polishing a shotgun. A flatscreen TV had Fox News on in the background.

"Hey, big bro, what's up?" Travis said as he came down the stairs.

"Check this out," Blanton said. "It's a Mossburg with a damn built-in flashlight. Somebody comes poking around here, I'll blind 'em, then I'll blow a hole in 'em." He touched the side of the light attached under the barrel, and it began to flash. "Look at that. A strobe. Can't nobody see with that in their eyes."

Travis took the weapon and whistled. "That is something. What'd it set you back?"

"Got a good deal on it at the flea market. Four hundred dollars. Runs about a thousand online."

Travis handed it back. Blanton's fascination with guns had begun practically in infancy, and he was always buying, selling, and trading weapons. It was an interest Travis had never shared, not least because of the *blackbird incident.*

Blanton handed Travis a beer. "Did you hear about them black people at church last week?"

"No. What black people?"

"Ever since that deaf boy's been coming, they've been having a sign-language class so people can talk to him. I don't know why they don't just teach him to read lips instead of making a bunch of us learn to wiggle our fingers around. Anyway, last week that family brought some deaf, colored friend of his and his parents. You shoulda seen all them mouths drop open as them black sons of bitches walked down and sat on the front pew like they owned the place. Like there ain't enough colored churches or something."

"What did you do?"

"Nothing this time, but if they show up again, we'll run their black asses off. There's plenty of churches across the tracks for them folks; we don't need 'em stinkin' up ours."

"Ain't that the truth," Travis said, and they clinked beer cans over it. "Judge says *I* have to go to a colored church. Do my community service for that last DUI."

"That's bullshit."

"I know, right?"

"I was you, I'd rather go to fucking jail than do that."

"Yeah, but you ain't gotta look after Mama."

Travis sat back and listened to his brother continue to talk——monologue, really——about everything that was wrong with the world, usually boiling down to the Democrats, the immigrants, and the gays. He'd heard it his whole life, so he didn't really pay attention. Instead, he focused lazily on the centerfold directly behind his brother's head.

"And I swear, did you see that yard sign down the street in front of the Blankenships' house? 'Hate Has No Home Here.' It's like they want a bunch of Mexicans running all over the place taking all the damn jobs." He paused and, with a sigh, added, "Goddamn Episcopalians."

"They're gonna look mighty fucking stupid when they find out heaven's full of Baptists," Travis said. Blanton laughed hard at that.

But Travis, still gazing into the centerfold's cleavage, realized he couldn't even imagine what it was like not to hate. Without it, without the certainty that the world was against him, what would he do?

DEACON ELDER REACHED Somerton after dark and parked in the lot of the TLC-Mart. This was one of its 24-hour stores, so other cars were also parked there, and numb-looking shoppers wandered in and out through the automatic doors.

He watched it, thinking, *You have to go in. Nothing in there can hurt you. You know the truth about it. Just go in, do your business, and get out.*

The radio finished Jimmie Rodgers's "Honeycomb," and segued into a TLC-Mart commercial. First was the insidious instrumental jingle, and then the chorus sang:

You always find Tender Loving Care
    And the best prices anywhere
    at TLC-Mart!

Elder turned it off and went into the store. With each *whoosh* of the doors, the chimes played that same insufferable tune.

These stores had popped up everywhere across the south, cancerously killing off all the small, locally-owned businesses and even other chains. He understood the appeal: to people on fixed incomes, disability, or unemployment, the stores were a lifeline to goods and services they could not otherwise afford. He didn't blame *them*.

But the rest, the blindly avaricious, overstuffed on grease, Fox News, and self-serving interpretations of the Bible, were destroying their own culture without even realizing it. The owners of TLC-Mart, the seldom-seen Beleth family, knew just how to appeal to their customers' greed, laziness, selfishness, and total lack of empathy. Elder knew exactly *why* they did it. He also knew that no one would believe him.

He stopped inside the door, waiting to adjust to what he always found in the place. He'd told that sour judge the truth: he *did* have the ability to discern the presence of demons by their *odor*. He was certain a demon squatted inside little Jurnee Holscomb because he'd *smelled* it. But that was nothing compared with what washed over him here.

Each TLC-Mart was *filled* with devils: literally, not metaphorically. TLC-Marts collected them like the bugs around security lights, filling the cavernous store with an odor unnoticed by anyone else but nauseating to him. He had no doubt that many of the demons he faced in his deliverances latched onto their hosts somewhere in its wide, air-conditioned corridors. They swarmed the place, lurking and prowling, listening to thoughts and conversations, whispering words to people, and waiting for the invitation for more. Most often, the demons simply agreed with the worst tendencies of the shoppers, encouraging all their prejudices and fears and hatreds. It didn't always end in actual possession, but it did convince people that the store was a place that suited them, that sympathized with their view of the world. And so they came back, again and again.

It was also why Elder had to enter. If he arrived in a town to battle a demon, he had to let its compatriots know to stay out of it. A man who could stand up to them here was no one to trifle with.

That first whiff of concentrated demon B.O. was always the worst. His stomach lurched, he fought to keep down whatever he'd recently consumed, and his vision grew blurry and uncertain. Even now, it was like being gagged by caustic chemical vapors, and he grabbed the nearest shopping cart to keep from falling down.

"Are you all right, young fella?" a voice asked. Through watery eyes, he saw the face of an elderly greeter. His sympathy was mixed with contempt because he clearly thought Elder was on something.

Elder smiled and forced himself to respond. "No, I'm a little under the weather. Don't get too close; I'd hate for you to catch it."

The man stepped back. "Appreciate the warning. Would you like one of our motorized carts?"

"Oh, no, I'll be okay. Thanks."

The worst of it passed, and as he walked through the aisles, he recognized some of the smells. There was the demon Agares, the stink of swamp rot and bird droppings; he was often depicted as an old man riding a crocodile and carrying a hawk. Here was Morax, the odor of manure matching his image as a bull with a man's head. Passing close by was Penemue, a fallen angel whose distinctive stench smelled like nothing of this earth.

And those were just the ones he'd encountered before and successfully driven from hosts and dwellings. There were dozens more, *hundreds* more, just waiting for the opportunity to insinuate themselves into a shopper.

He walked down the toiletries aisle and palmed a travel-sized tube of toothpaste. In the men's room, he took the last stall, did his business, then washed his face and hands at the sink. The pungent disinfectant used in the restroom actually masked much of the demonic odor that permeated everything else.

He put some toothpaste on his fingertip and vigorously ran it across his teeth.

"You pay for that, champ?"

He looked up. A large-bellied man in a blue TLC-Mart vest, carrying a spray bottle and a paper towel roll, had entered.

"If I say no, will you shoot me?" Elder said with a nod at the bottle.

"Heh. You a vagrant?"

"I'm a minister."

"Hey, me, too." He extended a hand. "Horton Johnson."

"Nice to meet you. Deacon Elder."

"I'm at Christ is King Baptist. You?"

"I travel doing deliverance ministry."

He shook the spray bottle. "I hope that pays better."

Elder held up his finger smeared with toothpaste. "I wouldn't bet on it."

The big man guffawed at that, his voice echoing in the empty restroom. "So, what you doing in the TLC-Mart in the middle of the night?

"I just drove in from Mississippi, and I wanted to freshen up a little before I showed up at my friend's house."

"Uh-huh. Is she pretty?"

"No, it's another minister."

Horton sprayed one of the mirrors, then wiped it with a handful of paper towels. "Ah, don't worry about it. The good Lord probably wants more people to have fresh breath."

"Thanks." He put away the toothpaste and asked, "Tell me, Brother Johnson, how can you stand to work here?"

He sprayed another mirror. "It ain't easy. But pride's a luxury when you've got mouths to feed. Used to be a manager at the old grocery store, but when this place came in, it closed down in five months."

Elder looked up as the fluorescent lights began to flicker.

"Happens every night at 3 a.m.," Horton said. "Nobody knows why."

Elder knew. Three in the morning was the real witching hour, when the powers of evil were strongest. Christ died at three in the afternoon, and this was Satan's inversion of that. Three-thirty-three A.M. was the prime point, as close as a clock could come to 666, the Number of the Beast. The Catholics considered the entire hour between three and four to be the realm of the devil.

As he walked back down the center aisle, he saw an old woman struggle to get a roll of paper towels off a shelf. She fumbled and knocked a half-dozen rolls to the floor.

Elder went to help. "I'll get those for you, ma'am."

"Thank you, son. My back doesn't let me bend over too well."

He put the rolls back on the shelf. "How many do you need?"

"Oh, just one."

He placed the roll in her cart. "There you go."

He used the excuse to get close and take a deep breath. She smelled like stale bread, faded floral cologne, and a slightly bitter edge of strong coffee. But nothing like the odor of the demonic.

He knew that a demon might've knocked the rolls off the shelf just to frustrate her, to make her give in to anger at God for putting one more petty obstacle in her way. That was all the opening some of them needed. But she was untouched by the evil around her.

She looked up at him with sad, kind eyes. "Bless you, son. I come here so late because it takes me forever to do my shopping, and if I come during the day, I'm liable to get trampled." She looked around. "Truth is, I hate this place. I miss my old grocery store."

"I'm right there with you, ma'am," Elder agreed.

Back in his car, he turned on the air conditioner full blast, lit a cigarette, and looked down at his phone. He didn't want to wake Anthony out of the blue with tales of messages from beyond the grave from their mutual friend. But he also didn't want to spend the rest of the night in the TLC-Mart cataloging demonic smells.

His thoughts returned to little Jurnee Holscomb. He often wondered why girls were possessed so much more often than boys. Males were more common victims in undeveloped countries, but in America, it was almost exclusively women and girls. He thought it must have something to do with the way the culture viewed women because possession was never about the possessed. It was all about those *around* the victim, spreading the certainty that they were vile, repulsive beings forever separated from the love and grace of God. Attacking women and girls, already objectified and commodified, struck at the rancid patriarchal heart of this society.

Elder took another drag on his cigarette. Tomorrow he would visit Anthony and tell him about the message from Grove. Then he'd try to find the girl. Perhaps "Dandelion" was her name or a nickname?

He drove off to search for an all-night place to drink coffee and think.

LATER THAT NIGHT, Linda Scote tossed in her bed, sweaty and half-awake. Despite all her sexual flaunting and some heated experimentation, she was still a virgin, so the dark sexual dreams that tried to take hold in her psyche could not quite find a purchase. At last, she woke up frustrated and a little angry. She looked at her clock; the big red numbers announced 3 AM.

The Ouija board had continued to speak to them for another half hour. It told them secrets known only to the three of them, like the time Linda wiped her nose in Chris Inman's hair in fifth grade or when Bethany pretended to be her mother when that creepy girl Carlyss Bolerjack called to see if she wanted to hang out. It started to tell something about Susie, but the girl had freaked out so bad that they'd stopped and put the board away.

Linda looked at her friends, asleep on pallets on the floor. She felt sudden contempt for them: Susie, dumb as a post, and Bethany, fat as a cow. Neither of them deserved a friend like Linda, but you had to take the friends you were dealt here in Somerton. At least in two years, she could go to college and move out, maybe as far away as Jackson or even Nashville. Then she could get a *real* boyfriend, not one of these overheated titty-gropers like Danny Blazer. Nothing made her despise a boy more than finding out how much he really liked her, and although Danny was cute and tough, he turned into a mewling little kitten at the touch of her boobies.

Still, this was what she had to work with for now, so she had to keep her true feelings to herself. She tossed back her covers and started to swing her legs over the side of the bed, intending to pee and maybe sneak a swig of her daddy's Jim Beam to help her sleep.

Then she froze.

A man stood in front of the closed bedroom door.

Well, it was most of a man. He was solid down to his waist, where he seemed to dissolve into a black shadow or mist.

There was something familiar about him, and at first, she thought it was her Uncle Travis again. It wouldn't be the first time he'd tried to spy on her since she started "riding the cotton pony," as her namesake, Aunt Linda, called the onset of menstruation. But the figure was shorter, slouchier, and radiated a confident sexuality that both excited and terrified her. She started to nudge Susie awake with her foot. Then with a start, she realized who it was.

Elvis.

The hair, the slouch, even the crooked lip snarled in a contemptuous grin all confirmed the identity.

Her first awareness of sexuality was tied to Elvis, specifically to an old album cover Linda's mother inherited from her parents. He stood in a gold suit, black hair disheveled, a simmering smile leering out at her. Before that, she had never thought about boys, or men, as anything other than disgusting; and then thoughts of *real* boys had quickly eclipsed her interest in this ancient figure from the past. But now, the shadowy form in front of her door rekindled that original stirring.

Then her head cleared enough that she remembered the session with the Ouija board. Raggedly, she whispered, "Are you...Jesse Garon?"

The shape nodded. Then it was gone.

She wanted to scream. She drew her legs up to her chin and stared, wide-eyed, at the space the apparition had occupied. She waited until the first light peeked through the curtains at 5:30, but it never reappeared.

3

As she always did, Haven Fields began the counseling session with, "So, Carlyss: what's new since last time?"

Carlyss Bolerjack sat in the chair with her knees and feet together, hands on the padded arms, head down and shoulders hunched. It was a submissive pose that deliberately gave Haven all the power in the room. But even after a year of these twice-weekly sessions, Haven still wasn't certain if it was all an act.

"What's new?" the girl repeated. "Not a damn thing. It's summer, I live in Somerton, and there's the sum of all my fears."

"That's an interesting turn of phrase," Haven said. "And it doesn't really answer my question."

"It's the answer I have."

Most of Haven's clients were troubled teens like this. They were into drugs or petty crime or just unmanageable behavior. Usually, it was simply a matter of finding the right code for the business office to turn in to make the insurance or the state pay the bill. These kids didn't care about getting better, and their parents were just marking time until their offspring turned eighteen and either moved out or were sent to adult prison. Haven used to genuinely care about them

26

all; now, though, she just did her job, head down, eyes straight ahead. She could ask the standard prompts in her sleep.

Except, that is, with the kids she somehow knew she *could* help. They were rare; at the moment, in fact, sixteen-year-old Carlyss was the only one.

Haven made a note on her pad. "And your grandparents? How are they?"

"Same as always."

Carlyss lived with her late mother's parents, who were elderly and good-intentioned but completely overwhelmed by their granddaughter's troubles. "Any boyfriends?"

She snorted.

"Girlfriends?" Haven asked, careful to use the exact same tone and inflection.

"You keep bringing that up. I'm not a lesbian. And I'm not 'bi-curious,' or 'gender fluid' or whatever they call it in those books of yours. I'm a 'she/her,' not a 'they/them.'" She shifted in her chair and mumbled, "This is just a waste of time for everyone."

Haven had to admit, she saw the girl's point on that. Not only were Carlyss's parents dead, but her initial therapist had dropped dead of a heart attack during their first session. There had been rumors—state employees were worse than housewives for rumors—that his death had been brought on by something Carlyss told him. But Haven assumed that hypertension, hard drinking, and being sixty pounds overweight had been more likely culprits.

In fact, Haven only got Carlyss's case after three other therapists flatly turned it down, one going so far as to threaten to resign. All three were dedicated churchgoers and heavily religious people, frightened of the events that led to Carlyss's court-mandated psychotherapy. Haven, who didn't believe in much of anything, took the case, and so far, the girl had not threatened her with anything. Including getting better.

Haven asked, "Given any more thought to getting a summer job?"

"No."

"Why not?"

"There are no jobs. This town is dying, haven't you noticed? They closed the skating rink, the movie theater, even the city pool. Pretty soon, there'll be nothing but the TLC-Mart."

"You could get a job there."

Carlyss looked at her with the hardest look Haven had ever seen. "Not on your fucking life. Besides," she continued, gesturing at her long-sleeved black blouse, pale skin, and black-dyed hair, "who the fuck around here would hire me? And for what?"

"There's that coffee shop downtown. I can put in a word for you, if you'd like."

"Would *you* like a pity job?"

"It depends on my circumstances. What makes you so sure it would be pity?"

Again, Carlyss gestured at herself. "Nobody hires a fucking loser like me for any other reason."

This was the core of the girl's trouble: self-esteem so low it could crawl under a duck. Somehow she'd gone from a perfectly healthy, vivacious fifteen-year-old to the sullen black-clad sixteen-year-old now seated before her.

Haven knew the ostensible cause: a botched religious ceremony performed by a doddering old minister who had convinced the girl and her grandparents that she was possessed by a demon. The minister had died in a fire that consumed his church, and firemen found Carlyss unconscious in the ruins just in the nick of time. The overzealous district attorney charged her with arson and second-degree murder, but there had been no real evidence that she started the fire or intended to kill the minister. Still, to avoid losing Carlyss to the state, her grandparents agreed to counseling, and thus Haven ended up with her.

And since then, very little had changed. Carlyss claimed not to remember the minister or the fire, but Haven didn't believe that. So, they talked about everything else, Haven constantly hoping she'd find a way in to the real problem.

"There's no need to swear quite so much," Haven said.

"There's no reason *not* to," the girl shot back.

"Maybe if you did it less, someone might hire you."

"But if I do more of it, more people might stay away from me."

"Is that what you want?"

The girl sat back and crossed her pale legs. This drew attention to the network of white inch-long scars across the tops of her thighs. Thankfully, none of them were fresh.

"What I want," Carlyss said with certainty, "is for everyone to forget I exist."

Haven sighed, not with impatience or annoyance, but just weariness. "Carlyss, I know you don't like being here. But you have to be, you agreed to be, and if you don't want to spend the next two years as a ward of the state of Tennessee—and believe me, Carlyss, you don't want that—then you'll start cooperating. A year ago, you believed you were possessed by a demon. That's an extreme belief in most places. I'd really like to know what convinced you that was the case."

Carlyss looked into the middle distance, her gaze unfocused and her expression blank. Haven knew the girl could do this indefinitely.

"Well," Haven said finally, "let's move on. Spend time online?"

"We don't have a computer. My grandpa's got a tablet, but he's always on it, arguing about politics."

"Spend time with friends?"

"What are those?" she said with dry sarcasm.

"You must do *something*."

"I go to church," the girl said.

"Really?"

"Really."

"So, do you consider yourself a Christian?"

"You can go to church and not be a Christian."

"I don't understand."

Again, the girl didn't answer.

Haven put down her pad and pen. She leaned her elbows on the desk. She wanted to go around it, kneel by the chair and take the girl's hands, but she'd tried that once with another client, and it took three people to pull that troubled girl off her. Sometimes a well-intentioned touch was a squeeze on a hair trigger. So instead, she said, with the most compassion she could muster, "I don't know how to help you, Carlyss. We both have to be here until you turn eighteen, but if you won't answer my questions or talk to me at all, I can't do anything."

"Maybe I'm beyond help," the girl said flatly.

"No one is beyond help. But you have to *want* help for it to work."

Carlyss met Haven's gaze. For an instant, the girl's defenses were down, and Haven saw the child behind all the bluster and ice. This was someone who needed the unconditional and steady love of a parent and had never gotten it. Yet it hadn't turned her cruel and heartless; it had made her hard, and separate, and alone. But under it all, that little girl's heart remained.

Then the shields reappeared, and Carlyss asked, "Let me ask *you* something. Do you believe in evil?"

"How do you mean?"

Carlyss leaned forward again. "I mean, evil. The opposite of good. I read somewhere that evil is 'a spiritual being, alive and living, perverted and perverting, weaving its way insidiously into the very fabric of life.' It's not just some abstract concept."

"Evil is not an absolute, Carlyss. It's a value judgment."

"If you don't believe in absolute evil, you and I have nothing to talk about. And you can't possibly help me."

"Why do you say that? Because of what happened at the church?"

But the girl was done. She folded her arms and stared at the closed window, as lost in what she saw as if the blinds were open. For the final ten minutes of the session, Haven's questions were totally ignored.

After the girl had gone, Belinda, one of the other therapists, came into Haven's office and closed the door. "Did you get anything out of her?" she asked conspiratorially.

"No," Haven said. "Well, that's not true. She asked *me* a couple of questions. But she didn't like my answers."

"I wanted to see you before your session with her, but I didn't get a chance. One of my clients mentioned her. He's living in a halfway house downtown. He sees her almost every day."

"Doing what?"

"You'll never guess." She paused for dramatic effect. "Going to church."

"Really?"

Belinda nodded. "Every day. Sometimes she stays all day. The halfway house is right down from the church, and my guy goes a fair bit himself. It's run by a Black preacher."

"Why did your client mention it?"

"He said because he'd never seen anyone so happy to be in the presence of God as she was. He was serious, too. He doesn't have enough functioning brain cells left to be ironic."

"I wish I *had* known about it before our session."

"I know. I'm sorry. But at least you'll have some more ammunition next time." Belinda paused, then smiled craftily. "So, how was your date with that lawyer?"

"Landon? Ugh." She shook her head. "All he wanted to talk about was football and himself."

"So, it didn't go anywhere?"

"There won't be a second date if that's what you mean."

"You know it's not. Come on ..."

"Look, he was as exciting in bed as he was at dinner, all right? I think he wanted me to yell 'touchdown!' when he finished."

Belinda snort-laughed. "I'll never look at him the same way again."

"That makes two of us," Haven assured her.

When Belinda left, Haven looked at Carlyss Bolerjack's file. She loved the physical presence of all that paperwork; she could rest her hands on the manila folder as if it were a talisman—no, an *icon*—of the girl herself.

Carlyss had asked about evil, and now Haven knew she compulsively attended church. The mystery was deeper than Haven suspected. Now she just had to solve it before the girl turned eighteen and aged out of the juvenile system, because Haven knew she'd be gone forever as soon as that happened.

If she wasn't *already* gone, she thought sadly.

4

The old Black man muttered, "Howdy, Rev'rend," when Anthony Acred came into the McDonald's. His nickname was Lucky, but he was definitely not: he was missing a finger, one entire foot, and his left eye was milky and useless. Diabetic, overweight, unemployed, and unmarried, he sat at a table by the window every morning, usually with a bit of Egg McMuffin stuck on his unshaven chin. The kids avoided him, although they snickered when his hand shook so much he couldn't drink his coffee.

"Good morning, Lucky," Anthony said. He was also Black, middle-aged, and resigned to the grey now showing up in his hair. He put his cup down on the counter. "Maria, can I get my morning fill-up?"

"You bet, Reverend," the Latina behind the counter said. She poured his cup as he put two dollars down beside it. Every few days, the manager—a middle-aged white man named Curtis who spoke no Spanish despite an almost exclusively Hispanic crew—would warn the employees to stop filling Anthony's personal cup. They would give him a serious *Sí, señor*, then refill it anyway.

Anthony looked around as he sipped his coffee. Two heavy kids wheezed their way through the tunnel in the play area while their equally overweight parents loudly consumed breakfast.

The McDonald's had been robbed three times in the past year, each time by unemployed white folks desperate for drug money. Anthony had even spoken to one of them at a Narcotics Anonymous group held at his church. He said, "There ain't no jobs for people like me since everything's closed down. Fifty bucks won't make my car payment or my rent, but it'll at least let me forget about 'em for a while." Anthony could not refute that logic.

"Oh, hey, Rev'rend, before you run off," Lucky called.

Anthony returned. "Yes?"

"You gonna be at that tent revival coming up?"

Anthony shook his head. "First I've heard of it."

"Out in that empty lot going toward the TLC-Mart."

"I don't think it's really my scene, Lucky."

Lucky lowered his voice. "And also, I seen that white girl poking around your church earlier, before you got there."

"She's helping me with some renovations."

Lucky looked up at him, desperation in his one clear eye. "Pray for me, too, would you, Brother Acred?"

Anthony patted him on the shoulder. "I always do, Lucky. You take care."

As he left the McDonald's, the air was already hot and sticky despite the early hour, and it didn't bode well for the rest of the day. Eventually, he hoped to be able to afford to get the church's central air conditioning fixed. Until then, he dressed in shorts and a baggy, light t-shirt: he looked like a middle-aged guy warned by his doctors to get in shape or else. In truth, he was in the best shape of his life, in large part because of the building he now approached.

The New Shiloh Methodist Church was on the corner of Main and Bedford, in a part of town once considered middle-class residential. Now there was no middle class in Somerton, and the houses were given over to the meth dealers who brewed in their windowless bathrooms, or the working poor who struggled to pay mortgages or rent far beyond their means.

The majority of his congregation now came from the halfway house down the street. At any given time a dozen men lived there, but many more came for meals, AA meetings, and the occasional visiting doctor. Church attendance could not be required, but it was certainly encouraged, and truthfully most of the men were so near the end of their ropes, or lives, that they needed little encouragement to come hear about the paradise in the next world.

Anthony missed the neat families he'd had at his old church in Smyrna, and especially the small, scrubbed faces of the children. But here, he never had any doubt that his words were heard. They may not have always been comprehended, but he couldn't fault the sad, desperate, defeated men for their attention.

He found Carlyss Bolerjack seated on the church's front steps. She was dressed in denim shorts and a black long-sleeved boy's shirt. He said cheerily, "Good morning, sunshine. How are you?"

"Fine," she said.

He fished for his keys. "Ready for a big day's work?"

She nodded.

"Fella at McDonald's said he saw you here earlier," he continued. "I don't mind you hanging out here; it's the Lord's house, not mine. But I'm the caretaker, and if you're doing something you shouldn't, I'll have to deal with it. Now, if there's a good reason—"

"I don't sleep," she said without looking at him.

"You don't sleep?"

"No. I mean, no, sir."

"At all?"

"No, sir."

"What do you do, then?"

"This and that. I can find stuff to do until about two AM, but then town shuts all the way down except for the TLC-Mart. I sure don't want to go *there*. So...I wander."

"That doesn't sound safe for a young girl."

She shrugged, tucked a strand of black hair behind her ear, and looked away. "I'm safe."

"Didn't you have a therapy session this morning?" He knew that she was supposed to go twice a week, Monday and Wednesday.

"I did," she confirmed. "I went."

"And?"

She shrugged.

Anthony knew that ended the conversation. Time and experience had taught him that confronting teens outright seldom got to the truth; you had to simply establish a line of communication and wait for the truth to come out on its own. It was similar to fishing: you put out the bait and waited for the fish to decide to bite.

He opened the door. The vestibule was insulated well enough that it retained the night's relative cool. He turned on the box fans that moved the air around in the sanctuary.

Carlyss walked past him, straight down the aisle to the riser where the podium stood. Above that, slightly in front of the choir, hung a cross with a three-quarters-life-size Christ nailed to it. It was painted realistically, but so long ago that the colors had faded to a uniform mix of yellow and brown. Anthony honestly found the thing a little creepy and far too Catholic for his tastes, but he didn't want to take it down and risk offending any of his parishioners. They expected to see it, and more than one had told him that the icon's strange, sad eyes had directly influenced their decision to accept Christ.

Carlyss knelt, clasped her hands, and bowed her head. Anthony couldn't make out the words of her whispered prayer. They didn't really matter, he figured; what counted was the girl was asking Christ for help and clearly needed it.

He waited in the doorway, in full view of the street. He didn't feel safe being alone in the church with a teenage girl, given the way people talked. That was why he always made sure someone else joined them for the renovation work. He had a list of people sentenced to community service, and on days when they didn't show, he sent the girl home—or wherever she went—right away.

And that realization made him sad. He had no sexual interest in her, and in no woman since his wife died. He was content to minister to his ever-shrinking flock and try to keep his church's body and soul together.

"What's up, big man?" a new voice said behind him.

Oh, no, he thought, *Travis Scote. Lord, give me strength.*

35

ALEX BLEDSOE

Anthony managed a smile, but inwardly he fought the surprisingly strong urge to punch that smug grin right in its shoddy teeth. He knew he'd get no actual work out of Travis; it wasn't the first time he'd burned off part of a DUI sentence here. Travis would hem and haw, complain about his back, his wrists, his allergies, anything to keep him from physical labor. He'd be sent on a five-minute task and disappear for an hour. And the whole time, he'd be smiling, certain there would never be any real consequences. Because there never were.

"Good morning, Travis," Anthony said. "So, you showed up. How are you?"

"Any better, and they'd throw me back in jail," he said. "Gonna be a hot one today, though. Ain't got the air conditioning fixed here yet, have you?" Then he spotted Carlyss, still kneeling beneath the cross. Quietly so only Anthony would hear, he said, "Hey, speaking of hot, who's *that?*"

"She's underage," Anthony said, although he doubted it would deter Travis. "Her name's Carlyss."

"Carlyss? Weird name."

"Yes, well, I'd appreciate it if you'd steer clear of her and simply do your job. She's got a lot on her mind."

"Lot goin' on everywhere else, too, from what I can see, and in all the right places. Right, big man? I mean, you're not one of them Catholics; you can appreciate a woman, right?"

Anthony's fists clenched. He knew Travis was baiting him; that's how he operated. People like Travis drove someone to the point of fury, then claimed it was all a joke, turning it back against their target. Anthony said, "I can appreciate that she's a young lady who's here for her own reasons, very different from yours. So, if you're going to spend the whole day flirting with her, I'd just as soon you turn around and go back home. I'm perfectly willing to call your probation officer and explain why you didn't put in your time."

"Okay, big man, there's no need to get your holy ghost all twisted," Travis said and patted him on the shoulder like they were old friends. "I'll treat her like the Virgin Mary."

36

"I'd appreciate it," Anthony said.

"Yep, she'll be laying there going, 'God, that was amazing!'" Then he laughed so loudly that Carlyss turned to look.

Anthony gritted his teeth. "Why don't you go bring in those pieces of paneling from the bed of my truck?" He seriously hoped Travis would take all day to do this simple task.

"Sure thing, big man," Travis said and, whistling, walked back out the door.

Carlyss rejoined Anthony in the vestibule. He dug some money out of his pocket and said, "Here, run down to the McDonald's and get me a sweet tea. Get yourself something, too, if you want."

"You already have coffee," she pointed out.

"By the time you get back, I'll be ready for something cold."

"You don't have to send me away. I know what that man is."

"Do you?"

"Yes. He's evil," she said simply.

"He's bad news, that's for certain," Anthony agreed.

"No, he's evil. Sneaky, whiny evil."

There was something in her voice that got his attention. "Why do you say that?"

Carlyss started to explain, then thought better of it. "I just don't like guys like that."

"In this case, I'd follow your instincts," Anthony agreed. But he wondered what the girl saw that made her so certain.

LATER THAT MORNING, Travis held a piece of paneling in place so Carlyss could drive the nails. He blatantly watched the way her slender body moved, the way her breasts and ass pressed against the fabric covering it. He said over the fans' drone, "You know, our names rhyme. Travis and Carlyss."

"That's not a rhyme," she said around the nails held in her teeth. "That's assonance."

"Sure it is. Like the way you rhyme 'good' and 'food' when you pray. You know, 'God is great, God is good, thank you God, for this food.' But hey, if you want to talk about your ass, I can find a few choice words for it. Like, 'sweet.'"

Carlyss did not look at him. "Yeah, well, so what?"

"How about I give you a ride home when we're done? Maybe we can split a beer."

Carlyss pounded the next nail. "I'm only sixteen."

"I ain't gonna tell nobody." He wished she'd look at him. He knew his smile did most of his work for him.

"No thanks," she said.

"Aw, why you got to be so stuck up? We've already been talking about your ass."

She did look at him now, and her eyes zeroed in on him like the laser on his keychain. He couldn't look away, and the anger that blazed from her felt like it could scorch him to the bone with its intensity. It didn't even seem like *human* rage, but something bigger and more primal.

She took the nails from her lips and said, "Because I know what you are. I know you use your .22 rifle to shoot holes in your neighbor's shingles, holes so small they can't see them, but that make their roofs leak and cost them a fortune. I know you once cut a baby possum open while it was still alive and tried to get it to eat its own insides. I know you once raped your neighbor when she was eleven, and you were fifteen. So, I really don't want to have anything to do with you, and I'd appreciate it if you'd just fuck off." She bowed her head and said softly, "Sorry for my language in your house."

Travis stared at her. Everything she said was accurate, but even if she'd somehow heard about it from someone else, the possum incident was something he'd never told *anyone*. "What the *fuck?*" he whispered.

"Evil knows evil," she said. "You think you're unique, but you're *so* not." Then she resumed hammering.

Travis just stared. He only held the paneling because he was too shocked to release it and walk away. When she finished, he stepped back and bounced on the balls of his feet, the urge to flee so strong he couldn't even pick a direction. Carlyss seemed not to notice.

Anthony joined them and said, "How's it coming?"

That broke the moment. Travis ran from the sanctuary out the front door. A moment later, they heard his car roar off.

"What's wrong with him?" Anthony asked.

"The truth hurts sometimes," Carlyss said. "Can you bring me some more paneling?"

Anthony went outside just as an old Chevy Nova pulled into the spot beside his truck. Deacon Elder got out, stretched, and grinned at Anthony. "Good morning there, young man. Hot enough for you?"

Anthony just stared for a long moment before finally saying, "Ho-lee shit."

Deacon grinned. "Language, Reverend."

"It ain't cursing, just an accurate description."

"Ouch. Tell me *that* don't sting."

"Truth's like a snapping turtle sometimes. It grabs hold and don't let go."

"That mean you're not glad to see me?"

The two men looked at each other for a long moment, Anthony musing and Deacon quietly waiting. Then Anthony let out a sigh and came down the church steps. Deacon met him with a hug.

Anthony asked, "So how are you, Deke?"

"Gettin' by, gettin' by." Elder looked up at the church. "You replaced those old gutters, I see."

"Yep, somebody donated them. All I had to do was the manual labor."

"Ain't that always the case."

"Let's get out of this heat before we melt."

"You got that air conditioner fixed?"

"No, but I got some big fans."

"That must be nice. *Nobody* likes me." They both laughed.

"You still got that old snakeskin jacket," Anthony observed.

"Course I do. Skinned it off Satan myself."

"Careful he don't come back to claim it some cold night."

"He can try."

Inside, Anthony called, "Carlyss, come here; I want you to meet an old friend. This is Deacon Elder. Deke, this is Carlyss Bolerjack."

Elder smiled at the girl and offered his hand. "Hello. It's a pleasure to meet you."

"That's a cool jacket," Carlyss said, admiring the snakeskin sport coat. She looked at his hand. "Is that a tattoo?"

"It is." He put his hands together so she could see the words.

"So, you like opposites."

He smiled. She didn't ask for an explanation; she simply understood it at once. "That's right.

"What brings you to town, hoss?" Anthony asked.

"Can we speak privately?" Elder said.

"Sure. Let's step outside. Carlyss, you call me if you need me."

They stood in the shade of an old oak that sheltered part of the church's graveyard. Elder lit a cigarette and offered one to Anthony.

He shook his head. "Doctor made me quit everything I used to enjoy. That's what 'healthy' means at my age."

After a long drag, Elder said, "I'm going to tell you a story. Just let me finish before you ask me anything, okay?"

"Sure."

Elder told him about the aborted deliverance in Mississippi. Anthony listened seriously. When Elder finished, Anthony said, "Deke, what do you know about how Grove Prosser died?"

"From what I heard, his church burned down with him in it."

"Do you know why?"

"Heard it was an accident. Are you saying it wasn't?"

Anthony chewed his lip for a moment. "Now, let me tell *you* a story. A young woman came to him begging for help, wanting him to pray deliverance over her. He asked me to come help him, so of course, I did. I don't have your gifts, Deke, so I couldn't tell you if there really was an indwelling spirit or not. But let me tell you, it was some shit. Screaming, thrashing, throwing stuff. Took both of us to hold her down a couple of times, But at the end, she said she felt better. That whatever had been there was gone.

"Then, the next night, I found that I'd gotten a text message with a picture on my phone. I don't know why it didn't ding earlier to let me know, I always have it on, but this time it didn't. And by the time I saw it, it was already too late." He held up his phone with the photo in question. "Earlier that day, the morning *after* our supposedly successful deliverance, Grove found this outside his church. He was absolutely sure that the young woman we'd prayed over did it."

Elder looked at the photo. "Lord a'mighty," he whispered.

"Like I said, by the time I saw this, he'd already tried to pray deliverance over the girl again, the fire had started, and he was already dead."

Elder said, "Then I need to find the girl."

Anthony silently pointed at his church.

Elder's eyebrows rose. "That's her?"

Anthony nodded. "She started showing up here and has been a regular ever since. I don't mind telling you, it makes me nervous. There's plenty of people around here that'd be glad to use a white girl in a Black church as an excuse for something."

"There's plenty of people like that everywhere," Elder agreed. He let out a low whistle. "So that's her."

"When you met her, did you get anything from her?"

"No," Elder said honestly. "Not a whiff."

"And I haven't seen any sign of anything since she's been coming around." He paused. "What do you think Grove meant by 'He's still there, still attached to the girl'? If he means the demon, you'd smell it, wouldn't you?"

"Yes. It's usually so strong I can't ignore it."

Anthony met his eyes. "Then do you think that really was Grove Prosser speaking to you, then? Or just something yanking your chain?"

"I think it *might've* really been him. Like Second Corinthians says, 'Even Satan disguises himself as an angel of light,' and that might work both ways. If someone was in real danger, Grove would've found a way to get help, even if it meant going through the devil."

A car passed on the street, and for a moment, the pounding music drowned out their conversation. When they could hear again, Elder said, "Any idea what he meant by 'Dandelion'?"

"Not a clue."

After a moment, Elder said, "I really need to talk to the girl. She's at the center of all this."

The two men went inside. Carlyss looked up from driving in the last nail but said nothing. Elder began with, "You know, I think we had a mutual friend. Reverend Grove Prosser."

"Really?" Carlyss said. "He was a nice old man."

Elder leaned close and spoke quietly. "I, uh ... I know what he and Reverend Acred did for you."

"Do you?"

"Yes." He inhaled as discreetly and deeply as he could, trying to sense if anything hid within her.

She did not look away the way a normal teen might from a steady adult gaze. She studied him in detail, with a cool, distanced quality that seemed both too mature for her age and too alien to be entirely human. He got no sense of fear or any demonic presence still residing inside her. He assumed the trauma of the possession and exorcism had, quite reasonably, both aged and matured her. At last, she said, "I owe him my life. And my soul."

Was something there after all? A faint tinge, an aftertaste almost? He asked, "How have you been since then?"

She shrugged, suddenly like a typical teenager. "All right. Especially when I'm here."

"Any—"

"I don't want to talk about it with you. I don't even know you."

"That's fair enough. Can I get to know you, then?"

Her lips twisted in a half-smile, half-scowl. "That's creepy."

"Not like *that*."

"It never stopped you before." She said this simply, without looking away.

He blinked. How could she—? But with a great inner flare of insight, he understood that denial would be pointless. "What stops me is knowing the difference between right and wrong."

She paused and cocked her head as if listening to some other voice. Then she said, "Why are you really here?"

He nodded at Anthony. "Visiting a friend. Seeing how his church is coming along. He speaks highly of you."

"I do," Anthony agreed.

"That's kind of you," she said to him. To Elder, she added, "He lets me hang around even when no one else is here. He lets me help." She gazed up at the plain plaster ceiling as if it were the painted vault of a cathedral. "I like being closer to God. I can pray here."

"Why can't you pray anywhere else?"

"It's easier here."

Elder glanced back at Anthony. She wasn't still possessed, but *something* encircled her, swirling around but not quite connecting with her. He had missed it at first the same way you might not smell a litter box over too many scented candles. He'd never encountered anything like it before. "I'll be in town for a few days," he told her. "I do hope we see each other again."

"Whatever," she replied with teenage dismissiveness. To Anthony, she said, "I'm going to go reorganize all those old hymnals down in the basement if that's all right. Do you want them alphabetical or chronological?"

"Chronological," Anthony said. "I'll check on you before I leave, make sure I don't lock you in."

"That'd be okay, actually," she said, then slouched off toward the door at the back of the sanctuary.

When she was gone, Anthony said, "She told you more about herself than I've gotten out of her in months. What do you think?"

"I think something is still hovering around her. Grove was right; he drove it *out*, but not *away*."

AFTER ANTHONY and Elder went back outside, Carlyss returned to the empty sanctuary and knelt to pray again. But *it* was too busy yammering.

...and he'll bend you over the hood of his car and flip up that little black skirt you like to wear and show you what a woman's for. Would you like that?

"I think *you* would," Carlyss said. She did not look at the source of the voice.

Hey, I'm just making sure you remember I'm here. If you're good, he might give you that snakeskin jacket too.

"Shut up."

Just take me back, and we can enjoy it together. His big ol' dick up your tight little--

"Shut *up*. I mean it."

Or what?

She began to sing "Amazing Grace." The voice cried, *Oh, for fuck's sake,* and then was silent. When it became clear that she was going to sing the whole song, the voice said, *He's still coming for you, you know, and your fucking Jesus Karaoke won't stop him.*

Carlyss finished the song, then closed her eyes, clasped her hands, and recited the Lord's Prayer. For the rest of her time in the church that day, the voice did not return.

5

Travis Scote roared home, the Camaro's engine echoing down the empty streets filled with abandoned houses. Once this had been a thriving neighborhood of good white people, but now the few residents were Black or Hispanic, and to him, they watched with the predatory eyes of people who hated him just for the color of his skin. He saw no irony in this.

He took the long way past the TLC-Mart. He passed the big vacant lot where they kept threatening to build one of those new liberal inter-denominational churches, but so far nothing had been done. Now a bus had parked there, and people were setting up a big tent. A hand-painted sign announced a revival beginning Friday night.

Just as he saw the sign for the store itself, the latest commercial came on the radio.

> You always find Tender Loving Care
>   And the best prices anywhere
>   at TLC-Mart!

Then a male announcer said, "Show your support for the Second Amendment by stocking up on ammo during our Shootin' Summer

45

Sale in sporting goods, now through July 15th. Only at the TLC-Mart!"

Travis screeched to a stop on the street outside his mother's house. A car he didn't recognize was parked in the driveway.

He debated what to do next. He wished now he'd been quieter on his approach because all he wanted to do was slip into his apartment over the garage, put on his old, huge headphones, and get high. But now, he'd have to go in and say hello to whoever was visiting; otherwise, his mother would come up and scream at him.

He ran a hand through his hair and checked it in the rearview mirror. He straightened his t-shirt, fluttered the fabric loose where sweat had stuck it to his armpits, and walked up to the side door, whistling. When he opened it, he stopped dead.

His parole officer, Carla Norman, sat across from his mother at the kitchen table.

"Hello, Travis," Carla said blandly. "I was just catching up on things with your mother."

"Er...hi," Travis said, shifting his weight from one foot to the other.

Carla Norman was a Black woman in her forties, with a short afro that told Travis she was probably a bulldyke. She'd certainly seemed immune to his charm, which made her sexuality instantly suspect; he could sweet-talk any woman, Black or white, out of her panties, and if not, it had to be *their* fault, not his. She dressed all citified, and at their first meeting, she told him she'd relocated from Atlanta to be near her mother. He hated her, in large part because she scared the piss out of him.

"Sit down," Carla said and patted an empty chair.

He did so, spinning it on one leg so he could straddle it. He'd learned that trick when he was twelve; it really impressed the girls back then. "So...what brings you around?"

"I just told you," Carla said. "I haven't spoken to Dottie in a while. And I knew you'd be doing your community service at Reverend Acred's church, so it seemed like a good time." She looked at the time on her phone. "Well, you finished early, didn't you?"

"We, ah...ran out of nails," he blurted, realizing as he said it that the excuse was completely lame. "Uh, you know, the special kind you need for paneling."

Carla wasn't fazed. "Really? I'm going by the hardware store anyway, so I'll pick some up and drop them by the church."

"That'd be nice," Travis said. He began to perspire anew, despite the air conditioning.

"Why *are* you home?" his mother Dottie asked, her heavy dark brows drawing close over her nose.

"Like I said, we ran out of nails," he said.

"And Reverend Acred couldn't find anything else for you to do?"

"I mean...he just said...I couldn't...no!" Travis wanted to flee, but Carla watched him with such steadiness, he didn't dare.

Carla said, "Travis, I think if you go back, you'll find that Revered Acred has plenty of tasks that need doing. And if not, well, I know a place where they always need help making license plates."

"You see?" Dottie said, her voice rising to a screech. "You see, you're going to end up in jail, just like I always knew you would! Blanton is my only decent child! You're worthless, Travis, you always have been, and you always will be!"

"Dottie, please," Carla said. "There's no need for name calling; we're all adults here. Aren't we, Travis?"

"Yes, ma'am," he managed past his dry mouth.

"So, why don't you run on back to the church and see what you can help out with. I might come by later myself. You know, to drop off those paneling nails."

He dug his fingernails into his palms at her words. He knew she'd deliberately said "might," so that he couldn't skip out again and yet also couldn't count on her showing up. And *she* knew the uncertainty would chew on him all day. "Okay," he said and stood. He stopped at the door and turned back, suddenly realizing she wasn't leaving.

"Oh, I'm still talking to your mother," Carla said. "Dottie and I were just in the middle of something."

Dottie glared at her son, but he couldn't tell if she was mad at him for skipping out on his community service or for getting arrested and making her put up with having a Black woman in her house. He started to say something, thought better of it, and left.

He did not go back to the church, though. Instead, he drove out to the Old Hickory Bowling Center, where the Ten-Pin Lounge would be open. It was the only bar in town that catered to the third-shift workers at the local Hungerman plant, and sure enough, a half-dozen of them sat sullenly at the bar, drinking so that they'd be able to sleep when they went home.

He took the seat at the far end, away from the others. People who had normal jobs always made him feel inadequate, and he felt their stares as judgments on his own slacking. He motioned for Vinton, the bartender, and made a beer-drinking gesture. Vinton brought over a bottle and said, "You can pay for this, right?"

"Of course," Travis said, digging out a $5 bill he'd stolen from his mother's purse that morning before she woke up. He slapped it on the bar, then turned up the bottle and began chugging.

Vinton immediately took the money; Travis had tried the oh-I-already-paid-you trick on him before. "What's wrong with you? You're drinking like you've seen a ghost."

"Tell me, you ever have somebody come up and know more about you than they should?"

"What?"

"You know, you're talking to somebody, and they bring up something there's no way they could know about? Like they been watching you in secret?"

"What do you mean, like a psychic?"

"No, man, just—"

"You got one of them webcams, don't you? You shouldn't never jerk off when you got one of those. Or at least put a piece of tape over the lens."

"No!" Travis almost shouted. A couple of the other patrons turned to look at him. More quietly he said, "I met this girl, you see? And she knew stuff there ain't no way she could know. I mean, stuff that had to have happened when she was a fucking baby, maybe even before she was born, and I ain't never told *anyone*."

Vinton's eyes narrowed. "You're already drunk, ain't you?"

"No."

"Are you high?"

"No!"

"Whoa, take it easy, calm down. Maybe you're just—"

"Don't tell me I'm fucking imagining things!" he said, not shouting but still drawing attention.

"Well, then, maybe she's into witchcraft or something. All the girls are these days, thanks to that Harry Potter stuff."

"Yeah," Travis said, nodding. That explained everything. "Yeah, maybe you're right. Except ..."

"What?" Vinton said with an impatient sigh.

"Well ... it happened at church."

Vinton said, "Well, then, maybe God just hates you, Travis. You ever think about that?" And with that, he walked away.

Travis stared at the wood grain on the bar top. Vinton's words rang in his head. He knew most people didn't like him once they got to know him, which was why he constantly had to make new friends. But the idea that *God* might hate him...he believed in God, and his contingency plan was a deathbed conversion, a last-minute born-againing that would ensure his entry to heaven. After all, God forgave everyone who asked him, right? That was his *job*. But Travis hadn't been to church in so long he couldn't really recall how he knew that, and he'd certainly never read the actual Bible.

Fuck you, God, he thought. *Just fuck you.*

———

ELDER AND ANTHONY sat at a table in the McDonald's. The screech of children in the play area punctuated their words. Anthony occasionally waved to people he knew; as they passed, they stared, not at Anthony, but at Elder. The other minister cut such a strange, compelling figure that Anthony knew gossip was already spreading about him.

Anthony first met Elder in the Marines, longer ago than he cared to remember. Anthony had been a chaplain, while Elder, using his birth name then, had been one of those slick, good-looking types who always got away with things. When he heard Elder had become a minister, Anthony's first thought was, "lock up the collection plates and the preacher's daughters." Even now, Elder remained a contradiction: for all his womanizing ways, he was serious about helping people needing deliverance, and his gift of discernment was genuine.

"So," Anthony asked, "what did you think of Carlyss?"

Elder sipped his tea. "Interesting. Surprising."

"She's safe around you, right?"

"Come on, Anthony. I'm old enough to be her father, maybe her *grand*father if her folks got an early start."

"That's not an answer."

"*Yes*, she's safe around me. I'm here to help her, remember?"

"Thank you." Now it was Anthony's turn to sip his tea. "Sometimes I hear her talking when she thinks nobody's around. At first, I thought she was talking to herself, but then I realized she was talking to someone else. Somebody only she could hear. How does that match up with what you said earlier?"

"If something's still attached to her, she might be able to converse with it. It wouldn't have any real power except that."

"How did that happen, though?"

"What if you and Grove hadn't quite finished driving the demon away? What if you'd only gone through the pretense, the breakpoint, and the clash, but hadn't gotten all the way through the expulsion? What if you knocked the thing *out* of Carlyss but not *away* from her?"

Anthony's frown deepened. "That's something I've never seen or even heard of."

"Me, neither." Elder looked out through the window at the little patch of grass at the edge of the parking lot. It was green and vibrant despite the heat, no doubt due to the sprinklers that came on every few minutes. A collarless dog ran out of nowhere and began snapping at the sprays of water. "And what the hell is 'Dandelion?'"

Anthony looked at him closely. "You sound tired, my friend."

"I *am* tired, Anthony. I'm mostly hole, not much donut these days.

But I can't just walk away from this." He paused and drank some more tea. "If you'll put up with it, I'll hang around and get to know her a little better. Help y'all with the remodeling." Then he smiled. "Mind if I borrow your couch while I'm here?"

"Long as you don't desecrate it with your carryings-on." Both men laughed.

But even though he appeared to agree, Anthony wasn't sure about this at all. Despite his good intentions, Elder tended to leave chaos behind him, and what Anthony had seen the prior summer when he assisted Grove Prosser still gave him nightmares. He had no desire to ever experience any more of that.

———

AFTER WORK, Haven stopped at the TLC-Mart for a frozen pizza. The sight of all the shambling, blank-faced shoppers did nothing to lighten her mood. This was the only place in Somerton that was ever crowded, and she suddenly wondered, with all the closed and departed businesses in town, how all these people could afford to come here. Other than shop at the TLC-Mart, what did these people *do* all day?

"Haven," a man said behind her.

She turned, dread rising in her stomach. Landon Marks, the lawyer she'd gone out with the previous weekend, stood there. He carried a twelve-pack of Michelob and smiled with the certainty of someone who knew he'd be welcome.

"Hi, Landon," she said, trying to force her own smile.

"How are you?"

"I'm good. Tired."

"Listen, I meant to call you, but I was in court all day. I had a great time the other night, and I was hoping we could get together again."

Oh boy. She was too tired for this right now. "Look, Landon. It was fun, but I don't think there's any future to it, okay? We're both busy; we don't have time for a relationship."

"Who needs a relationship?" Landon said brightly. He clearly

51

thought he was being smooth and sophisticated, but it only made him look sleazy.

"I'm sorry, Landon, but no."

His smile gradually fell, and that masculine anger Haven knew so well rose in his eyes. Coldly, he said, "I guess you're just the whore everyone says you are, then."

Now Haven got angry. "Hey. I have just as much right to say no as I do to say yes, to whoever I want, whenever I want. You want to apply those outdated good-ole-boy standards, then go find a choir girl at the Baptist church."

His fury grew, and he opened his mouth to reply, but Haven was having none of it.

"*Fuck off*, Landon," she practically shouted. Heads turned toward them, and she added forcefully, "I mean it."

"Well, I guess there's some things even Ajax can't clean," he snapped, put down the beer, and stalked off toward the door.

When she got home, her fifteen-year-old son Troy was at the table working on his homework. She had no illusions that he'd been doing so any earlier than five minutes before she was scheduled to arrive, but she accepted the illusion for the truth. He was re-taking algebra in summer school, and it was no easier for him the second time around.

"Evening, Mom," he said. "Make any delinquents cry today?"

"Only you, if you don't watch that mouth," she teased as she put down her purse and briefcase. She stepped out of her shoes and sighed with relief.

"What's for dinner?" Troy asked.

"I got you a frozen pizza. You know where the oven is."

"I think that's called child abuse."

"You'd be wrong, but keep talking and you might end up right."

She changed into scrub pants and a faux-ancient Black Oak Arkansas T-shirt she'd bought on a whim at the TLC-Mart. As she took off her jewelry, she realized she could not recall a single Black Oak Arkansas song; they were just before her time, enough so that she was aware of them without actually knowing anything about them.

She'd have to remedy that; it seemed silly to wear a shirt from a band you didn't know.

She came back downstairs to find Troy packing his backpack. "I'm going over to Sam's to study," he said without looking up. "Be back at nine."

She didn't kid herself about what he was going to do; her experience with teen junkies made even the slightest presence of drugs in her son as plain as a black cat in the snow. But so far, he'd only tried marijuana, and she figured that was a battle she couldn't fight with a clear conscience since she had a small bag and a supply of rolling papers hidden between her mattress and box spring. "Be careful," she said as he went out the door into the sunset. "Wear a condom."

"Always am," he called back.

Alone in the house, she poured a glass of wine, sat at her kitchen table, did her best to put the unpleasant encounter with Landon out of her mind, and took out the file marked *Bolerjack, Carlyss Anne.*

Up until age fifteen, Carlyss's grades were fine, her conduct either very good or so far under the radar, it got no official notice. There was a succession of school pictures, all of a bright smile, eyes crinkled with delight.

The year she turned sixteen, though, was entirely different. The smile was replaced by a sullen slouch. Although she tried for anti-social belligerence, it felt more like a desperate attempt at defense.

But against what? The loss of her parents? That didn't jibe with what Haven knew about the family situation. Even before then, Carlyss had lived mostly with her grandparents. Those two elderly people provided her only consistency, and while they meant well, their age and health issues kept them on the periphery of the girl's life. Whatever had turned Carlyss Bolerjack from a sweet girl with a future to a teen about to go off the rails, she didn't think it was abuse at home.

It had to be the church.

How did this fairly normal girl become convinced she was possessed by a demon? And how had the elderly minister, the one who'd died in the fire, come into her life? The family wasn't Lutheran;

when they did go to church, which was seldom, they went to one of the Baptist churches, like most people in Somerton.

And there may have been no evidence of Carlyss starting the fire, but there was the photograph of the *thing* Carlyss had made, found on her own phone and somehow, miraculously, not leaked onto the internet. If it had, the girl might be even more ostracized than she was now. The actual item had burned in the fire, but the image was enough.

And the most compelling thing was that Carlyss had taken the picture as a selfie. She stood in the foreground, grinning, her tongue dangling insolently.

Haven held up a print of the photo, amazed anew by the incredible cruelty of what the girl had done. This was not the act of a bored teenager, one left alone by preoccupied caregivers to find her own moral compass from TV, the internet, and her friends. It was the act of someone proud of what they were doing. It was, in a sense, an artistic statement.

An artistic statement, she added, made of flesh, blood, and pain.

The girl had asked about evil. And here it was.

THAT NIGHT, Linda Scote got out of the shower and took down the towel she'd used to protect her hair. She was tired and irritable and ready for the day to be over. She walked to the mirror and was about to wipe the steam from it when she gasped.

Someone stood behind her.

The distorted reflection made it clear it was a man with dark hair and slender shoulders. His face was a blur, but his masculinity burned through with laser clarity. Except for the towel in her hand, she was naked; the miasma of vulnerability and excitement threatened to overwhelm her.

She turned. But of course, no one was there.

She made a little choking sound. Her feelings now had no way to express themselves, at least no way that seemed capable of channeling their awesomeness. Is this, she wondered, what real women felt when a man turned them on? Was she finally, at long last, growing up?

She sat on the closed toilet, sucking in the damp air, letting the sensations tremble their way through her. She knew who she'd seen, of course: the ghost of Jesse Garon Presley, dead twin of Elvis, as beautiful and sexy as the King but all hers. All *hers*. Her hands began to roam over her body.

Then she remembered the Ouija board.

Without dressing, she locked her bedroom door, made sure the blinds were closed, and turned off everything but the little reading lamp over her bed. Outside the window, lightning bugs fluttered across the lawn, and a crescent moon hung low in the sky. As usual, her mother was watching one of the *Real Housewives* shows, and her dad was drinking beer and cleaning his guns. He must, she thought, have the cleanest guns in Tennessee, because from the time he finished dinner to whenever he went to bed, he was in the basement with them.

She pulled the Ouija board from the closet where she'd hidden it and opened it with religious reverence. She placed the board on the bed, then carefully lifted the planchette. Just touching the white plastic sent a shiver through her.

She put her fingers on the plastic, took a deep breath, and whispered softly, "Jesse Garon? Are you there?"

The planchette twitched beneath her fingertips. She waited, holding her breath. At last, it slid to the word, YES.

She felt the same rush of emotion she'd once felt about her first boyfriend, Terry. "Do you have a message for me?" she sighed.

Again, it replied, YES.

"What?" she said, almost shouting it.

And then an image popped into her head. It was something so outlandish, so far from anything she'd usually think about, that she had no doubt it came from the ghost. It was so simple in its beauty that she held it at the front of her consciousness the way an art student might absorb the Mona Lisa. She knew with certainty that not only could she create it, she *had* to. It would be the first monument to her new spirit friend.

"Oh, I can *do* this," she whispered.

The planchette moved again. YES.

CARLYSS SAT on the edge of the old railroad bridge, her feet dangling over the chasm, the stars shining above her. The bridge remained, although the tracks had long since been removed, leaving an over-grown two-mile stretch of old tar-stained wooden crossties extending from either end. Below, she saw a small fire, where some of the older kids, the ones out of high school but not really suited for college, drank beer and smoked dope. She knew some of them and could probably have joined them. But she did not want to be tempted.

Instead, she watched the glow of the TLC-Mart above the neighborhood that lay between the railroad and the store. She wondered how the people who lived in its shadow—or rather, its halo—slept with that constant, artificial glow. It never went away: they would never again experience the true dark of night, see the stars or even the moon unless it was particularly bright and full. They lived in a perpetual artificial twilight, hiding behind expensive window shades and blackout curtains. Or they moved.

Mosquitoes were drawn to that light as well, along with all the moths and other night-flying insects. Bats swooped around the lamp posts, diving out of the darkness to snatch their confused and disoriented prey. At the edges of the parking lot, great toads lurked in the grass for the same reason, their tongues snagging crickets and other creatures that, although they didn't fly, were still drawn to the light.

Beautiful, isn't it? the voice said. And she felt the presence beside her; for an instant, she glimpsed its own misshapen feet dangling off the edge at the corner of her eye.

She did not turn for a better look. "Shut up," she said quietly. "It's hideous."

But it makes so many people happy.

"It's killing the town. It's killing the people. It makes them hateful and selfish."

That's the same thing as happiness.

"Maybe where you're from." She took a deep breath. "I'm not talking to you."

Yes, you are, it mocked. *And you need me. If I hadn't told you what that Travis boy had hidden in his soul, he'd never stop pestering you.*

"I didn't ask you for it."

But you used it just the same.

She said nothing else. She knew better than to engage the voice. It had no power that she didn't willingly give it.

She stood and walked along the ties across the bridge. She smelled the fire, and above that, the sweet smell of pot. The humid night made the black shirt cling to her skin, and she closed her eyes, feeling her way with her toes. She knew that if she got off course, she might tumble sixty feet, landing in the middle of the stoners' party. That would sober them up.

But she sensed the solid ground around her after a bit and opened her eyes to see that she'd successfully crossed the bridge. The empty track stretched ahead into the night.

6

Nicely done," Anthony said the next morning as he examined the installed paneling. "Don't you think?"

"Good job," Bernard Jones agreed. Bernard was Black, middle-aged, and part of Anthony's congregation. He was also the only Black police officer in town and seemed like a good one to call after Travis fled in such a hurry the previous day. He could put the fear of God into Travis without involving his parole officer; Anthony hated to imagine anyone in the Tiptonville prison, even Travis.

Carlyss smiled shyly at the praise. She'd used more nails that were actually needed, but the new section was flat and smooth, and the seams between it and the older panels were pretty well hidden. If no one looked too close, they'd never see the row of nails that, like rivets, ran up the edge.

"Why don't you go get a drink and one of those donuts in the kitchen," Anthony said, "then I'll take you to McDonald's for lunch."

"Okay," Carlyss said. "But I'm not tired."

"Oh, I've got plenty of work for you," Anthony said. "Right now, I need to chit-chat with Bernard to get out of some parking tickets."

They both chuckled. In middle age, both had settled into careers that let them help others, and they kept in touch to keep each other from growing cynical about the world. Most days, it worked. Some days, not so much.

After Carlyss left them in the sanctuary, Bernard said, "She's still on probation, ain't she?"

"Technically. But as long as she sees her therapist twice a week and stays out of trouble, she'll be fine. And she can't get into any trouble here."

"Unless that damn Scote boy's around."

Anthony chuckled. "She's got *his* number. I don't know what she said to him, but he lit out of here like he'd seen a ghost."

"Well, I'll stop him next time I see him driving that damn Camaro around and give him a warning." He paused. "She should be with her friends, though, shouldn't she? That Bolerjack girl, I mean. And I know what them long sleeves are hiding. Girl wears long sleeves in this weather, it's to hide that she's been cutting herself."

"I don't ask her about it," Anthony said honestly. "I want her to feel safe here."

Bernard nodded. Then he said, "Who's that other car belong to out there? The old Nova?"

"Friend of mine who's staying with me for a while. Another preacher."

"Doing that tent revival?"

"No, nothing like that. Just visiting."

"The tags are expired."

"Well, you can write him a ticket if you want, but I'll be the one who ends up paying it."

"You need a better class of friend, Reverend."

"Don't I know it, Officer."

———

CARLYSS STOOD by the door in the church's tiny kitchen. She knew Anthony and the policeman were talking about her. *The cop thinks you're pretty. He's got handcuffs, you know. You'd like that.*

She ignored the voice, took a donut from the open box, and gazed at the old, faded picture of Christ on the wall. Jesus had luxurious, wavy hair, a sharp nose, and a cleft in his full beard. He gazed slightly upward with his dark eyes as if caught in the middle of looking at God.

Her grandparents had the same picture in their house, on the wall beside the fireplace, and it was just as faded and worn. It had become her mental image of Christ, despite now knowing that, as a Middle Eastern Jew, he likely had dark skin, curly black hair, and a prominent nose. After all, if God could appear as one man, why couldn't he appear as any man?

This anthropologically incorrect Jesus also had the quality she'd come to associate with Christ more than any other: kindness. There was nothing overtly masculine—or, for that matter, feminine—in his demeanor. Just a gentle acceptance of people as they were, flaws and all.

She wished she could believe that this Jesus, if he met her on the street, would accept and love her as well. She fantasized about being enveloped in his arms, feeling the texture of his robes against her, of putting her face to his chest. He'd be a thin man, ascetic, and she'd be able to feel his ribs through his clothes and hear his heart beating in his chest.

But she knew that what hovered near her forever kept her from that embrace. All she could do was try to keep it from hurting anyone else again, show it that her love for God was greater than its hate for him.

She fervently hoped that was true.

———

LINDA SCOTE TOSSED on her bed. She had dozed off after lunch, and in her dreams, she was being touched and fondled in ways that both scared and excited her.

She awakened to the sound of a baby softly crying. She sat up, still half-asleep, and tried to make sense of it. There was no baby in the house unless one was visiting, but this one sounded as if it was right there in the room. She looked around until she noticed one of her American Girl dolls had fallen to the floor.

Saige lay on her back, in a shaft of sunlight that peeked through the drawn curtains and cut a dust-lined slice through the room. Linda knelt beside the doll and stared at the little plastic face. She shook her head twice to clear it, convinced that she couldn't be interpreting what she saw correctly.

Yet no matter what, the image remained. Tears welled in Saige's plastic eyes and trickled down those manufactured cheeks.

This was not a doll designed to cry. This was a doll purposefully created to give white suburban girls a harmless role model. Yet as Linda gazed down at it, fresh tears bubbled from its eyes, and the soft crying continued.

"Jesus Christ," Linda muttered.

And the sound stopped. The tears evaporated.

Linda carefully picked up the doll. Had it only been two or three years ago that she'd taken this elaborate plaything so seriously? She placed Saige back on the shelf with her other remaining dolls and, for an instant, remembered the happy feelings associated with them. She smiled all the time then, something she seldom did now.

Her head grew woozy again, and she stumbled back to the bed. In moments she was again asleep, and when she awoke, she would be convinced that this whole thing had been a mere dream inspired by the heat and humidity.

THAT EVENING AFTER WORK, Haven Fields stopped at the coffee shop that had just opened near the public library. It was a real gesture of faith, opening a place like this in downtown Somerton, where half the businesses were closed and the rest were junk stores labeled as "antique malls." It was a quiet little place, decorated with taste and style and filled with gentle decor and soothing music. When she entered, she jostled the wind chimes over the door. The low sun bathed the place in amber light.

Three couples sat sipping their drinks, but at one table sat a lone Black woman tapping on her iPhone. Haven took the seat across from her and said, "Hi, Carla."

Carla Normand looked up over her half-glasses. Her ferocious intelligence blazed out of her eyes. "You're late."

"No, I'm not," Haven said.

Carla checked the time on her phone. "Oh, I guess you're not. I'm not used to people being on time."

"That's because they're so frightened of you they wait until the last minute and then some."

The Black woman smiled. She didn't do that often, but Haven could always get it out of her. "If they're not frightened of me, then I'm not doing it right. Yesterday I scared the shit out of some dumb redneck who still lives with his mother. So, what can I do for you?"

"I need some off-the-record advice. Do you remember last summer when the Lutheran Church burned down?"

"Of course. The minister was killed, right?"

"That's right. But there's things that didn't make the paper." She leaned closer. "He died in the middle of praying deliverance over someone."

"What's that?"

"Basically, it's a Protestant exorcism."

Carla's eyes slowly widened to show her surprise. "Really?" she said, her voice heavy with a mix of sarcasm and doubt. "People believe in that here."

"Yes, but that's not the important issue. When the firemen got there, they found my client beside the body, inside what they called a ring of fire. No Johnny Cash comments, please. They determined that the only way she could've gotten there is if she'd set the fire herself, even though they never found any actual proof. That's what she's on probation for, and that's why she's my client."

"I can certainly see why she'd need psychological treatment," Carla said.

"I've been seeing her for a year. I haven't done her any good. She won't open up to me. She'll talk if I ask her questions, but she's an expert in going in circles without revealing anything."

"She'd be set for politics if she didn't already have a record."

"I'm serious. I'm thinking of doing something...rash. To get through to her. To crack that shell."

"What did you have in mind?"

Haven hesitated. "This is just between us, right? If you repeat it, I'll deny it."

"Of course. You've seen me do drunken karaoke; I don't have the high ground."

Haven smiled a little. She sipped her coffee, then said, "I'm thinking about staging another exorcism."

Carla's eyes widened again. "Really."

"My client may believe she's still possessed, or invaded, or whatever the Lutherans call it. After all, the exorcist died in the middle of the show."

"I don't think they call it a 'show.'"

"Well, whatever. Ceremony, then. If we can complete it in a controlled situation like my office, then it might convince her to open up to me and let me help her."

"It's theatrics, Haven," Carla said with disdain.

"Of course, it is. I know that. But otherwise, I'm looking at another eighteen months of not doing her any good at all. Then she ages out."

Carla took her time before speaking. "Are you planning, then, to use a real priest? Or someone acting as one?"

"I hadn't thought it out that far yet."

"I don't know that you'd find a real priest or minister willing to conduct a phony ceremony for you."

"In that case, maybe I'll see if the community theater can recommend somebody." She meant it as a joke, but Carla didn't smile. "You don't like the idea?"

"No, I don't like the idea. It's playing with someone's deeply held beliefs."

"Do you have a better idea, then?"

"No," Carla said. "But I really think you should take a deep breath before you bring in the amateur theatrics. This girl, and I assume her family, clearly believes in some basic Fundamentalist things: the existence of the devil, the reality of demons, and the power of the Lord to drive them out. You risk destroying all that, and I don't know what might fill the space once it's all gone."

Haven nodded. This sort of insight was the reason she sought Carla's advice in the first place.

"On the other hand, it might work. If the girl believes it."

"What should I do, then?"

Carla chuckled. "Proceed with caution."

They chatted about nothing for a few more minutes, and then Carla departed. Haven remained, drinking her coffee and pondering her friend's words. Then she realized that, when she thought she'd been staring at nothing, she'd actually been gazing at a flyer tacked to the community bulletin board. The paper showed a picture of a circus-like tent surrounded by cars and trucks. Across the top, in huge letters, was the word REVIVAL.

CARLYSS WISHED SHE HAD A BIKE.

Truly, she wished she had a driver's license. She was old enough now, but her...*history* kept her off the streets. She had to get a form signed by both her doctor and her therapist saying she was ready before she could even take driver's ed in school.

Still, a bike would be so much faster to get around town, especially on a hot summer evening like this, when the humidity was through the roof, and no breeze stirred the syrupy air. Her black blouse clung to her, making her claustrophobic, and she could smell her own sockless feet in the old tennis shoes she wore.

Even the shade under the heavy trees was no relief. She realized she'd have to either go somewhere like a store or the bowling alley or back home if she wanted to get out of the heat. There was always the TLC-Mart; it would take half an hour to walk there, but it would definitely be cool inside. Cold as a frosted frog, in fact. Her grandmother always wore a sweater when she shopped there, no matter what time of year.

A car passed her on the street, music thumping from its cool interior. She saw two girls turn to look at her from the back seat. She didn't recognize them, but she envied them just the same: they were friends, they could *have* friends. But her envy was as wilted as everything else in this heat. Why would anyone be friends with her? They all could tell just by looking. She was certain of that. Even if they couldn't put a name to it, even if they thought they didn't believe in such things, they could tell. So, she really didn't expect anyone to be her friend.

She leaned on a stop sign pole and waited for traffic to clear so she could cross the street. A convenience store waited two blocks down; that would do for now. She had enough change for a Coke, and if she bought something, they wouldn't care if she spent an hour looking at magazines.

What she didn't expect, though, was the boy doing the exact same thing.

She knew him in passing: Jason Stein. His family had moved to town three years earlier when his father was transferred in to work at the Hungerman artificial flavoring plant. He was shorter than Carlyss, stocky and soft, but with kind eyes that his deliberately long bangs did their best to hide. He glanced up at Carlyss, blushed, and quickly put the issue of *Maxim* back on the shelf. He took down a gaming magazine instead.

Carlyss got a Sprite from the cooler; Coke was just too heavy for such a hot day. The clerk, a middle-aged man who barely looked at her, said, "Thanks," without moving his lips.

Carlyss went over to the magazine rack and said, "Hey, Jason."

"Hey," he said without looking up from the magazine.

She took down the latest *Rolling Stone.* Her grandfather had a box of ancient issues, printed on the same type of paper as the local newspaper. When she looked through those, it seemed that she was seeing into a special world of giants and magic, where musicians were different from regular people. The current incarnation looked like the women's magazines her grandmother read.

She snuck a glimpse at Jason. He wasn't actually reading; he was thinking about her. She needed no special insight to know that. "How's your summer going?" she asked.

"All right," he said. "Kind of boring. I'm supposed to go to camp in a week. Not looking forward to it."

"What kind of camp?"

"Computer camp."

They both fell silent for a moment. Jason was a sweet, innocent boy who wanted her in the way only a virgin could want a girl: with desire but no knowledge of expression. Oh, sure, he knew what went where, but he'd never experienced it like she had and had no idea what could be unleashed by it. She knew all this with the same certainty she knew that the man Travis was evil. Only in this case, the voice wasn't also shouting out the particulars.

"What else have you been doing all summer?"

He snorted. "Getting beat up."

"Seriously? Who beats you up?"

He started to reply, then looked down. "Nobody."

"Somebody," she insisted.

"Danny Blazer," he said. "Mostly."

"Why does he do it?"

"'Cause he can." He slipped into a heavy drawl. "'Cuz there ain't nothin' good on TV,' that's what he says."

"I'm sorry."

"Me, too." He put away his magazine. "Well...nice seeing you."

"You, too, Jason." She watched him bump into the *Free Shopper* rack on the way out. The last glimpse she had of him was of the back of his neck turning bright red.

He'll never love you, the voice assured her. *No one will. And if they do, they'll burn for it. Just like you will.*

She looked around sharply, in time to see it...*him*...duck out of sight at the end of the candy display. She'd never seen him whole, all at once, just parts of him at a time. Just now, she'd glimpsed his face and one side of his torso, along with a single foot.

His head was too small and rose to a peak with a tuft of hair at the very top. His eyes were small but always open wide, as if perpetually startled. His nose was merely a bulbous blob, and his rubbery lips often formed an expression she was unable to match to any emotion. His skin was a strange color, a high-pink tone that she'd never seen in nature. She knew he wore clothes, but she could never remember what they were. Even now, moments after catching sight of him, she couldn't recall anything about, say, his shoes, only that his feet were as narrow and pointed as his head.

But this was all he could do now: whisper, chide, mock, and hide. He couldn't make her do anything, undress or piss on herself or offer herself to men or any of the things he did before. He was just a voice now, and a presence. But that, she realized, might be plenty.

7

The next morning, Friday, Deacon Elder walked out of a different convenience store with a fresh pack of cigarettes. As he started to light up, he paused to read a flyer tacked to a telephone pole outside.

Come hear the man of God preach! read the banner across the top. *World-famous Brother Knode brings you the Word! Signs and wonders will follow those who believe! An 'ole-fashion' gospel revival!*

In smaller print, it declared, *Devils driven out! Disease and mental struggles cured! Prayer tent available!*

"Devils driven out," Elder murmured to himself. The hairs on the back of his neck stood up, and he caught the faint but unmistakable whiff of brimstone mixed with bullshit.

ELDER PARKED his Nova at the end of a row of large, shiny SUVs. The revival tent rippled in the slight wind. It was a dingy brown color in the daylight, but Elder knew that with lights, music, and a charismatic preacher, after dark it would be as lively as a state fair.

He looked at the plates on the SUVs. They were from Alabama

and read KNODE1, 2, and so forth. This was a level of minister he tried never to associate with, the ones who combined preaching the gospel with the showmanship of professional wrestling. They drew immense crowds, sent thousands away thinking they'd been saved, and hardly ever effected an actual conversion. Like many preachers throughout history, they were all about the collection plates. And most of them drove the fanciest vehicles, just like the ones in front of him.

Elder paused under the tent to let his eyes adjust to the shadowed interior. There was already a stage set up and rows of folding chairs on the grass. A dog rushed up and jumped on him, lapping furiously at his hand. Elder scratched the animal behind the ears, which made it whimper in delight.

By then, he could make out the people working around the stage. Most seemed to be local teenagers; with desperate adults filling the jobs teens used to get at groceries, fast food restaurants, and other seasonal businesses, kids like these were plentiful and worked cheap.

Supervising them was a tall man in cargo shorts and an Ole Miss t-shirt. He had a pompadour and sideburns and dangled a cigarette from the corner of his lips. He seemed to enjoy directing the boys and made them laugh with his comments.

Elder cleared his throat and said, "Excuse me, sir. I'm guessing you're Brother Knode?"

The man offered his hand. "That's me, son. Don't believe I've had the pleasure."

"Deacon Elder," he said, and they shook hands. Both had firm, bone-crushing grips. Both noticed.

"You're a deacon, eh?" Knode said. "What church?"

"No, sir, that's my name. You can call me Deke."

"Pleasure to meet you, Deke. Have you received Christ as your personal savior?"

"That I have, praise the Lord."

"Well, praise the Lord, indeed." He turned to the boys. "Y'all watch those clasps between the stage sections. Get your hand caught in one, you'll lose a finger." To Elder he said, "What can I do for you, son?"

"I was wondering if you prayed deliverance over people in your service?"

"We do indeed. We try to help anyone who needs to find his way to Jesus. Do you know someone who might need it? You yourself, perhaps?"

If he was asking seriously, Elder knew, it meant he had no gift of discernment. If it was a trick, a verbal trap to get Elder to give something away, it was smarter, but Elder still wouldn't fall for it. "I pray every day for Jesus to keep the devil at bay, and so far, he's seen fit to do so."

"That's a blessing."

"It sure is."

"So, if you don't mind my cutting to the chase, what *can* I do for you? I've got a lot to get ready before tonight."

"Well, I get asked about deliverances and such a fair bit. I just wanted to make sure if anybody asks about you, I know what's what."

"You tell them folks, whoever they are—Black, white, speckled, striped—that the Lord is here for everyone, and so am I."

"That's good to know, Brother Knode. Look forward to your preaching."

The men shook hands again, and Elder strode back the length of the tent, down the central aisle. He knew Knode watched him and was careful to keep his shoulders down and his head low. Body language was a skill every preacher should know, and he wanted Knode to underestimate him. He didn't know *why* yet, but he was sure.

Just as he reached the edge of the tent and was about to step into the sun, another car parked beside his. A woman got out, dressed in a dark skirt and a professional jacket and blouse. She wore sunglasses, and her hair was pulled back from her face. She strode with the businesslike purpose of a lawyer or process server, two types Elder knew better than he wanted to. But there was something about her that held his attention.

Elder waited until she reached the tent. She said, "Hello. I'm looking for the minister."

"I'm *a* minister," Elder said. "Will I do?"

"I'm Haven Fields. I'm with the state, and I need to talk to Brother Knode privately."

"About what?"

She smiled. She was quite attractive when she did that. "Something private."

"I assure you, I can keep secrets."

Her smile broadened, and he saw a flicker of interest. "I'll bet you can. But I'd still like to talk to your boss."

"My boss lives up there," he said, pointing at the sky.

She sighed, amusement and annoyance battling for supremacy. "You're funny, Reverend...?"

"Elder."

"But I have limited time, and I need to stay on task."

"Then you should probably catch up with Brother Knode. This is his dog and pony show, and you'll find him down there setting up the stage. You can't miss him: he's got the tallest hair in the tent."

That made her chuckle. "Thank you."

She walked past him down the aisle. He watched her until she turned and glanced back to see if he was watching.

He smiled. So did she.

———

HAVEN WONDERED who that handsome man really was; he certainly didn't look at her the way a minister should. But she put it out of her mind and focused on the reason she was there. The more she pondered her therapy idea for Carlyss, the more she liked it. An exorcism ceremony, even a pretend one, might shake the girl loose from the sense that she was still "possessed." At worse, Carlyss would see right through it, and it would do no harm.

"Excuse me," she said. "Are you Brother Knode?"

The man said, "Yes, indeed, ma'am. What may I do for you?"

"I'd like to speak to you in private, if I may."

"Certainly. Follow me. Boys, just keep working. If you have any questions, save them until I get back." Before Haven and Knode had reached the back of the tent, the boys were all sitting on the half-completed stage, checking their phones.

In the shadowy corner where more chairs were stacked, Knode asked with practiced concern, "Now, what seems to be the problem?"

Haven handed him a card. "I won't beat around the bush. I have a patient who believes she was once possessed by a demon. She's Protestant, not Catholic. Another minister attempted to exorcise her, but he failed to complete the ritual for personal reasons. That makes my client believe he was unsuccessful. I wondered if you might agree to come to my office and perform the ritual again for her."

Knode's slightly aloof attitude turned serious. "You don't believe in demons, do you?"

"I don't believe this girl is possessed by one, no."

"That wasn't what I asked. The devil counts on disbelief. What better camouflage can there be?"

Haven had a prepared response for this, developed over years of caring for people with religious fixations. "I'm a Christian, Brother Knode, and I believe the Bible. Not literally, but as revealed truth. Jesus cast out demons, and so did his apostles. I wasn't there to see what happened, but I also know that mental illness can look a lot like demonic possession. Does that answer your question?"

"You're telling me the girl believes she has a demon, and you think that if I put on a flashy show, she'll either believe it's gone for good or see it for the nonsense it is."

Haven hoped the shadowy tent hid her blush. "Well...yes, actually, that's it."

"What if it turns out to be a real possession?"

She smiled wryly. "I'm willing to take that chance."

"Because you think it's impossible."

"I think it's unlikely in the extreme, we'll say."

Knode rubbed his chin thoughtfully. "I can do that. My powers are from the Lord, to aid in the care of his creation. But it costs a lot of money to get a tent this size dry cleaned. What can the collection plate expect from this?"

"You want me to *pay* you?"

"If you called in a throat specialist or a cancer doctor, they'd get paid, wouldn't they? I assure you, I am a poor man, Ms. Fields, because I am a river to my people."

She waited for a smile to break through the false sincerity, but it never did. At last, she said, "I get $120 an hour for treating her. For that hour, I'll pay you what I would make."

"And if it takes longer than an hour?"

"My sessions always end on time." She stuck out her hand.

He smiled shrewdly and bent over her hand to kiss it. She fought the urge to yank her hand away. He said, "We have a deal. Let's talk particulars. When do you want me to do this?"

"Monday would be ideal. My client has a regular appointment."

"That sounds agreeable. I'll be done here after the weekend."

"And this has to be discreet. As I said, I work for the state, and I don't need the ACLU hassling me about bringing in religion."

"Oh, I assure you, I'm totally discreet."

"Right. Just so we're clear, by 'discreet' I mean no shouting, no throwing the furniture around, and no slamming people to the floor."

"That's entirely the devil's doing, not mine."

"I'll take that up with the devil, then, if he shows up."

"And I have one requirement for you as well. The possessed cannot know that we're going to be there."

"I wasn't planning to tell her."

"Good. Because the devil forewarned is the devil forearmed."

"Doesn't the devil automatically know everything? Just like God does?"

He frowned. "You're puzzling me, ma'am. You don't seem to be taking this seriously at all, and yet it's all your idea."

"I take my patients very seriously, Reverend, I assure you."

"And I take my job seriously too. I'll see you at the appointed place, then."

───────

CARLYSS STOPPED as she realized she'd gotten close to the TLC-Mart.

The new sidewalk went past vacant lots stripped of all trees, and thus with no shade. The plan had been for more new businesses to sprout up, mushroom-like, in the shadow of the vast new big-box store, but the economic "downturn," as the people on TV called it, had stopped that. One parcel of land had gotten as far as installing concrete outer walls for a strip mall, but the company went broke, and they now stood roofless and empty, like the great Glastonbury Abbey she'd seen in pictures on the internet.

And so, hot, tired, and with nowhere else to go, she went home.

The street she lived on with her grandparents had once been a residential neighborhood, where everyone knew each other, the kids were all welcome in anyone's house, and on holidays there were mass cookouts in the middle of the blocked-off street. Or so her grandparents told her.

Now a third of the houses were empty, and the people who lived in the others kept to themselves, being seen only when they left for work or mowed their lawns. Fences separated many of them as well, eliminating the great collective backyard that children once roamed. In the blazing sun, it all looked faded, like the houses in Florida where her grandparents kept saying they were going to move each winter. She knew they never would.

They hate you, the voice said. *They wish they'd never taken you in. They only did it to try to hang on to the memory of your mother, and you're nothing like her.*

Her grandfather sat in the garage in an undershirt and khaki shorts, smoking. He refused to smoke in his own house, but he also refused to quit, just as he never admitted he was wrong or changed his mind on anything. Carlyss knew he loved her, but it was a small, bitter love that was only slightly different from selfishness. The voice was actually right about that: he loved her because she was the last tangible connection to his dead daughter.

"How's it going?" he drawled, smoke puffing from his mouth with his words.

"Okay," she said. She just wanted to go inside but stopping to talk to her grandfather was part of their shared ritual.

"Where you been?" he asked with no inflection. It was not ominous or threatening; her grandfather just liked to pretend he was a disaffected alpha male when she and everyone else knew just how weak and beta he was in a real crisis.

"Helping at the church," she said.

"That old trashy Methodist church?"

"Hopefully, it won't stay trashy with all the work we're doing."

"Do you get paid, at least?"

"I don't want to get paid. I just want to help out."

"That's foolish. They'll take advantage of you. They're trying to get something for nothing, just like everyone."

"Not everyone, Grandpa. Some people really do want to help others."

"You just wait, you'll realize it one day that all these people you think are so wonderful are just out to get something from you."

"I'll keep my eyes open," she promised. Then, having done her part by letting her grandfather tell her how wrong she was, she kissed his cheek and went inside.

As always, the TV was turned to Fox News. No one was watching it, but it was a constant presence in the background, spreading its influence like sticky filaments of black bile. Oddly, the voice never spoke when she was actively listening to it, and she'd finally realized because nothing it said to her could possibly contain as much hate as what the talking heads on TV spewed forth.

The air conditioning made the sweat on her skin turn suddenly cold, and she shivered as she got a Coke from the refrigerator. Her grandmother was napping, as she always did this time of day, her body worn out from cancer and a lifetime of hard work and bad relationships. She hadn't married Carlyss's grandfather until she was 45, after two other marriages that had involved drinking, drug abuse, and physical violence.

Carlyss slipped quietly into her room, then closed and locked the door. She put in her earbuds, turned on the music on her phone, and crawled under the covers of her bed. Sleep would never come, of course, but if she was lucky, the music—the bouncy, optimistic music of the Beatles—would keep the voice at bay long enough for her to drift into a kind of liminal state where her body, at least, could rest. She draped an old t-shirt over her eyes, enjoying its silken touch and cold presence.

Because Carlyss had not exaggerated: ever since the exorcism that had only partially worked last year, she had not slept at all.

8

A re you supposed to have your parents' car?" Bethany asked, clutching nervously at the oh-shit handle above the door. The sun blazed off the back window of the car in front of them, making her wonder how Linda wasn't blinded by it.

Linda snorted. "I got my license; what are you worried about?"

"Well, you had a wreck the very first time you backed out of your own driveway by yourself."

"Hey, Mr. Lippin should've been paying more attention; that was *not* my fault. His damn car's as big as a battleship anyway. Besides, old people shouldn't be allowed to drive if they can't see someone coming out of a driveway."

Bethany said nothing. Linda never took responsibility for anything, so it wasn't a surprise, but her vehemence was new, as was the level of contempt she seemed to have for everyone lately. Bethany was so startled when Linda invited her to go to the TLC-Mart that she accepted without really thinking about it. Now she wished she hadn't.

The radio, moments earlier blasting the latest auto-tuned hit song, suddenly bleated:

You always find Tender Loving Care
And the best prices anywhere
at TLC-Mart!

A woman's voice practically purred, "Ladies, get ready for those revealing summer fashions with our Smooth as Glass home waxing kit, now on sale for only $29.95. Everything you need to be set for swimsuits, shorts, or skirts. Only at TLC-Mart!"

Bethany didn't like the store, especially on Saturday when it was always packed. It stayed too chilly even in the summer, she could never find what she wanted, and the shoppers seemed dead-eyed and sedated, like the Alzheimer's patients in her grandmother's nursing home. She'd been knocked down by an old lady in a motorized cart, who had neither stopped nor apologized. But she also felt obligated to hang out with Linda, who was the closest thing to a cool friend she had. Now, though, she began to wonder if "cool" was a worthwhile quality.

Bethany saw the huge tent set up in the field near the abandoned strip mall. She didn't need to see the REVIVAL sign to know what it was; when she was little, her aunt and uncle would take her to every revival that came through. Her memories were of sweat, screaming, and people flopping on the ground when they were "slain in the spirit." She was glad she was old enough to no longer need them to babysit her. "Anyone you know going to that revival?" she asked.

Instead of answering, Linda abruptly changed from the right lane into the left. The car she cut off blared on its horn. Linda screamed—not shouted or yelled, but screamed—*"Fuck you!"* and flipped off the driver.

"What the hell did you do that for?" Bethany cried, grabbing the oh-shit handle with both hands now.

"Shut up," Linda snarled.

Bethany stared at her friend. It seemed for all the world that Linda had changed lanes to get as far away from the revival tent as possible. It seemed even more like that when, once they were past the tent, she swerved back into the right lane.

"How come it's so hot?" Bethany said, drawing out the last word into an extended, multisyllabic whine.

"Because it's summer in Tennessee," Linda said cheerfully.

"Look at you. You ain't even sweating. How come?"

"Because I'm the coolest person you know," Linda shot back.

The TLC-Mart parking lot was packed, and they'd parked near the far end of a row, so their approach looked as long as a jet's landing strip. Other cars crept past, seeking closer parking spaces without luck.

"Danny Blazer has been tomcatting around me," Linda said out of the blue. "What do you think about that?"

"He's very cute," Bethany said, unable to keep the sadness from her voice. No boys ever noticed her.

"He is that, all right. He thinks he's got what it takes to get in my pants too. Think I should let him?"

Bethany looked sharply at her friend. Linda talked a big game, but Bethany knew she'd never done much of anything, and this was no doubt just her latest bluff. But there was a new quality in her voice as she said it that made Bethany say, "You know once he does, he won't want nothing to do with you."

"He might. If I'm really good at it," Linda said with a lascivious smile.

"Don't talk like that," Bethany mumbled. Linda laughed.

As they passed the final corral for the shopping carts, Linda stopped. "Look!" she said. Between the corral and the first of the handicapped spots, there was an open parking place.

"Wish we'd seen that," Bethany said, blinking sweat from her eyes.

"I'm gonna bring my car down here," Linda said. "You stay here and save it for me."

"But—" Bethany started to protest.

"Just stay here!" Linda said and walked quickly away.

Bethany sighed and took up her position. There was an extra-tall van in the handicapped spot, one of those that had a small elevator for getting wheelchair-bound people in and out. It cast a shadow, so Bethany moved gratefully into it. She hoped with all her might that no one drove up to challenge her, because she wasn't sure which she feared most: the wrath of a stranger or Linda's scowling disapproval. Again, she wondered why she stayed friends with a girl who so clearly had nothing but contempt for her.

Then the hairs on the back of her neck stood up, and she turned.

Directly behind her stood a young man, handsome and dark-haired, with a sly smile. He also looked completely familiar. Later she would not be able to remember what he actually looked like, or what kind of clothes he wore, but his presence startled her so much she gasped.

She was staring at him, not watching for Linda's approach, when the driver of an enormous Cadillac DeVille, Mr. Lippin, decided at the last moment to swing into the parking place. Mr. Lippin hadn't noticed the empty space until he was on top of it and did not expect anyone to be standing in it. Bethany, with her back to the car, never saw it coming. She just had time to turn and face the Cadillac before it pinned her between its grille and the front of an SUV in the facing parking spot.

She screamed as the impact crushed both her femurs.

She fell across the hood of the big car, which was scalding hot from the sun, and stared through the windshield at the face of the old man driving it. Mr. Lippin looked totally confused and more than a little put out. But past him, through the windshield and the back window, she saw Linda. Standing, not driving the car she'd gone to fetch.

And laughing.

LINDA COULDN'T UNDERSTAND why the sight of one of her best friends in agony struck her as funny, but it did. Hysterically so, in fact. She didn't want to laugh out loud, but she couldn't help herself. Bethany looked so ridiculous, sprawled across the hood like a broken Barbie doll. Didn't she know? Didn't she *care* that she made herself look so fucking stupid?

People ran up to see what had happened. Many of them had cell phones out, no doubt calling the proper authorities. The old man in the car just sat there, engine still running, hands on the steering wheel. He hadn't even tried to back up.

Linda felt someone move up next to her. At once, she recalled the glimpse of Jesse Garon in the steamed-over bathroom mirror, and her body responded to the thought just as it had then. Combined with her inexplicable but real elation at seeing Bethany injured, it got her so turned on she was certain everyone around could tell.

She turned, already forming the word, "Jesse," and was surprised to see her uncle Travis standing there instead. He had on cut-offs and flip-flops, along with his typical redneck-themed t-shirt, this time a Confederate flag that said, *Malcolm Don't Mess with This X.*

"What done happened here?" he said casually as if it was nothing more serious than a spilled drink.

"That dumb bitch got herself cut in half," Linda said.

"That's your long-legged little friend, isn't it?"

"Yeah, that's her. She ain't so long-legged now."

Both of them laughed. Then Linda looked up into her uncle's eyes and saw something so unexpected she almost gasped in surprise. There was an *affinity* she'd never noticed there before as if something in him looked back at something in her, and they both realized in the same instant that this thing, whatever it was, was identical.

Travis stepped away to take a picture with his phone. Linda, realizing she was on camera, impulsively lifted her shirt and exposed her bra. She stuck out her tongue. Travis took the picture before he even realized what she'd done and then stared at the frozen image of his niece flashing him. He was still staring at it when the first responders arrived two minutes later.

9

fter being urged away from the accident, Travis and Linda strode into the TLC-Mart, against the tide of people who rushed out to see the accident in the parking lot. As if nothing unusual had just happened, they moved down the store's suddenly-abandoned center aisle.

Linda asked casually, "Why are you here, Uncle Travis?"

"I need some paneling nails." He figured if he showed up with the nails, he could convince both Brother Anthony and that bitch parole officer that he was just making a hardware store run, not ignoring his community service. Of course, he'd need a reason why it took him twenty-four hours to do something that might take twenty minutes at best, but he'd think of something.

"You're doing actual work? Daddy says you ain't done an honest day's work in your miserable, worthless life."

Travis felt his face burn. His brother always took any chance to run him down, especially to family. "Yeah, well, your daddy don't know everything about me. So, what brings *you* here?"

"I need mousetraps."

"Got mice, huh? Man, your daddy must be having fits, mice getting around his guns."

"We don't have mice in the house. I just need dead mice."

"Why does anyone need dead mice?"

"You'll see," she teased.

They reached the hardware department and began looking for the traps. Travis admired the way his niece's shorts and tank top accented her curves and showed off little bits of forbidden skin when she bent over. He wondered if he was sensing her response correctly, though; his brother would kill him if he made a move on Linda that she didn't want. Of course, if she *did* want it, his brother would still kill him if he ever found out.

He risked putting a hand on her shoulder, feeling her skin around the tank top strap. She didn't shrug away or shout at him as she'd done in the past. "How many you gonna get?"

"Two dozen."

"You need that many dead mice?"

"I sure do."

He pulled his hand away when she stood up. Did he imagine it, or was she arching her back so that she pushed her breasts out at him? He forced his eyes up to her face, where she gave him a knowing smile far too mature for her years.

"Uncle Travis, are you checking me out?" she said in a low, almost purring way.

Travis felt his face flush again. "Naw, what're you talking about?"

"You know what I'm talking about, Uncle Travis."

The discrepancy between her tone and the way she kept reminding him of their familial relationship confused him. He said anxiously, "I'll be over in the gun section, all right? You come get me when you're ready."

"Why? We didn't come together." When she spoke, she accented the word, *come.*

He scurried away as she laughed at him.

He went to the gun section of Sporting Goods and asked to see a Bushmaster AR-15. The clerk, a pimply boy with black hair and a slack expression, unlocked the rack and took down the weapon. Travis felt the weight in his hand, and it took him back to his boyhood when his father was alive. *I don't know if you're big enough for this,* his father had warned as he handed him the heavy double-barreled shotgun. Blanton had snickered knowingly. His father said, *Now, point it at that tree full of blackbirds.*

Travis did, aiming the way he'd seen cowboys on TV aim. When he fired, he accidentally pulled both triggers, since his father had not warned him against that. The recoil knocked him flat, and he banged his head on the cold ground.

His father laughed. So did Blanton, who was twelve then. It wasn't good-natured laughter, either. It was cold, and mocking, and cruel. It was the way they always laughed at him, like his incompetence delighted them. Later, *much* later, he'd understand how they'd set him up for things like this by not telling him about the two triggers. Or how to use a gas pump. Or a million other everyday things that a real father would've taken the time to teach a son. He didn't follow this idea through, though. He only saw himself as their victim, and by extension, everyone's victim. Nothing was his own fault.

Now he sighted down the barrel and swung it slowly toward the end of the aisle, where Linda suddenly appeared, clutching a handful of mousetraps. She stopped, eyes wide.

He should've lowered the gun. Common sense, common decency demanded it. But he didn't. Instead, he met her eyes over the bead at the end of the barrel, smiled, and whispered, "Bang."

Then he almost dropped the gun when she silently mouthed, "Okay."

CARLYSS SAW THE AMBULANCE, police car. and fire truck as her grandfather's car entered the TLC-Mart parking lot. Her grandfather, driving in his slow, methodical way, said, "Well, we won't park down *that* row."

"Wonder what happened?" Carlyss said.

"It's down at the handicapped parking. Probably two old people with a fender-bender. They call 911 if you look at a car too hard nowadays. Back when I was your age, we'd just exchange phone numbers, and the one who was in the wrong would just pay for the repairs. Now you have insurance, police, lawyers..." He sighed, an expression that Carlyss knew well. It signified his disappointment in what the world had become.

It's a friend of yours, the voice said just behind her. *She'll never walk again.*

Carlyss clenched her jaw and resisted the urge to look in the back seat. She knew accompanying her grandfather was a mistake, but it was too late now. He'd looked so lonely when he asked.

They parked in front of the entrance at the opposite end of the huge store. Once through the automatic doors, Carlyss fluttered her t-shirt to break its sweat-hold on her skin. "I'll meet you back here in fifteen minutes," her grandfather said, and headed toward the pharmacy. He didn't want anyone to know what medication he was actually picking up; Carlyss assumed he was ashamed of the pills for his incontinence.

It's his Viagra, the voice said. *He can't get it up without it. Then he has to jerk off because your grandmother is dried up and useless.*

Stop it! Carlyss thought harshly and was rewarded with that maddening chuckle. She hated giving in to the taunts because that's what the demon wanted. Her only recourse now was ignoring it and hoping it went away.

Fat chance, the voice said, responding to her thought. *I'm on you like white on rice, baby.*

Carlyss made her way to the back of the store, where the small sign said PUBLIC RESTROOMS. A security turnstile blocked the way, and even though she'd never stolen anything in her life, she always feared it would go off when she went through. With her record, it would definitely become an incident.

A large woman glanced up from washing her hands, then looked quickly away. All the stalls were empty. Carlyss went down to the last one before the handicapped stall and stepped inside. She slid the lock and waited until she heard the bathroom door close.

She looked at the divider walls. Graffiti covered them, with no attempt made to remove it. She knew the stalls got painted every six months, but between those times, no one seemed to care.

The graffiti was as vile as anything in the men's room or the boy's bathroom at school. Below the purse hook on the door was written, *Fuck you all, one day you'll all die, and you can't take any of your shit with you.* Beneath that, another hand had scrawled, *Oh, yeah? Watch me.*

Above the handle were two crudely drawn breasts and the words, *Milk cannons,* arching over them.

Carlyss sighed. On her last visit, she'd written, *Everything has a purpose, even you.* Beneath it, someone wrote, *Shut the fuck up, bitch, this ain't Facebook.*

It didn't deter her, though. She found a reasonably clear spot, took out her Sharpie, and wrote:

You are enough. No matter what anyone says.

She did this every time she came to this store. It wasn't much, and she certainly never knew if it made any difference, but she had to put something good out into the world, to balance all the awful things she'd done, and said, and thought. And it seemed especially important in this cold, heartless place, though she couldn't say why.

She opened the door and risked a glance into the handicapped stall. There wasn't as much graffiti—the walls, being bigger, took more to cover—but one jumped out at her and made her throat tighten.

God is great, but the devil does that thing with his tongue. Beside it was a little drawing of a mouth with a thick forked tongue protruding.

She quickly wrote *Be strong* in big, swirly letters beside it. She finished just as the main door opened, and a store employee came in. Carlyss passed her on the way out, but the woman paid her no mind.

Carlyss wandered back toward the women's clothes. She wasn't planning to buy anything and actually had no interest in them. But it was something to do, and her grandfather would know where to find her if she lost track of time. So, she checked out the t-shirts featuring the latest boy bands and rappers, wondering again what the people on the shirts, with such vast income and influence, *did* all day.

She turned in time to see Travis and Linda emerge from the sporting goods department and head down the central aisle.

She recognized them both, of course, but had no idea they knew each other. How did Travis, the evil scumbucket who'd propositioned her at the church, connect up with Linda, one of the most popular girls in school? Suddenly she didn't want either of them to see her, so she stepped behind a rack. Through the tops of the hangers, she watched them.

Hey, what are you looking at? the voice said. *You have any idea what you're seeing? No, of course, you don't.*

Carlyss's eyes narrowed. Did the voice sound…scared?

Travis and Linda passed without noticing her, although she saw the way Travis stared at Linda's butt as she walked. That was creepy; somehow, it was even creepier than what he'd said to her at the church. He was old enough to be her father, but Carlyss knew *him:* heavy-set, with a crewcut and a bellowing voice. Everyone in school remembered the day he burst into the principal's office, yelling about how if he was a crazed gunman they'd all be dead, and demanding to know the details of their security plans. The police came and got him that day, and nothing else was heard about him. It didn't seem to damage his daughter's social standing, either, especially among the boys.

Linda looked different somehow. She had a confidence, an adult sense of her own physicality, that was new. Was it just the result of growing older? If Carlyss had been lucky enough to have a normal life, would she, too, now walk that way?

Would you look at that? the voice said admiringly.

"Stop it," she said. "You're disgusting."

Oh, honey, you ain't seeing what I'm seeing.

"I'll agree with that."

The voice sighed the next word as if it was a magical incantation. To Carlyss, it sounded like, *Dandelion.*

"What did you say?" she asked before she could stop herself. "Dandelion?"

She waited for the triumphant mockery that always came when

the demon managed to engage her, but the voice began to chant instead. Instead of the usual high, whiny voice it used when speaking to her, this was guttural, barely distinguishable as speech. It sounded like, *Dan-DEL-ion, UH! Dan-DEL-ion, UH!* repeated over and over. Carlyss wanted to cover her ears but knew that wouldn't make any difference. After a few agonizing minutes, the voice faded without weakening, as if the demon was twirling away into the distance. She didn't look for it; she had no interest in seeing it dance.

Carlyss saw what Linda carried: mouse traps, at least a dozen of them, in a bundle clutched against her chest and tucked under her chin. What did anyone need that many mousetraps for?

The voice stayed silent as Carlyss returned to meet her grandfather. He stood just inside the door, the bag from the pharmacy gripped tightly in his big fist. Linda and Travis had already gone through the checkout and departed, which filled her with relief. But her grandfather looked worried.

"I found out what all those sirens were about," he said. "Some girl got hit by a car. Do you know the Horner girl?"

"Bethany Horner?"

"Yeah, that's who it was. Pretty bad too. They say it cut her legs off."

Carlyss went cold and waited for the voice to crow its triumph. But it remained silent, which was as odd as seeing Linda with so many mousetraps.

"Such a pretty girl, too," her grandfather continued. "Her father used to date your mother; did you know that?"

"No," Carlyss said numbly. She struggled with the urge to run, to get back to the church where she could be safe, where she could pray. But instead, she followed her grandfather into the heat, tried not to look toward the flashing lights and the crowd gathered around the accident, and prayed as best she could—for herself, but also for Bethany, who had once, back in third grade, been her friend.

10

Travis, the nails forgotten at the TLC-Mart, arrived home and found his mother dressed in one of her hideous old sundresses, which made her look like a floral tablecloth draped over one of those big red balls outside Target. Before he even had time to say a word, she announced, "We're going to the revival tonight."

He recalled seeing the tent on his way to the TLC-Mart. The last thing he wanted to do was sit outside on a summer night, under a bunch of lights that would draw every mosquito in the county, listening to preaching. In fact, he just wanted to get high and jerk off to thoughts of his niece. "Aw, do we have to?"

"I need to be in the presence of the Lord, and I can't wait until Sunday," she said. Her normal shrill disdain was replaced by another tone he knew very well, that weird religious fervor that periodically took her over. "The world is trying me, son; it's trying me and finding me wanting. I need to be prayed over, to be slain in the spirit."

He knew there was no talking her out of it once she'd made up her mind. She saw religion as something similar to gasoline that required periodic refilling, and more so if she'd been under stress. Travis's parole officer showing up out of the blue certainly qualified as stress. He should've seen this coming.

"Now go put on some britches," she snapped, indicating his shorts. "I ain't taking you out looking like that."

"It's too hot," he whined.

"You ain't going before the Lord with your knees hanging out," she said. "Now you go do what I told you."

"Yes, ma'am," he said, slouching out just as he'd done all his life. He went into his apartment over the garage, pulled out a pair of jeans with holes in the knees (*that'll show the bitch!*), and took several quick tokes off a joint.

He looked at himself in the mirror. "Fuck God," he said to his reflection, smoke coming from his mouth like he breathed pitiful fire. "God ain't done a damn thing for me."

Then, numbed enough to endure it, he drove his mother to the revival.

AT SUNSET, Deacon Elder sat on the porch steps of the New Shiloh Methodist Church, reading the local paper in the glow from the security light. Another business, this one a bakery that had opened in 1974, had shut its doors for good. Eleven people were out of work. The owners blamed it on competition from the TLC-Mart.

Poor flour-covered bastards, Elder thought. *Even a blind baker should've seen that coming.*

Anthony came out, locked the door behind him, and said, "Ready to go? I'm beat."

Elder stood. "I think I'm going to go to that revival tonight."

"Checking out the competition?" Anthony said with a smile.

"Just one of those things," Elder said. "Getting the sense that I need to be there."

"Well, don't fall on the ground and flop like a fish. Unless nautical nonsense is something you wish."

Elder looked at him.

"It's a TV show theme," Anthony said.

"I don't watch much TV."

"Yeah. I'll leave a key for you under the doormat."

"Thanks. I appreciate it."

"*I* appreciate you putting in that new faucet in the ladies' room sink. Where'd you learn plumbing?"

"You pick up things if you pay attention."

"I must not, then, because I watched you, and I couldn't do it."

"Want me to grab anything before I come over?"

"Nah, I'm stocked up. Just ..."

"What?"

"Be careful. You tend to attract the wrong kind of notice, especially with other preachers you don't approve of."

"How do you know I don't approve of this one?"

"Heh. That's funny."

"I promise I'll just sit and watch."

"Uh-huh." Anthony paused, then said, "Deke, can I ask you something personal?"

"Sure."

"You ever thought about just settling down with your own church somewhere? Like I've got here? Someplace small, where you can do things the way you want, and everybody leaves you alone. Then you could have a wife and some kids, even."

Elder drew deeply on his cigarette before answering. "Yeah, I've thought about it. It ain't for me. I *know* I'm doing what the Lord wants." He grinned a little. "Besides, can you imagine the kind of woman who'd put up with me?"

"You ain't never had no trouble getting 'em that *I've* seen."

"Gettin' 'em is one thing. Keepin' 'em is a whole other ball of wax. I had a wife once, right out of high school. I wasn't a good husband."

"That was a long time ago. You're different now."

"She might not say so."

Anthony let it drop. He patted Elder on the shoulder and said, "Well, have fun. But I don't want to get a call from the jail tonight. I have to preach in the morning." He said it lightly but with an under-tone of seriousness.

"Anthony, I'd never call you and drag you into my troubles. What the Lord gives me to handle, I handle with His help, no one else's."

Elder drove through the unfamiliar town. He tried not to fixate on the woman he'd seen earlier, the one in the tight professional skirt who'd smiled when she caught him watching her ass. *Haven,* she'd said. A beautiful name. He wondered if it was really her name and if she might be that very thing for him. And if the possibility of seeing her again wasn't his real reason for going back to the tent where they'd met.

As Dion and the Belmonts finished "A Teenager in Love" on the radio, that damned jingle began.

"You always find Tender Loving Care
And the best prices anywhere
at TLC-Mart!"

Kids laughed in the background, and one boy's voice said, "What's summer without fireworks? Come to TLC-Mart for the biggest, baddest selection in the area! Now through July 4th!"

When he finally reached the revival site, Elder had to wait twenty minutes in a line of cars while listening to music from the rock band under the tent blasting into the dusk. He had no use for this sort of cacophonous noise and recognized it for what it truly was: marketing at best, the "false prophets" of Matthew 7:15 at worst. Sure, they might've drawn in more teenagers than traditional hymns, but the content of the lyrics was secondary to the atmosphere in the music. Like all rock music, it was about rebellion against authority, the very antithesis of how a sinner should approach God. A preacher who didn't understand that was not a preacher he trusted.

A young man in a sweat-soaked dress shirt directed him to park in a line of vehicles that rapidly filled the rest of the enormous lot. He got out of his car just as a half dozen people, four of them small chil-dren emerged from a battered old Ford LTD. The kids' hair gleamed with some sort of substance designed to hold it in place, and they wore stiff-collared long-sleeve shirts. The mother, her uncut hair piled high, called to one, "Xerxes, you spit out that gum right now!"

Elder lit a cigarette and joined the mass of people filing into the tent. He was the only one smoking and got disapproving looks from several others, most of them fat from diets of fast food and greasy cooking. Elder did a hundred situps and pushups every morning, so he indulged his lone vice with a clear conscience.

He took a seat at the back, where he could see both the stage and watch the people without having to blatantly rubberneck. A teenage girl in a lace-necked dress put her hand on his shoulder and said, "Sir, I'll have to ask you to put out that cigarette. The Lord's house is no-smoking."

"The Lord's house is a tent from Real Value Hardware," Elder said.

"That may be, but if the Lord's in it, there's no smoking," she shot back.

"The Lord tell you that Himself?"

"He did, when He made sure I found out the truth about cigarette smoking and lung cancer. Did you know that second-hand smoke is actually more dangerous?"

"Guess I made the right choice, then." But he ground out the cigarette under his heel.

She looked coquettishly up at him as she turned away. He shook his head; not only was she young enough to land him in jail, she thought this behavior was harmless. If she only knew what lurked in the shadows, waiting to accept an invitation from a young, pretty Christian girl who believed such flirting meant nothing.

The band, a standard four-piece rock and roll combo, finished their upbeat number and segued into Larry Norman's post-Rapture classic, "I Wish We'd All Been Ready." Elder recalled meeting Norman when he'd played for the Marines once just before his death. His long hair had perfectly suited the times, but there was something in the man's eyes that put Elder—or rather, the man he'd been back then—on his guard. He never found out what it was, but after his dedication to the Lord, he'd read up on Norman, unsuccessfully looking for something to put that feeling in context.

The song settled the crowd, and the talking dropped to a murmur as people sang along with the depressing chorus. When it ended, the tent was as close to silent as it was likely to get.

Elder studied the faces of those around him. They were uniformly white, mostly Pentecostal, and without a doubt, most of them secretly assumed they were damned to hell. The rest had a smug false certainty in their own salvation and were there to enjoy the show as the others tried to convince God they were worthy. Not more than one or two, Elder knew, genuinely understood what it meant to be a Christian.

And none of that even counted the demons that he *knew* were there. He could smell their simmering, sulfurous odor underneath the sweat, aftershave, and perfume.

Before he could focus his gift of discernment to identify them, Brother Knode appeared onstage. He grabbed the microphone like a rock star and said, "How many believers we got here tonight?"

There was a roar of *Amens* and *Hallelujahs.*

"That's not enough! I say again, how many believers we got here tonight?"

Another roar, even louder.

Knode looked pleased. He probably always looked pleased, Elder mused, standing up there receiving this adoration. For although he was ostensibly channeling praise to God and speaking for Him, Elder knew a lot of it was his own ego. Certainly, the money that came in would not be sent to heaven.

Elder crossed his arms and sat back to watch the show.

The music began again, and Knode led the congregation in a rousing, upbeat rock-and-roll version of "What a Friend We Have in Jesus." He came down off the stage and shook the hands of people in the front row. Already his shirt was dark with sweat, and he dramatically wiped his forehead with a handkerchief.

He kept glancing at one back corner of the tent. Elder followed his gaze and saw a teenage boy manning a video camera on a tripod. He smiled; Knode was playing to his real audience, the one online that would watch this performance for years. It had nothing to do with the Eucharist and everything to do with YouTube.

When the song finished, to a round of applause mixed with more shouts of praise and a few of the nonsensical ravings people believed God put in their mouths, Knode got back onstage, put the microphone on its stand, and said loudly, "There's only two things I want to talk about tonight that will make you even stronger in your belief. In Ephesians 2, Paul tells the church to take up the helmet of salvation. Do we need that?"

A huge affirmative cry went up.

"And he tells the church to take up the sword of the spirit. Do we need that?"

Another affirmative cry.

"Yes, we do. For the sword of the spirit is the Word of God, and we need that helmet and that sword to wage the battle raging in our world today. It's a war, just like the war against the Islamists over in the Middle East. And people, I believe that Satan has God's Church on Earth trapped in a corner. We should be winning, we should be triumphant, but I tell you true, the Devil has the upper hand over the Church today. That's because we don't believe in the enemy. (*Amen!*) We don't believe in the Adversary (*Amen!*) We believe our enemy is our next-door neighbor, or the Islamists, or the Buddhists, but that is *wrong!* Your enemy is *Satan!* The Apostle Paul tells us plainly, 'we wrestle not against flesh and blood, but against principalities, against powers, against the rulers of the darkness of this world, against spiritual wickedness in high places.'

"A lot of you people think the Devil's in Hell, but he's not in Hell; he's right here in Somerton. He's all around us! He's 'the prince of the power of the air, the spirit that now worketh in the children of disobedience,' that's what the Apostle Paul tells us. But thank the Lord Almighty in Heaven for not leaving us helpless and defenseless against Satan's works."

WHILE ELDER WATCHED Knode do his schtick, across town Linda Scote prepared for her own form of worship. She wore black yoga pants, a black long-sleeved blouse, and had her dark hair loose around her face. She thought about using shoe polish to cover her skin but figured that if she got caught, that would be almost impossible to explain. Besides, she wasn't doing anything wrong or illegal, just...weird.

She'd had to fake a great deal of distress all afternoon, pretending that Bethany's accident had horrified her so much that she had to hide in her room. The truth was, she simply couldn't care less. Bethany was a cow, and a whiny one at that, and for Linda, it had been worth the sacrifice of her friend to see something as wondrous as the wreck. Jesse Garon had promised he could do it, and he'd been as good as his word.

Now it was time for her to make a gift for him. She set the mouse-traps about five feet apart at the edge of the vacant lot down the street from her house. The lot, like her own backyard, abutted a field that was still farmed. There was a streetlamp right in front of it, but it sputtered and went out as she worked, leaving the lot in total black-ness. The house to the left of the field was dark, and to the right was an empty house with a REDUCED sign pasted over the FOR SALE notice. If anyone did spot her and report her to the police, it would be simply bad luck. And she suspected she had protection from that now.

She knew mice from that field must use this overgrown, neglected lot, so she figured this would be the easiest place to catch some. She'd thought about driving to the pet store in Jackson, where she knew they sold feeder mice for pet snakes, but then she'd have to watch them die, and she didn't know if she could do that. *Of course, you can,* Jesse Garon said in her head. *You can do anything you want.*

She stood back and watched the fireflies as they shimmered across the tops of the weeds. In the distance, light glowed above the trees. At first, she thought it was the TLC-Mart, but then she realized it was too close. It had to be that revival she'd driven by. Instantly she gritted her teeth in fury and wanted nothing more than to set that tent on fire and send those stupid mock-Christians scurrying into the night. She found that looking at the glow sent a shock of pain through her head, straight from her eyes to the back of her skull. She looked down and away.

Then she impulsively stepped into the waist-high weeds, knelt, and took off all her clothes. Naked, she stretched out, ankles crossed and arms flung wide. She closed her eyes and felt the insects and vermin frightened by her passage calmly return. Chiggers burrowed beneath her skin, mosquitoes plunged their needles into her, and ticks dropped from their perches on the weeds to slowly swell as they fed. Normally, the touch of any bug, even something benign, sent her screaming for the house, but she luxuriated in it now.

Only the fireflies gave her a wide berth. Had she been able to see herself from above, the great round shadow that covered her would've been obvious. As it was, she lay there, letting the worst of nature have its way with her, imagining as much as she could the way Jesse Garon would feel if he took her right there.

I am *taking you,* his voice said in her head. *Every bite, every touch, is me. You belong totally to me. We're almost the same person.*

The rush that went through her made her moan and writhe against the ground. She tried to move, but it seemed something held her ankles and wrists fixed in their mock-crucified position. She wanted to touch herself, to put her hands where she knew her Uncle Travis wanted to put his, but she could only lie there and endure wave after wave of delicious sensation, her carnal feelings mixed with the maddening pain and itch as the night's denizens literally devoured her a tiny bit at a time.

11

B y the time she got there, Haven had to park her car in the massive TLC-Mart lot and walk half a mile back to the revival tent. She was glad she'd changed into her running shoes after work.

The music and crowd response blared out at her the whole way, and she suddenly second-guessed her entire plan. If this was how Brother Knode conducted his day-to-day business, she wasn't about to let him do it in her office, where other people might hear. Then again, she *did* want a show.

The mosquitos were out in force as well, and she realized belatedly they were attracted to the dregs of her perfume. It promised to be a miserable evening.

She threaded through the parked cars and reached the side of the tent, where the mosquito-net flaps had been dropped. This close, the noise was as loud and raucous as any concert, except possibly the Rush show her college boyfriend insisted she attend. The band, a full-on rock combo, tore through a power chord version of "The Old Rugged Cross" while Brother Knode, with his jacket off and shirt untucked, exhorted the crowd. Some of the watchers screamed and bellowed in nonsense syllables, speaking in tongues they believed were a sign from God.

Brother Knode was entirely different than he'd been that morning. Instead of the smooth, sharp good ole boy, he was now sweat-drenched, his pompadour falling carelessly over his forehead, and his tie dramatically askew. His expression changed from rapt to agonized to scolding, all the while in time with the music as he led the crowd in singing along.

She'd never seen anything like this, although she'd always assumed tent revival ministers were as much performance artists as theologians. Her own experience with church was negligible as an adult, and her memories of childhood Sunday school were innocuous and boring. But she understood the appeal of this: Knode was clearly certain, and certainty was a powerful drug to those riddled with doubts.

She moved along the tent, looking for an entrance. She passed a teenage girl standing hunched over a small video camera on a tripod. She was inches away on the other side of the netting but had no idea Haven was watching. On the small screen, Haven glimpsed Knode's sweaty face in extreme close-up.

"Say you love the Lord!" he screamed over the music to a woman before him, who seemed to be in the throes of either a panic attack or the second phase of a grand mal seizure. "Say you love the Lord!"

Haven's doubts about her plan increased. She was glad she'd decided to visit the revival tonight to see Brother Knode in action before he came to her office to confront Carlyss. Perhaps it would be best to forget the whole thing.

And even as she thought this, she looked around for the big, handsome man she'd met that afternoon, but didn't see him. He'd said his name was "Elder," hadn't he? Or had that merely been his position in the Knode organization? There was something in his smile, his voice, a kindness mixed with...

She shook her head. She did *not* need a man in her life right now, certainly not one tied to a charlatan like Brother Knode.

Finally, she reached the entrance, accepted the one-sheet program from the small boy handing them out, and went inside to stand at the back behind the rows of packed chairs. The music stopped, the twitching woman was led away, and Knode began to preach.

"I'm about to throw this microphone and run outside this tent, praise be to God," Knode said, striding the edge of the stage like Bono. "Just last week, I prayed deliverance over a woman who'd been baptized a Catholic. That's right, she was raised in a church that said you can't talk to God unless you go through the Pope and pay your money!"

The crowd booed.

"A demon of sexual deviance had taken up inside this woman, driving her into the arms of other women! That Catholic priest had told this woman, it's too late for your immortal soul, but how many of you know it's never too late?" The crowd shouted its assent. Knode bellowed, with all his force, "Hallelujah!"

Haven looked at the crowd near her. With a start, she recognized the handsome man she'd met at the tent earlier. He sat with his muscular arms folded across his solid chest, his head tilted in skepticism.

The woman seated beside him, bone-thin and dressed for Easter Sunday, suddenly jumped to her feet and began shouting out nonsense while reaching for the sky. The man glanced at her, then looked away as if he saw this sort of thing all the time. The woman pushed her way to the end of the row and ran down to join the faithful in the press before the stage,

Impulsively, Haven made her way past all the sweaty knees and took the now-empty seat. The man glanced at her, then did a double-take. "Well...hello."

"Hello," she said. "Have I missed anything significant?"

"Not really. He's been telling them they're going to hell, and they've been rushing to agree with him."

"Don't you believe in hell?"

"I do. But I don't believe in using it to raise money."

"You think that's what he's doing?"

Elder shrugged.

"Well, I'm here to judge for myself," Haven said.

"And why is that?"

The question struck her as impertinent, but then she realized she certainly didn't seem like a typical believer. And the way sweat shimmered on his rugged face made her think more carnally than she'd done with any man lately. "I'm just curious," she said, knowing that a partial truth was better than an outright lie. She tried to keep her mind on the job.

Then suddenly Knode said, "I have to tell you, though, I know there's some of you here who are..." And then he bellowed again, *"Afflicted.* You are host to demons that turn you away from the Lord. But tonight, with the Lord's help, I will *drive* these demons from you, praise Jesus. I will leave you clean, and pure, and ready for the presence of the *Lord!"*

Someone in the crowd screamed, "He's lying! Don't listen to him!"

Immediately two big young men ran to grab the heckler. He was a young man, too, clad in a similar short-sleeved dress shirt. As he was hustled out of the tent, he continued to shout, "Don't believe him! He's lying to you!"

Knode stayed on track. "That's what happens when the truth comes out: Satan don't want you to hear it!"

Knode climbed down from the stage and prowled the center aisle, before he finally stopped next to a young man in glasses who trembled in his seat, eyes closed, mouth silently working.

"The spirit of God has moved on me to call you to come to God and make a choice," Knode said. "You must decide to be free of this demon inside you. Hiding in there the devil, watching and waiting for his chance. Well, he don't get no chance tonight, does he?"

The congregation shouted and clapped their approval.

Two more heavy, strong-looking young men in white dress shirts and ties appeared, took the supposedly afflicted boy by the arms, and pulled him to his feet. He did not resist, but his eyes rolled back, and he said, "Jesus I know, and Paul I know, but who are thee?" Then he laughed, loud and obnoxious.

Knode got right in the young man's face. "You in there, demon? I know you're in there! You let this child of God go! Turn loose of him!"

The young man spewed out nonsense syllables, but with a decidedly venomous tone.

"The devils of hell have tormented your mind. Look!" He held up the boy's arm to display a friendship bracelet made out of string and various little danglies. "This once belonged to a witch! The Lord has just told me that."

He tore the bracelet from the boy's arm and pinched one of the baubles between his thumb and forefinger. He shoved it in the boy's face, right under his eyes. "See this right here? That is a Satanic symbol, whether you know it or not. In Joshua, the Lord says, 'keep yourselves from the accursed thing, lest ye make yourselves accursed.'"

"That ain't nothing, shit-cock!" the boy said distinctly. Gasps, murmurs. and calls of prayer came from the congregation. Elder stood up, to get a better view.

Knode grabbed the boy's head with his free hand while making sure the microphone picked up everything. He shook the boy's skull like a housewife checking a melon's ripeness, so hard the boy's glasses flew off. "Come out of him! Come out of him! You come on out of him, you vile spirit!"

He struggled, but Knode's grip didn't loosen. Then the boy began to cry.

"You come out!" Knode continued. "I command you! Come out of this boy! Demon, leave this child of God."

Despite the vividness of the spectacle, Haven found herself watching Elder. He was neither horrified nor offended; if anything, he seemed amused, as if he got the joke being played on everyone else, including her.

"In Jesus's name, I say come on out of him!" Knode cried. "The rest of you, you better get your minds on God so that this demon don't find somewhere else to hide."

Then the boy screamed and went limp. The two men holding him almost fell on top of him. Knode stumbled back, like a weary gladiator after delivering the *coup de grace*, and the congregation began to murmur prayers of thanks.

Knode put the microphone to his mouth so that his labored breathing came through the speakers. He reminded Haven of near-the-end Elvis, heavy and out of breath yet still plowing ahead. "'And the spirit cried, and rent him sore, and came out of him.' Praise God! Hallelujah!"

The two handlers dragged the semi-conscious boy away behind the stage. Haven quickly stood. "Excuse me," she said to Elder, "but I've seen enough. I have to go."

He stood as well to let her pass. Their bodies slid against each other, and both looked straight into the other's eyes. "Pleasure seeing you again," he said. "Ma'am."

She skirted the shadows around the tent until she reached the back of the stage. Hidden in the darkness, she watched the formerly possessed boy sit on a camp chair, head down between his knees, while the handlers leaned against the trailer. One lit a cigarette.

The boy reached up for it, and the handler gave it to him without a comment. It read like the gesture of old friends enacting an oft-repeated ritual. As the music began again inside the tent, Haven turned away in disgust and began the long walk back to her car.

***

INSIDE THE TENT, near the front, Travis sat with his mother. He desperately wanted a beer, and a joint, and a cool breeze to dry the claustrophobic sweat from his face. But his mother had taken the car keys once they'd arrived, and unless he wanted to walk home, he was stuck.

He wasn't paying any attention to the sermon or the supposed deliverance from evil spirits going on mere feet away. It wasn't the first time he'd experienced either. He didn't believe in demons, because nobody possessed by the devil would either act in such a goofy manner or be foolish enough to come to the one place where the devil might be cast out.

His mother, meanwhile, had her knobby hands clasped together and murmured prayers into her knuckles, eyes tightly shut. She believed her prayers aided the minister in his efforts and felt the deliverance's success or failure as something personal. All around him, in fact, people prayed or spoke that gibberish that passed for prayer, joining in a great religious circle-jerk that, to Travis, was more funny and pathetic than powerful.

He looked around the tent, hoping one of the pretty girls might have on a tight dress or be leaning down to display sweaty cleavage. But none were seated anywhere near him. He was surrounded by the old, the fat, and the pathetic. Hell, some of them were all three.

Brother Knode climbed back on the little stage, mopping his face with a handkerchief. "That was the Lord at work, good people. But that young man ain't the only one here harboring the devil. No, there's many more of you who have invited demons into your lives. The demons of..."

He raised his hand, and with each word, he brought down his fist, and the drummer hit a punctuating beat.

"Alcohol!"

"Drugs!"

"Pornography!"

"Acupuncture!"

"Witchcraft!"

"Atheism!"

"Role-playing games!"

"And streaming videos!"

Again, he wiped his face. "Now, I extend to you the strong right hand of the Lord, of Jesus Christ, of the Holy Spirit! Bring yourselves before me and feel the might of our Lord and Savior! He can drive these demons from you! He can do it this very night if you truly in your heart want it!"

"And give me a twenty," Travis muttered.

His mother grabbed his wrist. Her gnarled fingers felt like iron. "You go on up there, Travis," she said urgently. "I know the devil's in you. I've known it since you were a little boy. This may be your last chance. Go on up there and ask for deliverance."

Travis felt his face burn. "Mama, stop it. I ain't—"

"Get up!" she screeched, her face as red as his. "Get up there and ask the Lord for help before you burn in hell!"

Her expression was vulturous, wide mouth open and eyes bulging. The loose skin on her neck swayed with her words. Those seated around them turned to look, and at once several of them reached out and put their hands on Travis, simultaneously closing their eyes and praying.

Travis's heart raced, and he jumped to his feet, the hands trying to alternately hold him down and push him forward. "Y'all get off me!" he yelled, but his panicked cry was drowned by the other voices, his mother's shrill "Go up!" over and above them all. He pushed past the people in his row, trying to get to the aisle and get some free space to run.

But when he reached it, Brother Knode waited for him.

Travis was frozen to the spot. The minister's bulk, his reeking sweat, and the energy blazing from his eyes transfixed the younger man. Knode's breathing echoed through the loudspeakers before he finally said into the microphone, "This boy needs our help."

Assenting prayers and cries went up.

Travis realized he was surrounded, in the center of a circle of transfixed believers. He was trapped.

As if to emphasize this, Knode grabbed him by the head, the same way Travis used to palm a basketball in high school. The fingers dug into his scalp and made him grimace.

"What demons afflict this child of God?" Knode called out.

"Drink!" his mother's voice shrieked. "And drugs!"

Knode pulled Travis close to him until he could drop his arm around the younger man's shoulders. "Come here; I'll pray for you, precious brother. Lord, I humbly ask you to look all through the sex organs and functions of this boy's body for any evil spirit. I ask that the Holy Spirit search his bones, his blood, nerve circuitry, muscles, tissues, glands, hair, skin, and each and every cell in his body for any demonic activity. Root them out, Lord, and then *cast them out*, praise the lord!"

Another cry went up. Travis felt the same way he had on the roller coaster at Six Flags, terrified beyond belief but helpless to make it stop. Was his dead father watching this and laughing, the way he always did when Travis was scared?

"I feel the demon within you, fighting the power of the Lord," Knode said, his eyes scrunched shut. "Satan has held onto you for years now, sending his thoughts into your mind, telling you falsehoods, turning you from the path. Do you want to be shed of this demon?"

Travis couldn't answer.

"The demon will not let him speak!" Knode cried. The congregation wailed in sympathy. Knode released the almost-headlock and put the heel of his free hand against Travis's forehead. "I charge you, demon, let this man acknowledge his sin before the Lord our God! Nod for me, son, if you want this demon from hell sent from you!"

Travis, numb and almost too scared to stay on his feet, couldn't move.

But it didn't matter. Knode said, as if he'd received assent, "He does want this demon gone! I felt him nod! Oh, you demon, you think you're strong, but you ain't nothing compared to the power of Jesus Christ! In His name, I tell you, begone! Leave! Back to hell with you!"

Knode pushed down on his head, and Travis's already-weak knees buckled. He hit the ground, making a splat where the former grassy field had been pounded into mud by the humidity and the passage of so many feet. He could feel only the hand on his head and the wet soaking through to his shins. The noise around him was deafening, and above it all, he heard three distinct voices.

One was his mother, shrieking her approval of her son's ordeal. That didn't surprise him.

The other was Knode, amplified so that his words seemed to come from both near and far.

The third was his own voice bellowing, *"Fuck Jesus! Fuck you! Fuck God!"*

12

H ours later, just past ten o'clock, Brother Knode stood drinking iced tea inside the smaller tent that served as his mobile office. Instead of the netted sides of the main tent, it had opaque flaps suited to the task within: counting the take. No, he corrected his thoughts, the *love offering*. Because these people loved him.

An oscillating fan, carefully positioned so it wouldn't scatter the bills in their neat stacks, provided what little cooling there was. They could've done it back at the hotel, or even in one of the air-conditioned RVs, but he didn't like to take a chance on the money going uncounted any longer than necessary. After all, if he didn't know how much they'd taken in, how would he know if any had gone missing?

One of the big security men sat at a folding table with an old-fashioned calculator and new laptop before him. Another took the bundles of bills and slapped binders around them for quick identification. The take wasn't great, but it was only the first night. Now, word would spread through the town's target community and Knode expected a healthy percentage rise through the rest of the week, culminating in a weekend take that should pay their expenses for the trip and nestle a healthy profit into bank accounts only he could access.

"Trice," he said to the man bundling the bills, "how's it looking?"

"Long about four thousand so far," Trice said, looking over his glasses. They were the same glasses that had fallen from his face during his pretend "deliverance."

"You did good tonight," Knode said. Trice's performance had primed the pump for the others to come forward. The boys who worked for him took turns playing the role on a carefully-charted schedule that ensured they never did it in the same place twice. It helped that he insisted they all keep the same identical, close-cropped haircuts and wear similar, nondescript dress shirts and jeans, so it was hard to tell them apart. It was little details like this, he knew, that kept the business afloat. "I especially liked the way you called me 'shit cock.' That kind of thing really gets the people going."

"Thank you, sir," Trice said. "I was hoping you'd like that. Next time I'll have me a piece of Alka-Seltzer ready, so I can foam up."

"Now, now, let's not overdo it. It's better to just do it with your face and your words, not with a lot of tricks and stuff. Make it too much, and folks won't trust it."

"Yes, sir." Trice beamed at being treated like an equal. He was essentially a good kid, Knode knew, but with an impossibly soft and malleable moral center that Knode could redirect with ease. It was a quality he looked for and cultivated in the people who worked for him. Fortunately, it was an extremely common commodity.

A new voice said, "Never been sure how to knock on a tent."

A muscular, good-looking man with black hair stood at the tent flap. He looked familiar, but Knode couldn't place him at first. He saw Trice's hand move toward the automatic pistol that lay hidden by the laptop screen.

"What can we do for you?" Knode said neutrally, moving to shield the money from view.

The man was physically big, and there was a swagger to his walk that Knode immediately disliked. He disliked it even more when the man lit a cigarette.

"I'd prefer you didn't smoke in here," he said.

"Well, I'd prefer you didn't sell good-hearted idiots the load of total bullshit you peddle," the man said through a puff of smoke. "Don't look like either one of us are going to get what we want tonight, does it?"

"Who are you?" Knode demanded.

"Deacon Elder. We met this afternoon."

"Oh, yes. Now I remember."

"I saw your show tonight. I saw that boy—" He pointed at Trice. "—do his little song and dance to give the prod to everyone else. I also got a few minutes of cell phone video through the tent flap just now showing him counting your money, and you complimenting him on his performance."

The other young man, who'd eased around while Knode spoke, suddenly grabbed the gun and leveled it at Elder. "I'll be taking that cell phone, sir," he said with the exaggerated politeness of a rookie highway patrolman.

"Metcalf!" Knode bellowed. "Put that gun away." In a perfectly reasonable tone, he said to Elder, "Now, why in the world would you be doing that, sir?"

Metcalf did not put the gun away. Elder continued to stare evenly at him until he finally lowered it. Then he said to Knode, "Because we're working the same side of the street, except I do it for real, and you just put on a burlesque show. You couldn't tell a demon from diarrhea if they both came out of your ass, and you know it. You ain't got no sense of discernment."

"And you do?" Knode said, the mockery just below the surface.

"I do. And you had some people there who really had indwelling demons. They could've used a real prayer of deliverance."

"That still doesn't explain why you made a video of me talking to my associate. Or what you plan to do with it."

"Well, I've already sent it to some of *my* associates. If anything should happen to me, they'll make sure it goes public, along with links to the video your staff posted an hour ago of this young man getting exorcised. We'll let people make up their own minds."

Knode's eyes narrowed. "And to keep that from happening—?"

Elder smiled. "I'll take about a thousand dollars of your cash right there."

"Oh, we hardly made that much."

"I believe your young exorcee there told you four thousand a few minutes ago, and you ain't finished counting it yet. You can give me a thousand now and send me on my way, or you can keep counting, and I'll revise my figure accordingly."

Elder smoked quietly while Knode frantically tried to think of a way out of this. It was a simple scam, one that Elder had plainly spent some time perfecting, and the only downside Knode could imagine was that he couldn't easily pull it more than once on the same people. If the video *did* reach the public, it would be a tiny tempest, to be sure, one that his reputation would have no trouble weathering. But it might impact the bottom line on a more immediate basis and end his ability to work in Somerton for at least a few years. So, he smiled, took a stack of bundled twenties, and extended it toward Elder. "I trust you're a man of your word, and that video will never see the light of day."

"You won't find a trace of it," Elder said, flipping through the money.

"That could be," Knode mused, "because you didn't take any video at all."

"Could be," Elder agreed. "Either way, you're safe now. As long as you don't do any more of them fake deliverances. You just pray over people; that's all most of them need anyway. They're just confused because they ain't got jobs, they ain't got healthcare, and they got people all around 'em yelling at 'em about what they should and shouldn't do. Demons love that sort of thing. And if you want to do some real good? Go down to that TLC-Mart and pray deliverance there."

"The TLC-Mart?" Knode said. "What's that got to do with anything?"

Elder smiled. "Boy, there ain't a legit bone in your big old flabby body, is there? If you can't tell anything about the TLC-Mart, you best find another line of work." Then he took a paper fast food bag out of his back pocket, put the money in it, and backed out of the small tent.

When he was gone, Metcalf said, "You want me to go get it back?"

"No," Knode said firmly. "But I do want you to find out everything you can about that man, so that if he ever crosses paths with us again, it will be to his eternal detriment."

———

ELDER DROVE SLOWLY AROUND SOMERTON, watching in his mirrors for anyone following. He'd taken a big risk: charlatan preachers like Knode weren't above using physical violence if they felt threatened. But Elder wasn't afraid of that and had the training and experience to give as good as he got. More importantly, he'd known the moment the gun swung his way that the boy holding it lacked the nerve to actually shoot.

Elder felt bad, in the broad sense, about blackmailing someone, but in the immediate world, he needed funds, and the money would be used for something legitimate instead of continuing a false and dangerous ministry. The devil was afoot in this town and not just at the TLC-Mart.

"Sorry, Lord," he said sincerely. "I know I'm playing fast and loose with your Big Ten, but it ain't just for me. That little black-haired girl you put in my path needs my help, and you know I'll do whatever I can for her. But a man's got to eat." *And smoke and take a drink now and then to settle his nerves.*

He watched a suspicious pair of headlights behind him finally turn onto a different street. If he was being followed, it was by multiple cars using a sophisticated grid, and that was so unlikely it made him smile.

He saw an illuminated Budweiser sign on the front of a small building and impulsively pulled into the lot. He knew Somerton, like many southern towns, kept a tight leash on its bars and taverns, and wondered how this one could stay open so late. There were only a couple of cars there, and when he got out, he smelled steak.

Inside was dim, with lights over the booths and tables turned barely high enough to see the food. Candles burned in the centerpieces.

"Are you a member?" the young woman at the greeter station asked.

"I'm not."

"This is a private club, I'm afraid."

Now he understood how they skirted the blue laws. "And how much is the membership?"

The girl smiled. "One dollar per year."

"Then sign me up."

He used Anthony's address on the little three-by-five form and had to pay his dollar membership with a twenty from Knode's money. Then she showed him to his table. As he opened the menu, he glanced around at the other patrons, then did a double-take.

The beautiful woman he'd seen at the revival tent also sat alone in a booth. She had a plate of appetizers before her, and a beer. There was no place setting for a companion, and her attention was focused on her phone.

Impulsively, he went over and said, "Hello, again. Haven, right?"

She looked up at him with her lips slightly parted in surprise. "Hello," she said after a moment. "And yes, it's Haven. And you're Mr. Elder?"

"Reverend. But call me Deke."

She gave him a once-over. "That is one shiny jacket, Deke."

"It's rattlesnake."

"Skin it yourself?"

"Charmed it right off." He paused. "You left the revival early."

"Yes. I saw what I needed to see."

"Which was what?"

She tilted her head skeptically. "Are you following me?"

"If I say no, will you believe me?"

"If it's the truth."

"It is. I stopped here on impulse. But since we're both here, and it's Saturday night, may I join you? Unless you're expecting someone—?"

She smiled slyly. "I bet rattlesnake skin isn't the only thing you can charm off, is it?"

"You can always tell me no."

"And you'll go away?"

"I will."

"Well, if you promise to be a gentleman and not do anything to make me get you thrown out of here, you may join me. That means hands to yourself, a minimum of flirting, and no attempts at religious conversion. And we're going dutch."

He sat, then asked, "So, what did you think of Brother Knode?"

"Honestly? He's a charlatan."

"Why do you say that?"

"Because there's no such thing as demonic possession, and even if there was, that first boy he supposedly helped was not possessed by anything except greed and a little community theater acting skill."

Elder grinned. Her spunk matched her beauty. "I don't agree with your first proposition, but you're dead right about the second. It *was* a total sham. The idea was to show people that Knode could do it, so they'd feel brave enough to come forward."

"So, you approve?"

"Hardly. He couldn't help a real person afflicted by demons any more than he could make it rain in the Sahara."

She sipped her beer, then said, "I take it you believe in demons, then."

"I'm a minister. If it's in the Bible, I sort of have to believe it. That's the operating manual."

"You really are a minister?"

"I really am."

She was silent for a long moment. He recognized the struggle in her eyes: her common sense battled with her very real attraction to him. He had to admit, he hoped the latter won. She was not only beautiful but there was something sharp and biting in her intelligence that he found immensely appealing. She wore no wedding ring, nor was there a crease to suggest it had been recently removed.

At last, she said, "I would not have pegged you for clergy. You seem too...secular."

"Now you know what *I* do. What's your trade?"

"I counsel juveniles and young adults who have been in trouble with the law. You know, the ones who might be turned away from a life of crime and misery."

"You don't sound sincere."

"I'm totally sincere. I do the best I can with what I have to work with because I believe it's an important job. But I've also done it long enough to be realistic about my chances of success. The percentage of my kids who end up in the adult legal system is..." She took another sip. "High."

"So why were you interested in Brother Knode?"

Again, she didn't speak right away, but this time he could tell she was thinking about whether to include him in her confidence. He could watch her mull things over for quite a while without getting bored; the minute animations of her face made every moment different, and all of them were lovely.

After another pause, she said, "I have a client who was the victim of a similar ceremony. It went awry and left her feeling...damaged. I had thought that exposure to another such ceremony, one done properly, might help her put the trauma behind her. I asked Brother Knode if he would be willing to help."

"And let me guess: for a fee?"

She smiled wryly. "He did mention that."

"Uh-huh. That's his kind."

"Anyway, I got second thoughts afterward. So, I decided to see him in action. Now I'm glad I did."

Now it was his turn to think before speaking because the obvious connection occurred to him, and he didn't believe in coincidences where God and the devil were concerned. "Look, I understand about doctor-patient confidentiality. It's not that different from minister-congregant, when you get right down to it. It's why Catholic priests can't testify about things they hear in the confessional. But I have to ask, and if you can see your way clear to answering, it might help us both. Is your client a girl of about sixteen, black hair and lots of cutting scars, who might be on probation for burning down a church last year? And before you freak out, I knew the minister who died in the fire. He was a friend. That's how I know about her."

Haven's expression shut down to neutral. "I can't talk about it."

"That's not a denial."

"It's not anything. I can't talk about it."

"I understand. And I respect that. We'll move on."

She took her napkin from her lap and put it on the table. "Perhaps you should move on entirely, Reverend Elder. Or I should."

"I'd appreciate it if you didn't. Not for professional reasons, either. I would just as soon talk about the weather or the price of tea in China. As long as I can keep talking to you."

"I warned you about flirting."

"You said a minimum, not none at all. Are you involved with someone?"

"No, I'm...aren't you a minister?"

"A minister, yes. Not a priest."

"Is there a Mrs. Elder hidden away somewhere?"

"No. There was once, but it didn't take. I'll tell you about it if you want."

"No, that's all right."

"If you want to Google me while I wait, you can."

She reached into her purse for her phone, then caught herself. "No, that's silly. We're adults, we're in public, and we're just talking, right?"

"Right."

"And we're not talking shop, right? We're talking about the weather."

"Right."

She drank some more of her beer. "Fuck it, then. Hot enough for you?"

He grinned. "Yes, indeed."

13

The Old Hickory Bowling Center had been the central teen gathering point in Somerton for fifty years. Part of the reason was its location, near both the main street that ran downtown and the bypass that allowed easy access to the interstate. The rest came from the total lack of viable alternatives, especially once the skating rink on the highway toward Milan shut down.

Cars drove slowly through the parking lot, looking for empty places or friends' vehicles. A police car sat at the service station next door, where an officer supposedly watched to make certain there were no fights or vandalism. In reality, he just played games on his phone and occasionally admired the teenage girls.

That officer, Bennie Jernigan, looked up as Carlyss Bolerjack walked past, drifting out of the night like a ghost. She wore tight black jeans and a long-sleeved black t-shirt with some band logo on the front.

"Honey," he said to himself, "the things I could show you." Then another pair of girls emerged from the gas station's bathroom and walked, giggling, across the lot toward the bowling alley. They each wore ridiculously tight short-shorts and tank tops with push-up bras.

"You got to shave to wear them pants, and I don't mean your legs," Bennie murmured.

ELDER TURNED on the motel room light. It did not make the place look any classier. Haven locked her car and joined him. They both looked over the bed with its pea-green comforter, the ancient TV with a dial to change channels, and the closed door to the bathroom.

"It's not much," she said. "But it'll do just fine."

He turned to her. "You've stayed here before?"

"Stayed? No." She looked at him. "Does that bother you?"

"That you know the best motel for a rendezvous?"

"That you're not the first man I've brought here."

He gave her a sincere, warm smile. "It'd be hypocritical of me to think less of you for it."

"You're a minister, isn't hypocrisy part of the job?" she shot back, then said, "I'm sorry. That was crass of me." She tossed her purse on the bed and put her hands on her hips. "Look, Deke, I'm a grown woman with a teenage son and a stressful job. I like sex, but I don't have time for a relationship. If that makes me 'easy' by your standards, then I guess I am. But I also don't have to measure myself against you or anyone."

"I agree."

"Besides," she continued, "how will you justify this to yourself? I mean, you're a preacher, and the Bible's pretty clear about premarital sex."

"Tell me, is this how therapists always set the mood?"

That made her laugh. "You have a point."

She closed the door, locked it, and put on the chain. On her way to the motel, she'd called home and left Troy a message that she was going into the office to finish something she forgot. She didn't like lying to him, but the truth was not something she wanted to talk about on voicemail.

She put her back against the door and slipped out of her shoes.

Elder stood between her and the bed, seeming somehow bigger indoors with normal furniture to give him scale.

She met his eyes. "I very much want to be naked. Is that all right with you?"

He smiled. "Only a fool would say no to that."

She shrugged out of the blouse, then slid her bra straps off her shoulders, all the while gazing right into his eyes. He gazed back at her almost tenderly, as if she were a treasure being slowly unwrapped for him.

Her bra fell to the floor, and she unzipped her skirt, leaving her in just her panties. She hooked her thumbs in the waistband, but his hands wrapped gently around her wrists.

He said huskily, "I'd like to take these off you."

"Why? You don't have to seduce me, Deke. I'm entirely willing."

"Maybe I enjoy it. The sensation of that last barrier sliding away..."

His hand slid to her behind and cupped it firmly. She closed her eyes and sighed. Then she began unbuttoning his shirt.

They didn't talk much. Really, they didn't talk at all. They guided each other's hands and mouths to their destinations and expressed their pleasure with animalistic noises of approval. Haven came three times under his powerful ministrations before he finally let go in her mouth, they lay atop the sweat-soaked bed—they'd never even pulled back the covers—beside each other but barely touching, the only sound their mutual gasping for breath.

With absolutely no irony, Elder thought, *Thank you, Jesus.*

CARLYSS WAS PUZZLED. After the weird encounter at the TLC-Mart, the voice hadn't spoken to her for the rest of the day, although she could hear it muttering indistinctly to itself as if from a great distance. And she had not glimpsed its presence at all. Something in the store, something about Linda Scote and Travis, had silenced it. That confused her more than anything because what could frighten a demon?

I'm not frightened.

Ah, she thought, I knew you weren't gone. "Yes, you are."

No, I'm not. I'm the prince of pestilence, I'm--

"You're doing the equivalent of hiding under the bed. What scared you so bad?"

Nothing.

"Fine. Forget it. But don't think I didn't notice."

She felt eyes on her as she approached the bowling alley's main entrance. It made her sad and drained. Some looked at her just because she was a girl, as they would any girl. But many of them knew her and her past. They thought she was an arsonist at best, a murderer at worst.

The girls that had tormented her all through school were now, at least, too scared to say anything directly to her face. But it also meant that no one tried to befriend her, no boys asked her out, and she moved through the world in a vacuum. Only Preacher Anthony treated her like a normal person, and even he watched her closely although he did his best to be discreet about it. There was nothing sexual in his scrutiny, just gentle love mixed with trepidation as if she were a bomb that might go off.

A group of girls near the door stepped aside as she approached, and their conversation fell to whispers. She went in, enjoying the blast of cool air after the humid walk. All the lanes were full, and she glanced around to see if she knew anyone.

You have no friends, the voice said. *Who do you think you'll see?*

Shut up, she thought in reply, or I'll take you back to the TLC-Mart.

I'm not scared of that place!

Then you were scared of someone we saw there. What does 'Dandelion' mean?

It's a stupid flower.

Then you're even more chickenshit than I thought.

Shut up!

"Stop it!"

This was a voice from the real world, and Carlyss turned toward it.

Jason Stein stood at a video game, trying to keep his attention on it. He was surrounded by three other boys, all older and bigger. She knew them, especially Troy Fields, son of her therapist. But he wasn't the leader.

That was Danny Blazer: seventeen, tall and muscular, with pimples on his chin and a hateful smirk. Everyone knew he was a bully, a racist, and liked to hit girls, but because he was big and strong and did well at sports, he was tolerated. And because he was big and strong and tolerated, he thought he could get away with anything.

Danny smacked Jason hard on the back of the head. "Do something about it, fat boy. Come on, show me how tough you are." His friends laughed.

Jason stared at the screen, his hands working the controls. "Just go away, will you?" he said, his voice not quite a whine.

Danny put his face right in front of Jason's. "Make me, fatso. Come on, you're so tough."

Again, his two toadies laughed.

Carlyss stepped up to them, looked Danny right in the eye, and said, "Leave him alone."

Danny turned to her as if she'd done the most ridiculous thing in the world. It took him a moment, but then he recognized her. His smirk became a smile, malicious and spiteful.

"Is this your girlfriend now?" Danny said. "That makes sense, two freaks getting together."

Carlyss turned to the other two. "Sam, I know about you and your little sister. And Troy, should I tell them what *you* jerk off to when you're home alone? As for you, Danny..." She locked eyes on him. "What happened to Helena?"

The boys all froze. Even Jason looked away from the screen to stare at Carlyss.

"Fuckin' bitch," Danny breathed. "You fuckin' bitch." He raised a hand to slap her.

"No," Carlyss said, with the certainty of someone playing on an entirely different level.

The three boys scurried away. Jason, frozen in place, said, "Wow. What did you just *do?*"

"Nothing. I just talked to them. You were here."

"You scared them to death. What did you mean by all that?"

"Just rumors. It's like the Republicans; if you say it like it's true, people'll believe it whether it's true or not."

Jason continued to look at her. At last, she said, "Your game's over."

"What? Oh." He started to fish out another dollar but then said, "I don't want to stay here anymore. You want to go somewhere else?"

"Like where?"

"Maybe a walk?"

"At night, in the middle of town?"

He shrugged. "Or not."

"What if they're out there waiting for you?"

"I'll take that chance," he said and quickly looked away, embarrassed by his blatant interest.

She thought for a moment. She'd come down here tonight to add more positive graffiti to the women's bathroom, but she didn't have to do it right now. The fact that Jason, soft and sweet and kind, wanted to spend time with her—and had worked up the courage to ask—filled her with an emotion very much like the way she remembered happiness feeling.

He just wants to get his hands on your titties, the voice said.

She said, "Okay. Let's go out the side in case they *are* waiting."

"Okay."

They walked out, past the same group of girls who'd earlier snickered at Carlyss. Now they stared, unable to find a way to fit what they'd just witnessed into their view of the world.

SAM AND TROY followed Danny outside into the night. Danny went straight to his car, climbed in, and slammed the door. The other two did likewise.

"Get the pipe out of the glove compartment," Danny muttered.

Sam, in the passenger seat, jumped to do so. Danny snatched the pipe from him, jammed a crystal into it, and snapped, "The lighter, too, you dumbass."

Sam handed him the lighter. "Dude, there's a cop right over there at the gas station."

"Fuck it, I don't care." He held the flame beneath the bowl until the crystal melted and began to smoke. He sucked in the fumes.

Helena. Helena was his cousin, and when they'd both been eight, he'd thrown her favorite doll into the street out of pure meanness. She'd rushed to get it and been struck by a car. Luckily the driver hadn't seen the doll so he simply thought she'd run out in front of him for no reason. She had permanent brain damage and hadn't spoken since. No one but Danny and Helena knew the truth, and Helena wasn't talking.

So how had that weirdo bitch known?

"Dude, can I have a hit too?" Sam mumbled.

"Fuck, no," Danny muttered, sucking every bit of fume from the pipe.

He was so thoroughly absorbed in his own situation that he didn't notice how Sam and Troy were also fixated on what Carlyss had told them. But none of them thought of sharing their feelings with the others.

ELDER AND HAVEN still lay side by side on the bed. Finally, she said, "That was a surprise."

"Pleasant one, I hope."

"Definitely. You seemed like you'd be...rougher. Quicker. More selfish."

"I wanted you to have a nice time too."

"Oh, I did. I appreciate you paying so much attention to me." She rolled onto her side and ran a fingernail along his jawline. "You're a mighty good-looking man, Deacon Elder."

"Thank you."

"Oh, like you don't know it," she teased. "I bet you check yourself out in every mirror you pass."

He cupped one of her breasts and said with a little grin, "And I suppose you don't stand up a little straighter to make these beauties stand out?"

"Vanity isn't a sin, is it?"

"Only in excess."

They kissed. When they broke for air, she touched the small metal cross he wore on a chain. "Do you get these when you finish seminary?"

"I never went to seminary. I'm self-taught. Well, that's not true. I'm lucky enough to have learned from examples, both how to do it right, and how to do it wrong."

She lifted the cross. This close, in the room's half-light, it seemed rough and ill-made. "Where did you get this, then?"

He ran a hand down her bare back. "That was made from the last bullets in my gun when I stopped being a Marine."

"How long ago was that?"

He moved his hand to her hair and grabbed a handful of it, loosely but firmly. "I can promise you, that story would kill the mood entirely. Can we save it for another time?"

She shuddered at the sense of his power and remembered how her own had left him sprawled helpless and moaning beneath her. "Of course. But can I ask you something else?"

"Sure."

She gestured at their naked bodies. "It's pretty clear you do this a lot. How *do* you reconcile this with your job as a minister?"

He turned his head to look at her, and she was surprised by the pain and sadness in his eyes. "The Lord asks a lot of me. I'm not saying he approves of this but I can only hope that when I stand before him, he'll take everything into consideration and not judge me too harshly for seeking a little solace."

She touched his chin, which was scratchy from stubble. It made her realize how late it was. "I'm going to take a shower."

"Really? Why not wait until you get home?"

"Because I have a teenage son, and if he's up, I don't want him to ask why I'm so sweaty."

She stood and walked across the room. When she turned on the bathroom light, it silhouetted her for a moment, and he was again struck by her beauty. It wasn't the garish kind that drew overt attention; instead, it was the sort that pulled you in gradually, enveloping you in a sense of completeness and acceptance.

When he heard the water running, he got up as well. He desperately wanted a cigarette, but he didn't want to set off the smoke alarms. He knocked on the door and said, "May I come in?"

"I don't think the stall's big enough for us both," she said.

"No, I just want to talk to you." He entered and paused for a moment in front of the mirror, straightening his hair with his fingers. Then he sat down on the closed toilet, still naked.

The shower curtain was opaque, so he couldn't see her. "What about?" she asked. She tried to sound casual, but inwardly she dreaded any sort of emotional content to this. It had been sex, and it had been *great,* but that was all. She didn't expect to see him again, and she didn't want any awkward goodbyes.

"I really intended to try to charm more information about Carlyss out of you."

She snickered. "No one's ever tried to charm information out of me. I wish you had so I'd know what it feels like."

"That's just it. I decided it wouldn't be right. I don't want to use you, Haven."

She felt a rush of shame at his words. She *did* want to use him. And she had, and that was that. "Well, no harm done. And I appreciate your honesty."

He wiped his damp chin. "But now I want to give you some advice. Brother Knode is a fraud and letting him near Carlyss would be a mistake."

She rinsed the soap from her still-tingling body, annoyed that her immediate response was to reflexively resist his comment even though she agreed with it. *Thanks, pal,* she said to the memory of her ex-husband. "I'd already decided that, actually. What I saw tonight... well, honestly, it was disgusting."

"Good. That makes me feel better."

She turned off the water and pulled back the curtain. She expected to feel self-conscious, maybe even embarrassed, but he was so accepting of her and so casual in his own nakedness that she stepped out in front of him and reached for the towel. He took it from the hook and handed it to her.

She saw the tattoo across his knuckles. "'Love' and 'Fear.' The two opposites."

"That's exactly right. You'd be surprised at how many people don't get that."

"No, I wouldn't. I live in the South. I'm surrounded by hate: racism, sexism, reds hating blues, homophobia, Baptists hating Catholics, everyone hating Muslims. I know hate isn't the opposite of love. Hate is its own thing, and it has no opposite. It's either there, or it's not."

"Wow. Most naked women aren't so erudite."

Then he was on his feet, and his hands went around her waist. He kissed her ferociously.

When they broke for air, he said raggedly, "I wonder if you'd mind if we did it one more time, and I did get a little rough?"

She felt his readiness against her belly. She could barely choke out the words, "Pull my hair and fuck me like you hate me, then?"

"Something like that."

And the next thing she knew, they were back on the bed.

———

ALONE IN HER OWN BEDROOM, Linda Scote experienced her first real orgasm. She knew where to touch herself, of course, and had brought herself to smaller climaxes many times. But this was the first time it felt like the ones described in romance novels or that she'd seen women have in the porn videos she'd spent the evening secretly watching. She had been prepared for the physical sensation but not for the emotional intensity; she didn't even realize she was crying at first.

It's wonderful, isn't it? the voice of Jesse Garon purred in her head. *Your body is made for this. All those people telling you to save it for marriage and only fuck your husband? They just don't want you to feel like this.*

She hadn't even thought about Bethany, who no doubt was in the hospital now, being plaster-casted from her ass to her ankles. It was as if the whole accident was nothing more than a TV show she'd watched out of the corner of her eye. Her friends had texted and posted about it, and Linda assumed she'd have to at least go through the motions of sympathy. But truthfully, she felt nothing but the same contempt she always felt for her friend.

When Jesse Garon's voice whispered, *Make her stand in that parking spot and watch what I do,* she'd done it without hesitation. She'd do anything Jesse Garon said at this point, especially after he'd suggested watching porn, followed by what she'd done to herself. But the strangest part was that Linda didn't picture Jesse Garon doing anything to her while she masturbated; she pictured her Uncle Travis, handsome and cocky and grinning.

She got out of bed and slipped into the bathroom. After she peed, she looked at her naked self in the mirror. The insect bites that covered her were all livid and swollen; some even oozed. Yet while they itched, she had no urge to scratch them. Nor did she find them particularly repellant. If anything, she saw them as love bites, hickeys from her non-corporeal but very real lover.

She returned to her bedroom. Somewhere in the house, her father slammed a door, and she heard his feet coming up the stairs. He would be drunk by now and probably enraged by whatever he'd watched on Fox News. He might wake her mother for sex or just pass out on his own. At least he'd never approached Linda, something she appreciated more and more as she realized the truth about people like Susie.

Susie probably asked for it, Jesse Garon said. *Probably paraded around in tight little shorts, showing off for her father. It's surely not his fault.*

Something deep in Linda's psyche winced at this. She knew it was wrong to blame the victim, no matter what. And she'd been friends with Susie forever and knew that she...

The thought trailed off. What had she been thinking?

She waited until she heard her father snoring. Then she dressed in black and slipped out to retrieve her mousetraps.

HAVEN QUIETLY OPENED Troy's bedroom door and peeked in. He was still awake, looking at his phone, his hair tousled. He looked so much like his father it gave her a start despite herself. "Hey," she said softly.

"Hey," he said without looking at her.

"You're up late."

"Just playing a game."

"Did you go out with Danny and Sam?"

"Yeah."

"What did you do?"

"Hung out at the bowling alley. Drove around."

"Okay. Well...good night."

"Good night."

She closed the door and went to her room.

She had not showered again after their second time. When they were done and she'd caught her breath, they lay beside each other, laughing like idiots. Then they both dressed, and he walked her to her car, even holding the door for her as she got inside. He made no inane promises and did not kiss her goodbye, but she saw in her rearview mirror that he watched her until she was out of sight.

She undressed and pulled on her old sleep shirt, then got into bed. She stared at the ceiling, tinted faintly green by the light from the TV power button. She had nothing to feel guilty about, she reminded herself: she'd been upfront, in control, and gotten exactly what she wanted. She'd also given as good as she got, which is what a sexual partner should always do. That was the advice she gave clients, and she'd followed it herself.

And she *didn't* feel guilty, not exactly. She felt...foolish. Not for what she'd done, but for thinking she could do it once and then walk away.

LINDA SNUCK BACK into her room, opened the cooler, and surveyed her harvest. Twenty dead mice, all with their little necks broken. Some eyes were closed, but many of the beady little black orbs looked up at her in what she imagined was surprise, dismay, and terror. That made her happy.

She'd had a pet mouse once when she was eleven. She'd named him, inevitably, Mickey. He lived for a year and a half and then died. He didn't get sick; he wasn't hurt; he just turned up one morning dead. She didn't know that mice had fairly short lives; she thought her father had killed him out of spite because he hated the noise Mickey made when he ran in his wheel at night. It wasn't true, but it was the beginning of her contempt for the man.

She pulled a paper bag out from under the bed. In it, she'd collected sticks, all around six inches long. She arranged a pile of them on her desk, beside several rolls of thread and a tube of Super Glue.

This will be beautiful, Jesse Garon said. *You're beautiful.*

She looked at the tiny, distorted faces, their whiskers limp. Some showed their little sharp incisors, but most of them looked so small and helpless that a stabbing pang of sympathy struck Linda's heart. Tears ran down her cheeks before she was even aware of them.

"They're so little," she said. "So cute."

They're filled with lice and diseases. They're vermin.

Unbidden, the image of little Mickey poking his nose through her fingers rose from her memory; his paws perched on her skin, his trusting eyes gazing up at her with the kind of wonder she'd never before experienced. The tears increased.

"I don't want to do this," she said.

We have a plan. And a deal.

"I don't care. I don't—"

Pain like she'd never felt before swelled within her. It started just under the skin, at the bottom of her ribs, and drew her body tight, as if trying to turn her inside out from a point just below her sternum. Her head yanked back as if her spine was shrinking and pulling her brain through the bottom of her skull.

We have a deal, the voice said again. And the pain went away.

She was more frightened now than she'd ever been in her life. "You're not Elvis's brother, are you?"

No.

The simple answer made her shiver. "Who...who are you, then? Are you..." She couldn't bring herself to say the name *Lucifer*.

I'm anyone you want me to be. Jesse Garon is as good a name as any.

Linda fell sobbing onto her bed. She lay there for a long time, purging all the self-doubt and revulsion that she'd tamped down and ignored since that night with the Ouija board. When she finally sat up and blew her nose, the dead mice again looked impossibly inviting.

And she remembered Jesse Garon. And her body came alive. She ran her hands over herself through her clothes.

No, not that, not yet. Work first. Remember our deal.

"Please," she whispered. She needed to feel him watching her while she touched herself.

Soon. And worth the wait, I promise.

With great effort, she took the first mouse from the cooler and got to work.

14

Dawn on Sunday morning found Elder sitting at Anthony's kitchen table, smoking and nursing a cup of instant coffee. When Anthony wandered in, he asked Elder, "What time did you get home last night?"

"About three-thirty."

"Are you drunk?"

Elder smiled. "No. Sober as Abraham."

"Is there a woman sleeping on the couch?"

"No. I promised, remember?"

"I appreciate it." He poured some water into a cup and put it into the microwave. "Are you coming to church this morning?"

"Of course, I am."

"Do you want to give the sermon?"

"No. I'll just sit in the congregation if that's all right."

"There'll be plenty of seats," Anthony said wryly.

"Yes, but the ones that *are* there will be the people who need to hear you."

The microwave beeped, and he carefully removed the cup. "Does that include you?"

"Always." Elder paused for a drag off his cigarette. "Will Carlyss be there?"

"She usually is. She's the acolyte."

Elder smiled slightly. "You trust her with fire in a church?"

"I trust her completely," Anthony said seriously. "Unless you tell me otherwise."

"I'm hoping to get a better sense of what's happening with her this morning."

"Don't let her catch you staring. She hates that."

"I can be subtle."

Anthony smiled sideways. "Right. Subtle as a car crash."

CARLYSS RETURNED to her bedroom from the shower and quickly dressed. She didn't like to be naked any longer than necessary; the voice was too mocking, too seductive, too carnal for her, and if she glimpsed his face, he would grin and lasciviously lick his rubbery lips. She also didn't like to see the scars on her arms, which filled her with more shame than anything else.

Lots of girls cut themselves; she knew probably a dozen who'd done it at least once. One girl cut criss-cross patterns into her thighs to the point it looked as if she'd been burned by a waffle iron (which was the story she told her parents). But Carlyss had done it for the most banal of reasons.

She had not been able to cry for her mom and dad.

At some point, the memory of her parents had stopped mattering. She reached a point where she understood that, while they may have loved her as much as they could, it wasn't enough. Not as much as they loved partying, and fighting, and doing the stupid risk-taking you were supposed to outgrow when you became parents.

On the first anniversary of their deaths, her grandmother had cried. Even her grandfather had teared up a little. But Carlyss felt nothing, and her grandparents noticed. They yelled at her about it,

131

called her unfeeling and cruel, and held up their own tears as examples of how she *should* have felt.

So she looked for those feelings in her own flesh. And hadn't found them. Which just made her feel worse about herself.

And as she just finished that thought, the demon spoke up. *Thinking about our artwork again?*

"Shut up," she said.

That was beautiful. We should do more.

"In your dreams."

The last time she'd cut herself had been under the demon's influence. Across her forearm, she'd carved the word RANCOR, which she didn't even know at the time. When she saw it, she'd had to look it up. Then she'd cut madly at herself, obliterating the word in a hash of bloody lines that only dumb luck and obliviousness kept hidden from her grandparents. Now she always wore long sleeves to hide her mutilated arms.

The demon wasn't done, though. *Did you feel that big fat cock of his get hard?*

"Stop it," she whispered, tired of the topic.

Jason had kissed her. It had been a quick, closed-mouthed, chaste peck on the lips, but a real kiss, done with affection and respect and possibly even love. He'd touched her hand when he did it, but that was all. And at the instant their lips touched, Carlyss felt the kind of peace she hadn't known since *it* showed up.

And *it* had been silent. This time, though, she understood that fear hadn't silenced it. And she had a sudden insight into the true nature of things. The ink on that strange preacher's hands had it exactly right. Hate wasn't the opposite of love; fear was. And Jason had conquered his fear with that kiss.

The voice wasn't silent now, though. *Your nipples got hard, too, didn't they? You wanted him to pinch them, then suck on them, didn't you?*

"You're childish," she said wearily. "Everything is not about sex."

Yes, it is. For you humans, it is. All about fucking and sucking.

She opened the closet and took out her Sunday dress. It was white, high-collared, and long-sleeved. She dressed, then put on small earrings and a simple bracelet. Her hair was parted in the middle and hung, still wet, around her ears.

There was a gentle knock at her door. Her grandmother said, "Are you ready, honey?"

"Yes, ma'am," she said.

Ready to get that boy's cock in between your legs, huh?

"You need a new topic," she said softly, with more annoyance than anger.

HAVEN LOOKED at herself in the mirror. Her reflection was, hazy through the post-shower steam. She'd had sex--*great* sex--with a total stranger last night. She barely knew his name and had no idea where he lived or how to contact him. It was the kind of thing horny college girls did, not professional women with a child and a mortgage. Yet she'd done it, and enjoyed the hell out of it, and refused to feel guilty for it. Unlike her dire night with Landon, she had no regrets.

So, what exactly *was* she feeling? And the irony that this was a question she'd ask a client was not lost on her.

Troy knocked on the door. "Mom, you done? I have to pee."

Haven put on her robe and opened the door. Troy, shirtless and in only his boxers, pushed sleepily past her. She stood in the hall and waited until she heard him flush.

When he came out, he said without looking at her, "Mom, can I ask you something?"

"Sure."

"Will you always love me, no matter what?"

This caught her by surprise. Troy hadn't asked her that sort of question since he was eight or nine years old. "What? Of course, I will."

He didn't look at her as he spoke. "I mean, even if I was a drug addict, or gay, or into bestiality or something?"

She put her hand on his shoulder, feeling the hard muscle over bone. His father had been built that way, at least in college when they met. It hadn't lasted. She said, "Yes, even then. If you have a drug problem, we'll get you medical help. If you're into animal sex, we'll get you psychological help. And if you're gay, there's nothing wrong with you, and you don't *need* help."

She pushed his bangs back from his eyes. He still wasn't looking at her, but she could sense he was relieved.

"Thanks," he said and went back to his room.

She watched his closed door for a long moment. Then she went back to her room and began to get dressed. She thought that parental worries had dissipated the lingering erotic memories of the night before until her own hand inadvertently touched one of the same places Elder had brought to quivering life, and then it all came rushing back.

God, she *really* wanted to see him again.

And she didn't even know how to reach him.

It promised to be a long day.

TRAVIS WOKE up on the floor of his garage apartment, clad only in his underwear, an ashtray and several empty beer cans beside him. His phone still blared away through the earbuds he'd tossed aside at some point during the night, so he turned it off, went to pee, and then dropped heavily on his couch.

It was Sunday morning, and his mother would expect him to take her to church. But he'd had enough churching the night before to do him for life.

The insane minister at the tent revival had shaken his head like a terrier with a rat, then screamed insults nose-to-nose for what seemed like an eternity. He wasn't insulting Travis, of course; he was after the demon that supposedly dwelled within him. Travis had witnessed deliverance before and always thought it worth no more than a giggle, but this had not been funny at all.

When the minister was done, two of his burly henchmen had dragged Travis out of the big tent and into a smaller one, where he sat with three other women who were also supposedly afflicted with demons. Young, earnest men knelt before them and prayed. The women prayed along, but Travis, out of breath and terrified, just sat there.

At last, his mother came to fetch him. She handed the young minister a wad of bills and thanked him profusely. She took Travis's hand and pulled him out to the parking lot, where most of the cars were already gone. She was blessedly silent for the ride home, but when they parked, she turned to him.

"I always knew the devil was in you, Travis," she said seriously, tears in her eyes. "You were so different from your daddy and Blanton. I pray for you all the time. I hope Brother Knode managed to knock some of the devil's claws loose."

He sure managed to knock some of the money out of you, Travis almost said out loud. But he was too numb.

Now he considered what he needed to do next. He didn't want to go to church, that was sure. He could drive his mother, drop her off and pick her up, but what would he do then?

He idly checked his phone and was surprised to see he had a text. Hardly anyone ever texted him except to try to sell him something, but this was a real message, and the source startled him as much as the words.

SKIPPING CHURCH THIS MORNING, Linda Scote said. COME OVER WHILE EVERYONE'S GONE?

He stared at the message for a long moment. He couldn't have imagined this happening a few days ago, yet after their strange meeting at the TLC-Mart, anything seemed possible.

He looked down and was surprised to see an erection pressing against the front of his underwear. Of course, he'd do his niece if she was willing, but she'd always hated him before; what made her change her mind?

Still, as he'd always said, never look a gift pussy in the twat. He got up and went to shower.

CARLYSS'S GRANDFATHER stopped at the curb outside the New Shiloh Methodist Church. A group of men, mostly elderly and black, stood smoking at the bottom of the steps.

Her grandfather said, "I really don't like you going to this church."

"It's fine," she said as she got out. "I'm safer here than at school."

"All right. Call me if you need me," he said, then drove away.

She walked past the men, all of whom stepped aside for her, and climbed the stairs. In the vestibule, the yard-long candle lighters hung in a rack. She took one down and extended the wick. By then, the men from outside filed in to take their seats, and one of them paused to light the wick from his lighter.

"Thank you, Mr. Johnson," she said.

He smiled. He was in his sixties, and his suit looked almost as old. "My pleasure, Miss Carlyss."

Once the organ music started, Carlyss walked slowly down the aisle, matching her steps to the organist's rhythm. She lit the two candles, pulled the wick back into the handle to extinguish it, and returned to the vestibule. By the time she had replaced it, everyone was standing to begin the first hymn, "His Eye Is On the Sparrow." She quickly moved down to her usual seat.

To her surprise, Revered Anthony's friend Deacon stood there. He moved aside and allowed her to enter. His physical size made her cautious as she passed him, touching him as little as possible. When she was past, he extended his hymnal so that she could see the words. It wasn't necessary because she knew this hymn by heart, but she appreciated the gesture and held one side of the book while he supported the other.

When the song was finished, there was a communal rustling as everyone sat down. There were maybe twenty people in the sanctuary, about evenly split between men and women. There were few couples, though, and except for Carlyss, no children.

Anthony said, "Today, I'm reading from Revelation, chapter 21, verses four and five." Carlyss heard pages turning around her as those with Bibles quickly sought the passage so they could read along.

"'He will wipe every tear from their eyes. There will be no more death or mourning or crying or pain, for the old order of things has passed away. He who was seated on the throne said, I am making everything new!'"

It's nothing like that at all, you know, the voice said.

Shut up, Carlyss thought back.

It's actually boring as fuck.

Without meaning to, she saw one big-knuckled hand resting on a knobbed knee beside her on the pew. She closed her eyes to avoid seeing the rest of her tormenter. "Shut up," Carlyss whispered aloud. "I mean it."

———

ELDER HADN'T DELIBERATELY PICKED the same pew; it was either serendipity or providence, and he was okay with either explanation. But he heard her speak softly as if to herself, and then once again, he caught the faintest whiff of the *smell.*

But only a whiff. Like a door briefly opened and then closed.

From the side, Carlyss's face was serene and innocent, with a tiny, upturned nose and a spray of freckles on her cheeks. Her hair was dyed black, but he suspected it was light brown beneath the artificial color. She had three piercings in the ear he could see.

What was missing was the tight-skinned, shiny quality possessed people had, one that made them look younger if they were middle-aged. In her case, it wouldn't have had that effect, but it would've obliterated the placid stillness with a rigid, artificial plasticity.

He was convinced anew that this was something unique in his, and possibly anyone's, experience.

———

TRAVIS LET himself into his brother's house. The lights were out, and the sunlight through the curtains turned everything a shade of hazy gray. "Hello?" he called.

"Up here," Linda answered.

Travis shifted his erection to a more comfortable position and climbed the stairs. Her bedroom door was open, and the light shone into the hall. He approached cautiously, ready for any trap, prepared to quickly and efficiently shift the blame to Linda if his brother suddenly appeared.

But when he got to the door, she sat at her desk, working over something he couldn't see. The desk lamp almost blinded him as he approached. She wore a tank top and shorts, and her hair was pulled back in a ponytail, exposing her neck and shoulders. Fresh, livid mosquito bites covered the skin he could see, and something that looked very much like a blue, swollen tick was attached to her skin right at the nape of her neck. He was too preoccupied with her lack of a visible bra strap to care.

He asked, "What are you doing?"

"Check it out," she said, and held up her handiwork.

Travis stepped back a second. "What the *hell* is that?"

"It's art. Why?"

"Well, I mean, it's…"

"Oh, come on, Uncle Travis, you're not grossed out, are you? That would be so disappointing." She turned and arched her back to high-light her figure through the tank top.

"I was wondering," she continued, "if you'd help me with these."

He then saw the cardboard box at her feet, where a dozen identical items were laid out in neat rows on a padding of paper towels. "Help you do what?"

"Well, I want to distribute them. I've got a couple of places in mind, but I'm afraid to go alone. But you're not afraid, are you?" She ran a finger along the tank top's neckline and pulled it down ever so slightly, revealing the tops of her breasts. A huge red mosquito bite marred one, but not enough to turn him off.

Travis had to swallow before he spoke. "How about you tell me *why* you want to do this first?"

She shrugged. "It's something to do. Ain't that a good enough reason? Ain't that all the reason you have for some of the shit you do?"

He chuckled. "That's true enough. But where is it you want to put these things?"

"Down at the high school. And there's a church I want to put them at, for sure."

"Kinda hard to get to those places without anybody seeing you."

"Not if you go late at night. And it's summer, so nobody'll be at the school."

"I don't know, Linda. This is kinda weird."

"Say you'll do this for me, Uncle Travis, and I'll let you put your hands anywhere on me you want for a whole count of ten."

Travis's lips went dry. He knew this was a big, dangerous line to cross—not only was she jailbait, she was family—but she was also deliciously hot. "Over your clothes," he asked raggedly, "or under them?"

"Oh, definitely skin to skin, Uncle Travis. I'm not a tease."

"Is that all I get to do, then? Touch?"

"It's all *you* get to do. I might do some other things." She formed her mouth into a blatantly suggestive O shape, then extended her tongue just slightly past them in a slow, languorous lapping motion.

His mouth went dry. He could feel no part of his body other than his erection. He watched her as she turned and bent to put the last item in the box with the others. The gap between her top and her shorts revealed the small of her back and the swell of her hips.

"Okay," he said.

15

After church, Carlyss went through the empty sanctuary and straightened the hymnals in their holders on the backs of the pews. Anthony and Elder stood in the vestibule, Elder blowing cigarette smoke toward the open door.

"I have *got* to get the air conditioner fixed," Anthony said, running his finger around his collar. He noticed Elder's gaze had not left the girl. "What is it?"

"I need to seriously talk to her," Elder said quietly. "Alone."

"I don't know."

"And *I* don't know what's up with her, but something went wrong with the deliverance, and I can't help her until she tells me what it was."

Anthony put his hand on Elder's arm. "She's not a suspect in a crime, Deke. She's a teenage girl, a *child*."

"That may be, but like it or not, she's now part of the battle between good and evil."

"Well...just don't be mean to her, okay?"

"I'm never mean."

"I remember what they said about you in the Marines, Deke. You may be on the side of the angels now, but—"

Elder turned to him, and Anthony was startled by the hurt and pain he saw in his eyes. He said, "Anthony, I can't change what I've done. I can only try to balance the scales by doing more good than evil now. This is part of that." His voice choked a little at the end.

Anthony sighed and nodded. "This is the perfect time, then. Go ahead. But remember what I said, okay?"

"Okay."

ELDER APPROACHED Carlyss as she finished at the last pew. He said, "Hi. I wondered if I could talk to you for a minute."

She looked up in surprise, then glanced at the vestibule, where Anthony stood looking out the door, purposefully not watching them. "I guess."

He gestured at the front pew. "Sit down."

She did. He sat beside her, an arm's length away. She looked down at her hands folded demurely in her lap.

"I'll get right to the point, Carlyss. I need to know what happened that night when Grove Prosser prayed deliverance over you alone. The night of the fire."

She looked up sharply and for an instant, appeared frightened. Then her mask of neutrality fell back. "I don't really remember."

Elder smiled skeptically. "Come on. You can convince a lot of people about that, but not me. I've done what Grove did for you for lots of other people. I've seen the aftermath. The one thing that's never left is blessed oblivion. On their way out the door, the demons make *sure* you remember all the debasement and humiliation they drove you to, especially if you secretly enjoyed it."

She looked back down. Her fingers twisted together.

"I *know* it didn't work," Elder said quietly. "At least, not all the way. To fix it, I need to know everything."

She sighed heavily, and her shoulders slumped. She didn't cry, though. After a very long moment, she said, "Do you know the four stages of exorcism?"

It was like asking Tiger Woods if he knew the basic rules of golf, but Elder only said, "Yes."

"My grandparents took me to see Reverend Prosser after my grades got bad and my attitude got worse. They thought I was on drugs, and since Reverend Prosser had been a social worker, they thought he could help. They also wouldn't have to pay him, which was a big deal to my grandmother, with all her medical bills. They couldn't afford anything like a therapist or a psychiatrist, and even if they could have, the wait was six months. Reverend Prosser was available right then, and he could see the truth about me. He knew what was really wrong, and it had nothing to do with sex or drugs like my grandparents thought."

Elder nodded. Grove Prosser had a true gift of discernment, which manifested visually; he could see the demons for what they were. When Elder met him, each had instantly sensed that the other was legitimate, and their respect was deep and mutual.

"He said he could drive the demon from me," she continued. "I agreed to let him try. We didn't tell my grandparents: they wouldn't approve."

"Why not? Didn't they send you to Grove?"

"Yes, but not for religion. They thought demons were only for Catholics. They thought Reverend Prosser would help me like a psychiatrist would." She paused and got her story back on track. "So, I came to his church one night, and he and Brother Acred began to pray over me. It was awful, like being stabbed with hot needles under my fingernails. But at the end, we all thought it was gone."

"But it wasn't."

"No. It was just pretending, just playing a joke. It was still there, still inside me. I called Revered Prosser, and he told me to come over the next night. I think he thought he'd have help again, but Brother Acred never showed up." She sighed. "I know why now. *It* blocked the text from going through. But I was so upset, Revered Prosser prayed over me alone."

Elder winced. No one, even a veteran like Grove Prosser, should do a deliverance alone. It was too much work, physically and spiritually. Had Prosser gotten cocky or just careless?

"It was awful. Worse than the night before. He battled through the pretense for hours. When the demon finally...finally came out and announced himself..." She stopped, her whole body trembling with emotion.

"What was the demon's name?" Elder asked gently.

"M-Merihem," she said, almost choking out the name.

Elder thought hard. That name seemed to be associated in his mind with rot, decay, and pestilence. "Merihem," he repeated.

"They began the clash," she continued, marking the third stage of the exorcism. "I...he hurt me. A lot. Merihem, I mean. He wanted to tear me apart, leave me a pile of torn flesh. But thanks to Reverend Prosser, I...I..."

She began to sob then. Elder put a hand on her shoulder. He wanted to embrace her, comfort her, but this was not the time. She needed to get through this on her own.

"Merihem was strong. He made me hit Reverend Prosser. Made me taunt him with...with my body. Made me..." The sobs began again. "Made me say the most awful things to him. But it was because he was scared. He was *losing*. Reverend Prosser ordered him to leave, and he did. But...before Revered Prosser could give me the final blessing, he had a heart attack and died. And then Merihem set the church on fire."

"Merihem did? He made you do it?"

"No! He did it. I was too weak. Merihem didn't let me burn, he wanted them to find me that way. The police thought...they thought it was some weird sex thing gone wrong, and that I deliberately killed him. They couldn't prove it, which is why I'm not in juvie. But...they made me promise to see a psychiatrist until I turn eighteen, or else I *would* go to jail."

Elder had never heard this sort of story before. "What happened to Merihem?"

In a quiet, almost childish voice, she said, "Oh, he's still around. He can't make me do anything anymore. But I *hear* him. Constantly. And sometimes, I see him out of the corner of my eye. He taunts me, laughing at my pain. He wants me to invite him in again. And…"

"What?"

"He's stolen my sleep. I haven't slept since that night last summer."

Elder's mind raced with the implications of this. If the girl was being honest—and he had to accept that she was—it meant the demon Merihem was right there, listening to them and whispering things only she could hear. He could not imagine how debilitating, how wearying that must be for her and how strong she had to be to resist the urge to invite him back in. He looked at her in outright admiration.

"Carlyss," he said after a moment, "I've never encountered this particular situation before, but I've cast out many demons. Merihem is terrified of me right now."

She chuckled like a man before a firing squad. "I don't think so."

"He won't admit it. They never do." He lifted her chin and turned her to face him. He looked into her eyes. "I'm not talking to Merihem. I'm talking to *you*. You've fought this by yourself long enough. The Lord never wanted us to fight and suffer alone. That's what *Satan* wants. Evil uses people and casts them aside; I'm here to stand beside you, and with you, against this pathetic creature until it's gone. If you'll let me."

Carlyss met his gaze with the eyes of someone who'd seen and suffered more than any girl should. She also regarded him with pity. "Reverend Elder," she said at last, "if you think you can, then I'll let you try. I can't tell you how much I want to be free of this…son of a bitch. But Reverend Prosser gave his very life for me, and it didn't work. He *gave* his *life*."

More than that, Elder thought, remembering how Prosser had gotten the message to him. *Maybe even his soul.*

She looked down and continued, "I'm not worthy of that sort of sacrifice once, let alone twice."

"He thought you were. And so do I, although I don't think it'll come to that. So, if you're willing, we'll do it."

"When? Now?" She looked so hopeful.

"No, I have to get some things ready. I'm not going to make Grove Prosser's mistake and do it all alone, unprepared."

"But this is Sunday. Isn't it the best day to do it?"

"God will help us any day of the week if we plead the blood of Jesus."

HAVEN COULD NOT CONCENTRATE. The memory of the previous night, of the incredibly wanton, unrestrained way she'd felt, kept intruding on her mundane thoughts. The sensation of hands, of a mouth, of a cock on her and in her just wouldn't let her alone.

Don't be an idiot, she told herself. *It had nothing to do with him, really. It could've been anybody. You were just horny, and after that godawful Landon,* anyone *would've been a relief.*

She knew that was at least partly true. But there had been something about Deacon, a strange dichotomy between his hyper-masculine appearance and the almost feminine way he'd approached her, that she couldn't deny. No other man, let alone one as muscular and virile as him, had ever spent as much time making sure *she* got off before attending to himself. And he hadn't stopped with her first climax: he'd made sure she was *satisfied.* Whatever else she felt about him—and the fact that he was a shady traveling preacher had set off lots of alarms in the common-sense part of her brain—there was no denying he hadn't taken advantage of her.

And now, she desperately wanted him to not take advantage of her again.

"Troy?" she called up the stairs.

"Yeah, mom?" he called back down.

"I'm going out for a while. Call me if you need anything or go anywhere."

"Okay. Where are you going?"

"For a drive. I need to think."

Troy appeared at the top of the stairs. "Is everything okay?"

"Oh, of course. It's a case from work. It's just bothering me, and I need a change of scene to think about it."

"Would you like to talk?"

He sounded so mature when he offered that she almost teared up. And his sincerity was obvious. "No, son, thank you, but it's about a patient so I can't talk about it."

"I can keep a secret."

"I'm sure you can. But it wouldn't be right for me to do it. I appreciate you offering, though."

"Okay."

She drove out to the revival site. She parked close, carefully picked her way across the muddy field, and went into the big empty tent. "Hello?" she called. "Anyone here?"

"Hi," a chipper voice said. A neat young man appeared from the back, smiling and offering his hand. "I'm Trice. May I help you?"

"I'm looking for Brother Knode."

"I'm afraid he's indisposed at the moment. Is there something I can help you with?"

Carlyss pulled out a card. "I spoke to him earlier about helping with one of my patients, but after thinking it over, I don't believe it's such a good idea. Would you please give him my apologies? He can call me if he has any questions."

Trice looked at the card. "Sure, Dr. Fields."

"Thank you." She left feeling relieved.

Trice was a simple, diligent man and had every intention of passing on both the card and the note. But when he went to slip the note in his pocket, he unknowingly missed, and it fell instead to the churned-up ground inside the tent. And just as easily, all memory of the encounter slipped from his mind, as if something had come along and erased it.

Haven drove out to Mulligan's, where she'd met Elder the night before, but he wasn't there. Then she went to the motel, but there was no sign of his vintage car.

She tried to think of anything he'd said about where he might be

146

headed, but all she really knew was that he somehow knew about Carlyss.

She sat at the red light, which took forever to change since it was on a timer instead of a sensor, then headed into the part of town where, as her father said, "you don't stop at the red lights." The church Carlyss mentioned was down here somewhere; Haven couldn't recall its name, only that it was a Methodist church.

At last, she saw it: the New Shiloh Methodist Church, a rather ramshackle building, in desperate need of a paint job and a new roof, but with freshly-tended grounds and other signs that the people who cared for it did the best they could. She pulled up beside a pickup, got out, and locked her car. Somewhere a big dog barked; she hoped it was chained or behind a sturdy fence.

The front door was open, and she stepped inside. It was incredibly hot and humid. She called out, "Hello? Anybody here?"

A Black man emerged from a door at the back. He looked tired and kind. He said, "Can I help you, ma'am?"

"I'm looking for Deacon Elder," she said, suddenly realizing how ridiculous his name was. Reverend, deacon, and elder were all roles in church hierarchy, and he'd probably just made up the name so she couldn't track him down. She was an idiot.

But the man seemed to know him. "Deke's not here right now. I'm Reverend Acred. Can I help you?"

Haven suddenly realized that if her patient saw her, it would lead to all sorts of awkward questions. "Uhm ... is Carlyss Bolerjack here?"

The preacher's eyes narrowed suspiciously. "No, she's not. How do you know both Deke and Carlyss?"

"It's complicated. Could you give this to Deke if you see him?" She handed over a business card. "Ask him to give me a call as soon as he gets this if he can."

He looked at the card. "You're Carlyss's therapist, aren't you?"

Oh, God, she thought. "Yes, but that's got nothing to do with this."

"Then it's a pretty big coincidence, wouldn't you say?"

She laughed with no humor. "I would."

"Listen, I don't want Carlyss to get mixed up in anything that's going to hurt her any more. She's been through enough. I know she likes you and trusts you."

"I promise you, Reverend... ?"

"Acred. Anthony Acred."

"Reverend Acred, my interest in Deke is entirely unrelated to my treatment of Carlyss. I shouldn't even be admitting I'm her therapist, honestly, so I hope I can trust your discretion."

Anthony thought this over, seemed about to nod, then blurted, "Look, I'm the one who called Deke in on this, so anything he does, I'm responsible for. He's a good man at heart, and I think he can help her, but I don't think you should be involved. She's going to need your help long after he's gone on his merry way."

"I'm not here to see Carlyss, or to arrange anything with Deke that has to do with her."

Anthony's eyes lit up. "Ah. Then you're the woman from last night, aren't you?"

Haven felt herself blush. "I don't know what he said, but—"

"He didn't say a thing. Just that he'd met someone. Now *that* is one super-sized fries-with-that coincidence." Anthony fought the urge to laugh. "I apologize for the confusion, ma'am. I'll make sure he gets your card."

"Thank you," she said with relief and got out of there as fast as she could.

LINDA SCOTE WALKED down the hospital hallway. It was Sunday afternoon, so the place was fairly packed with visitors, and she heard sniffling, sobs, and the occasional rare laugh from the other rooms. TVs blared baseball games. Nurses went about their duties.

The Somerton hospital was only three stories, and Bethany was on the top floor. Jesse Garon had promised Linda that Bethany would be alone, and sure enough, when Linda knocked, Bethany said weakly, "Come in."

Bethany was on her back, with both legs encased in plaster and

Frankenstein-like mechanisms holding the pins that kept the shattered bones together. Her hair was pulled back from her face in a greasy unwashed ponytail, and her eyes were red-rimmed and blurry. She wore glasses instead of her contacts. She said woozily, "Linda?"

"Yep," Linda said cheerfully. "Thought I'd come see you now that you were settled."

"Thanks," Bethany said mechanically. "Nobody else except Susie has."

"Well, it's summer. People have things to do." She walked around the bed and sat in the chair. "You look like shit, Beth."

"Hard to dress up with all this."

"Yeah, but you could make an effort. And it smells awful in here."

Tears ran down Bethany's cheeks, but her expression didn't change. "I'm sorry."

"Well, don't worry about it," Linda said flippantly and put her hand over Bethany's. "Just concentrate on getting well."

"They say that'll take a while. I'll probably miss the first half of senior year."

"Oh, bummer," Linda said. "No homecoming, no prom, no dates." She laughed. "That's awful."

Bethany looked down at the remote control that would summon the nurses. Linda slid it out of her reach.

"Why are you here?" Bethany asked in a small, timid voice.

"Why, to see one of my best friends, why do you think?"

"You set me up, Linda. I don't know how you knew, but you put me there on purpose so that old man would hit me. You never went back to get your car. I saw you. I saw you standing there, laughing."

Linda's smile faded, and she squeezed Bethany's hand until the girl winced and tried to pull away. She leaned close until she could count the tears caught in Bethany's eyelashes. "Listen, you stupid whore, I hope you've got sense enough to keep stuff like that to yourself because you're not in a position to be starting any shit with me. If I hear that shit from anyone else, I'll know where it started, and I'll come find you here one night, between the nurses' shifts, when no one can protect you." She looked down at Bethany's legs. "Wonder what would happen if I started tightening some of these bolts, huh? Or just shook you a little?"

She pushed the bed hard, making it rattle. Bethany gasped in pain.

Linda's voice dropped to a whisper. "Whatever happened to you, honey, you deserved. You're a waste of fucking bra and panties, you know that? Nobody likes you, that's why nobody's been to see you. Friends? You ain't got no friends. Better for you and everyone else if that car had crushed your skull instead of your legs."

She moved her hand down until she found the edge of the hospital gown, then slid it under, along her friend's skin. It was slippery with dried sweat, and her belly heaved with fear under Linda's fingertips.

Even softer, Linda said, "And don't pretend you don't like this, bitch."

Bethany's face contorted, and she began to sob.

Linda withdrew her hand and stood up, smiling. "Well, I've got to get ready for church tonight. I skipped this morning, so you know how my daddy is. You get well, Beth. I'll be back to check on you soon."

Whistling to herself, Linda left her friend crying. In her head, Jesse Garon said, *That was exquisite. You did that perfectly.*

Linda beamed with pride.

ELDER SAT in the booth at McDonald's, using their wireless to look up the demon Carlyss had named. The place was packed with teenagers, but the noise barely registered on him. He scrolled through the search responses on his phone before clicking one.

The entry read:

Merihem was once an angel who, in the Great War with Heaven, angered the Lord by bathing in the blood of the opposing angels. Formerly beautiful, he was cursed with ugliness and consigned to hell. This drove him mad, and now he spreads pestilence and degradation.

Other sources supported this. A minor demon, then, with an unbalanced mind and a rather pitiful demonic skill set. Grove should've been able to handle him easily, shake him loose from his host, and send him back to hell, where he belonged. That ill-timed heart attack, though, had prevented it. Had Merihem somehow caused it? Or had Grove, no longer a young man and foolishly working solo, simply collapsed from the pressure? Elder would never know, and ultimately, it didn't matter.

But he did know a bit more about the enemy, and he needed to call in his backup. He dialed the first number, and a deep male voice said, "Hello?"

"Pastor Woodson. It's Deacon Elder."

"Deke," he said noncommittally.

"I need your help with a deliverance tomorrow night. In Somerton, over near Jackson."

"Can't do it, Deke. Gloria's in the hospital. Might've been a heart attack."

He tried the next name on his list, Reverend McNally. But the number no longer worked

His last call was to Anastasia Brennan, a nondenominational officiant who nonetheless had the true gift of discernment. Her voice was weary when she answered.

"Stacy, I need—"

"I can't, Deacon. I'm getting chemo, and I'm just too worn out."

He made his condolences, then sat back and considered his next move. He remembered the stalled text that Grove sent to Anthony and wondered if all the misfortune was coincidence or the influence of that greasy little demon. But nothing in what he'd read, or sensed, implied that Merihem alone had that sort of power.

That was always the danger, he knew. Not that demons would interfere, but that the minister praying deliverance would see every accident as a deliberate act. And truthfully, like what happened to Grove, there was no way of knowing.

It looked like it would just be him and Anthony.

CARLYSS KNOCKED on the half-opened door. "Can I come in?"

Bethany's mother, seated beside her daughter's hospital bed, looked up and said, "Now's not a good time."

"No, it's okay, Mom," Bethany said. "Come on in, Carlyss."

She entered the room and waited at a respectful distance. Bethany's mother stood and said, "I'll take a walk and let you two girls talk." She gave Carlyss a hard, warning look as she left the room.

Carlyss stepped to the side of the bed and looked over the damage to Bethany's legs. "Wow, Beth. I'm so sorry."

"Me, too," she mumbled.

"Is there anything I can get you?"

"No, that's what the nurses are for. And Mom. I have to let them do everything for me."

"How long will you have to stay here?"

She shrugged as much as her position allowed. "Weeks. Maybe months. I probably won't graduate next year." Her eyes grew heavy with tears.

Carlyss took her hand and said again, "I'm so sorry."

Bethany snatched her hand away as if Carlyss's touch had burned her.

Carlyss's eyes opened wide. "Sorry about that too. I didn't mean anything by it."

"No, it's just ..."

Light sparkled on something. A piece of glass about the size of a quarter, broken from a drinking cup, lay just under the edge of the pillow. "What's that?" Carlyss asked as she carefully picked it up.

"Nothing," Bethany said quickly. "I broke a glass earlier."

Carlyss held it up. The razor-sharp edge gleamed. A cold jolt went through her as she realized what it meant. "Oh, Beth," she whispered.

Bethany turned away as much as her condition allowed. "Shut up, Carlyss. I don't need some weirdo's sympathy."

"Beth, I know you're hurting, but you can't—"

"What do you care?" Bethany snapped. "What do any of you care?"

Carlyss carefully put the broken glass out of reach in the trash can.

She was filled with compassion for her friend. "Jesus, Beth, you can't seriously mean to kill yourself over this."

She looked past Carlyss at the open door, then said, "Go make sure mom's not outside listening, then shut the door."

Carlyss did, careful to also keep an eye on her friend in case she had another hidden weapon. Bethany's mom was nowhere in sight. She closed the door, then returned to the bedside.

Bethany said softly, "How well do you know Linda Scote?"

"Not very. She's never been very nice to me."

"She's never been very nice to anyone, including her friends. But...I think she did this to me on purpose, Carlyss. I mean, I can't prove it or anything, but...I was with her, and she had me stand in the parking spot where that old man hit me. And when I was laying there hurt, I saw her *laughing*. She didn't try to get help or anything; she just stood back there with some guy, laughing."

Carlyss frowned. She had seen Linda that very day at the TLC-Mart. It must've been right after the accident happened, and sure enough, she hadn't looked upset at all. "That's awful, Beth."

"Yes. And she came to see me a couple of hours ago. She...she threatened me. And..."

"What?"

"I don't know how to say it. She came on to me. While I was like this."

Carlyss's eyebrows rose. "She did what?"

"She put her hand under my gown and t-touched me."

Carlyss's brain was rushing at a thousand miles an hour, connecting things and creating patterns. Merihem was totally silent. At last, she said, "I'm very sorry, Beth. She's always been a bitch; I guess she's a pervert too."

"There's nothing wrong with liking girls," Bethany snapped defensively.

Carlyss suddenly realized what that implied about Bethany. Gently she said, "No, there's not. But there's something wrong with groping them while they're in your condition, against their will. And there's something *seriously* wrong with laughing while your friend is hurt.

But none of that is your fault, and you have too many people who *do* care about you to let it drive you to..." She didn't say the final word, afraid to utter it aloud.

Bethany said nothing.

Carlyss felt a strange, overwhelming sense of peace come over her, tingling like goosebumps along her skin. She took Bethany's hand in both of hers. "I don't mean anything by this, Beth, except that you and I were best friends once, and I miss that. I miss *you*. And I care about you. I'm very sorry for what happened to you. I'll try to visit as much as you want me to, but you have to promise me you won't try to hurt yourself."

Bethany nodded at Carlyss's long sleeves. "You cut *your*self."

"I don't anymore. And I never tried to kill myself."

Bethany looked up at her. "That'd be nice," she said in a small voice. "For you to come visit. We could maybe watch TV together."

"Yeah," Carlyss said and smiled. She leaned close and kissed Bethany on the forehead.

The door opened, and Bethany's mother said with forced cheer, "Have you girls caught up on your gossip?"

"Yes, ma'am," Carlyss said and patted Bethany's hand where she put it back down. "I won't keep you, I know you must be tired. I'll try to come back tomorrow if that's okay."

"I don't know if Bethany is up to—"

"Yes," Bethany said, interrupting. "That'd be nice, Carly."

Carlyss smiled. She hadn't been called that since middle school.

As she walked to the elevator, Carlyss mulled over the inescapable but outlandish conclusion: Linda Scote was *also* possessed by a demon. It explained her new viciousness, as well as Merihem's response to her at the TLC-Mart. Had her demon been chanting the other one's name? Dandelion?

And what had Merihem said? *You have any idea what you're seeing? No, of course, you don't.* Was Linda possessed by an even more powerful demon?

As the elevator descended, Merihem said, *That was a waste of time, wasn't it?*

"Not at all," Carlyss whispered, still feeling the residue of the almost preternatural peace. "Kindness is never a waste of time."

THE AFTERNOON SUN blazed down on the lot where Grove Prosser's church once stood. The remains of the old building had been removed, and a chain-link fence surrounded the construction of the new church.

Elder stood at the fence, imagining the fire that had consumed the original church. *Grove, you dumbass,* he thought. *You knew better.*

"Hello," a new voice said. He turned to see an older woman walking a long, thin greyhound down the sidewalk. "Are you lost?"

"No, ma'am," Elder said. "I knew Reverend Prosser. I just came by to pay my respects."

"He's buried over there," she said with a nod toward the graveyard.

"Yes, ma'am. I'll stop by. Did you know him?"

"Oh, yes. We're members of this church. I mean my husband and me, of course, not me and the dog."

Elder chuckled. "Glad you cleared that up for me."

"It was a terrible thing that girl did. I can't believe she got away with it."

"I thought he died of a heart attack."

"Oh, that's what they *had* to say since they couldn't prove it. Everyone knows that girl did it."

"Well...nice meeting you," Elder said and strolled off to find Grove's tombstone. He felt the woman's eyes on him for a moment, then she continued on her walk.

Grove's marker was small and dignified, an appropriate monument to the man himself. As he stood over it, Elder prayed, *Lord, let me succeed where Grove failed. And please don't let his eternal soul suffer for the way he got word to me.*

A hot breeze stirred the air around him.

AT THE FIRST BAPTIST CHURCH OF SOMERTON, the evening youth services had finished, and it was time for the social hour, when the teens shared soft drinks and crackers in the fellowship hall. It was a tense, dangerous time, with groups and cliques of kids who never socialized anywhere else moving uneasily around each other.

Except for Danny Blazer and Linda Scote, the sharks in this goldfish pond.

Danny sat on a bar stool in a corner where he could survey the room, especially the girls. On a hot summer evening like this, they all tended to wear sundresses or shorts, and he watched for the sway of breasts or the flash of thigh. He sipped his Coke and luxuriated in the certainty that he'd had his hands all over the most desirable girls and could again if he wanted.

Linda sauntered over, her own Coke in hand, swinging her hips under the short sundress. Danny's friends stepped aside as she approached, allowing a clear path to their leader. She leaned against the wall near him and said, "Did you hear the commotion outside?"

"What commotion?" Danny asked.

"That Black couple tried to bring their little deaf boy back tonight. My dad, your dad, and a bunch of others told them to fuck off."

Danny and his friends looked up sharply. They all cursed, of course, but not in church.

Linda chuckled. "Shoulda seen that little boy cry. I thought deaf people couldn't talk, but he was howling like a bull getting his nuts cut off."

Everyone looked at Linda now. She ignored it and focused on Danny. "Can you give me a ride home tonight?"

Danny shrugged and belched. His friends giggled. "Sure," he said. He'd done so in the past, with slowly increasing increments of physical interaction. The last time, he'd cupped her substantial breasts behind the closed Shell station on Latimer, and his dick had stayed hard for an hour afterward.

"Something bit you," he said and indicated the red swollen circle on her shoulder. It was as big around as a silver dollar, with a firm head in the middle.

"Yeah, I'm delicate. Anything that bites me gets me all wrought up." She said it in a throaty, almost purring way, and ran her tongue around the top of her Coke bottle.

His dick solidified almost instantly. "Looks infected."

"It's nothing. Can we go now?"

"Yeah, sure, why not?" He stood and was glad his erection was positioned so that it wasn't too terribly obvious. His friends again stepped aside to let their informal king and queen pass.

He'll do whatever you say, Jesse Garon whispered to her. *As long as you make his dick hard, he's your puppet.*

Danny didn't look at Linda to see her smile. If he had, he might've had second thoughts.

DANNY HAD Linda's left nipple in his mouth and sucked hard, pinching with his teeth. She wrapped her arms around his head and held him close, luxuriating in the forbidden sensation. This was called "second base," and she wondered why she'd ever resisted it because it felt so good.

They were again parked behind the Shell station, in the dark spot where no streetlight reached. Her sundress was gathered at her waist, and his dress shirt was discarded on the floorboard. The air conditioner blasted coldly against them, but Linda didn't notice. His erection pressed against her through his jeans, and she rocked her hips over it. His hands cupped her ass through her panties.

She was glad the dim light didn't let him see the other bites that covered her skin, including one on her breast. Danny had been right: they looked infected. But Jesse Garon had said not to worry about them, and they didn't itch, so she did her best to ignore them, even the ever-growing tick under her hair at the back of her head.

Tell him now, Jesse Garon said.

Oh, not yet, Linda begged. As much as she enjoyed touching herself the way Jesse Garon told her, it was *so* much better being touched by someone else.

No, now, while he'll do anything you tell him. The voice was firm and no-nonsense.

She pulled his head from her breast and pulled him up into a kiss. When they broke for air, she said, "This is what that fat boy wanted to do to me, did you know that?"

Danny blinked, confused. "I don't...what?'

"That fat boy. Jason something. He keeps texting me pictures of his dick and messages about how he wants to suck my titties."

"You're kidding."

"No, I'm not. You want to see?"

"Pictures of his dick? No."

"I want him to stop, but he won't leave me alone."

"Did you tell your dad?"

"Of course not. He'd kill Jason, then he'd beat me senseless. Then he'd go to jail."

Danny was trying hard to keep up. "Wait, he *beats* you?"

"He has."

Danny shook his head. "My dad tried that with me, I'd shoot him in his sleep, make it look like a suicide."

"So, what do you think I should do about Jason?"

He smiled. "You want him to leave you alone?"

"Yes."

"Then I'll take care of it," Danny said. "I owe the little motherfucker for some shit, anyway."

Linda leaned close and whispered in his ear. "If you do, I'll get naked and touch your cock."

She felt Danny's erection twitch beneath her, and he gasped. She wondered if she'd just made him come.

The clock on the dashboard said 9:45 P.M. She had a date with her uncle in a little over an hour and needed to get ready. She groaned, not wanting this to end.

What's coming will be better, Jesse Garon said. *I promise.*

16

Bennie Jernigan yawned as he drove through Somerton. Third watch became exceptionally boring on Sunday nights, and he spent as much of it asleep as he could. But last night, there had been three calls to the TLC-Mart for shoplifters, and he dreaded the paperwork that each arrest had waiting for him at the station. The store chain had a reputation for prosecuting as far as the law would allow, so that also meant he'd be called to testify at some point, which would totally wreck his sleep schedule.

He turned by the high school. The loser kids attending summer school would be lined up here in a few hours, but right now the parking lot was empty. He thought again how much the school resembled the state prison down in Tiptonville, all concrete walls and newly-installed fences. Ostensibly it was to keep crazed gunmen out, but it also kept the kids *in*, where they could do no harm except to each other.

As he turned in the circle drive, he noticed something on the ground in the garden beneath the flagpole. He slowed, stared, and turned on the car's spotlight. He couldn't have seen what he thought he saw.

The bright, clear beam illuminated the area and left no doubts.

"Jesus Christ," he whispered.

LINDA CAME into her room and stopped dead. Her mother Ruby sat on her bed, her terry cloth robe cinched tight over her faded nightgown, the Ouija board box beside her.

"Where," Ruby said in her best highfalutin' manner, "have you been?"

"Church youth group," she snapped back.

"Until nearly midnight? And what," she said as she tapped the box, "is the meaning of *this*, young lady?"

To Linda, this seemed like the most idiotic conversation in the world. "Why are you going through my stuff?"

"Your stuff is *my* stuff, Linda Lynn, until the day you start paying your own way. Did *you* buy this?"

She thought fast. "No, Bethany did. She brought it when we had our last sleepover, but I told her no way, I wasn't messing around with anything like that. She must've left it here." She pretended to realize something. "I reckon that's why she got hit by that car, isn't it? You play with the devil, you have to pay the piper, don't you?"

Ruby stood up. Even if the half-full wine glass on the bedside table hadn't been there, Linda could tell by the way she wobbled that she was already lit, and the best tactic was to just agree with everything she said.

"You're lying to me, Linda Lynn," Ruby said. "I know you are."

"I swear to you, mama, I'm telling you the God's honest truth."

"You better be, young lady. The next time Bethany comes over, I'm going to ask her about this. She'll tell me the truth."

"You do know she's in the hospital, right?"

Ruby looked confused for a moment, then said belligerently, "Of course I do! But she ain't dead, is she? She'll be coming back over sooner or later, and when she does," Ruby jabbed Linda with a finger.

"I'm going to ask her about this. And if you're lying, I'm gonna tell your daddy. And he'll tan your hide six ways from Sunday, young lady. You just wait and see if he don't. I don't care how old you are!"

Linda imagined grabbing that fat little finger and bending it back until it snapped. "Yes, ma'am. But I ain't lying, I swear."

Ruby looked back at the board. "I want that thing out of this house. I mean it. I ain't having no Satan-worshipping games under my roof."

"I'll throw it out tomorrow, Mama. I promise."

"You better."

Ruby slammed the door as she left. Linda waited until the footsteps faded, then locked her door. She drank the wine her mother had forgotten, then sat down and opened the Ouija box. She sighed with relief at the sight of the board and planchette.

You don't need those anymore, Jesse Garon said. *We're much closer now.*

"Then I can throw it away?"

It was never that important. You would've found me anyway.

She closed the box and put it back under her bed. Then she turned out the lights, undressed, and climbed into bed. Within moments she was asleep, but her dreams were anything but restful.

THE NEXT MORNING, Monday, Haven was dressed for work by the time Troy stumbled downstairs. "Morning, Mom," he said as he went to the pantry and took out the box of cereal.

"Good morning," she said. She was already on her third cup of coffee. Between the conversation with Reverend Acred and her inability to find Deacon Elder, she'd slept very little.

"You look tired," Troy said.

"Got a lot on my mind. Work stuff."

"Same stuff as yesterday?"

"Yes. But it'll be taken care of today. What are you going to do?"

"I dunno. Mow the yard as soon as the grass is dry. Play some *Warcraft*. Maybe go hang out at the bowling alley."

"Don't you have summer school today?"

He sighed. "Yeah, that too."

"Well, behave like I'm always watching."

"Aren't you?"

The drive to the office seemed to take forever as she hit every single red light. She arrived ten minutes late, went in, and turned on her computer. As usual, the state system was down, so she pulled Carlyss's file from her briefcase and put it on her desk. Her first client, though, was a young woman trying to stay drug-free long enough to get her kids back. So, Haven did her best to focus on that.

"WHERE'D you go yesterday after services?" Anthony asked Elder as they drank coffee in his kitchen.

"Over to the old Lutheran Church. I wanted to see where Grove died."

"Why?"

"Wanted to pray for him. Wanted to ask his soul to pray for us. It's just you and me up against Carlyss's demon."

Anthony said nothing.

"She told me its name. Merihem. It's not very intimidating."

"It intimidated the hell out of me and Grove."

"I don't mean it'll be easy, just that now we know a lot more than you and Grove did. We know its name, its nature, and the fact that it's only attached to her by the slightest of threads."

"You say. Doesn't it bother you that Grove couldn't chase it off? He was no amateur."

"No, he wasn't. But he was old and tired. He had no business doing it."

"And you're young and strong and here to kick demon ass and chew gum, and you're all out of gum?" He held up his hand as Elder was about to reply. "I'm sorry, Deke. It's no time for snark."

"No," Elder agreed.

"Oh, and I forgot something." Anthony slid Haven's card across to him. "This woman came by looking for you yesterday."

Elder's eyes widened. "How the hell did she know to come here?"

"I didn't ask that. But I did find out she's Carlyss's shrink. Did you know that?"

"I did."

"Does she know about your plans for tonight?"

"Sort of. I didn't explain them in any detail."

"Do you think maybe you should? I don't think we should be working at cross purposes with her."

"No," Elder said. He tapped the card on the table a few times as he thought. "I'll go talk to her. It's the kind of thing that's better in person, I think."

Anthony winked. "I bet it is."

BENNIE JERNIGAN and Bernard Jones stood outside the school, staring at the tableaux beneath the flagpole. In the bright, hazy morning it looked even more absurd and more demented.

"What do we do?" Bennie asked.

"You asking me?" Bernard shot back.

"I mean, I guess this counts as vandalism, right?"

"I guess."

"Should we put up yellow tape before the kids get here?"

"We should, and then we should cover it up with a sheet or something. This weird-ass shit'll upset people."

"It kinda upsets *me*," Bennie said. "I mean, who *does* that?"

Bernard shrugged, but inwardly, he had a pretty good idea. "Tape it off, cover it up, and call Animal Control."

"Animal Control?"

"Those are dead animals. I ain't touchin' 'em."

"What are you gonna do while I'm doing the grunt work?"

"Hey, you called me, remember? I just have an idea I want to check out. If I'm right, we can stop this before it goes any farther."

"What do you mean, 'goes any farther?'"

"Just give me a couple of hours. I'll call you when I know something."

"A couple of hours? Dude, I'm on third shift. I should be home asleep by now."

"Go get yourself some coffee and donuts, then. Be a real cop."

"So do we call this shit in?" He was trying to think of what 10-code to use for it.

"I'm not going to. If you want, you can. But this is just some prank, and if we call it in, and it gets in the papers, then the little freak bastards get what they want, which is attention."

Bennie looked skeptical. "I guess. But if we get in trouble—"

"Bennie, if anybody says jack shit to you, point 'em toward me. I'll take the fall. I got seniority, anyway, and the union'll back me 'til doomsday. But if we can shut this down before they do something else, we need to do it. Everybody's too tense in this town already. Won't take much to set 'em off."

Bennie looked from the display on the grass to Bernard. "All right, I guess," he said dubiously.

"So just cover it up, keep it to yourself and wait until you hear from me. Okay?"

"Sure, Bernard. But I'm going off-duty in an hour, whether I hear from you or not."

As he drove away, Bernard felt a twist in his gut. Anthony Acred would take this harder than anyone. He believed the Bolerjack girl looked up to him and trusted him. He thought he was helping her.

But some people, Bernard knew, were totally beyond help.

WHEN ANTHONY PULLED up to his church, he immediately felt something was off-kilter. He got out and looked around, carefully checking for broken windows or a kicked-in door. Nothing seemed damaged. Somewhere in the neighborhood, that big dog barked, loud and angry, and its rage seemed to permeate the whole scene.

He walked down to the McDonald's, said hello to Lucky, and got his coffee. The manager gave him a dirty look, but this time said nothing. On the way back, Anthony noticed the eerie silence around his church. The dog had stopped barking, and none of the usual birdsong, sounds of motors, Spanish radio, or breakfast arguments could be heard.

As he approached the church, he spotted something in the little flower garden he kept along the street side of the building. He couldn't make them out at first, but as he got closer, he saw that they were little crosses. There were a dozen of them, stuck into the ground at awkward angles as if done in a hurry.

Then he stopped dead. That wasn't the strange part.

Tied to each cross—*crucified* on each one—was a dead mouse.

The stillness and quiet enveloped Anthony like cling wrap. He found he couldn't breathe for a moment and had to close his eyes and consciously inhale through his nose to bypass his clenched throat. *Please let them be gone,* he prayed. *Lord, when I look again, please let them be gone.*

But they were there, little forelegs stretched out and tied to the crosspiece, minuscule back feet lashed together and cinched to the upright.

He knelt before one of them. A tiny piece of wood was pinned to the top, with the words REX MURES written in what looked like black Sharpie. *Rex,* he knew, meant king; a similar sign had hung above Christ, marking him as *King of the Jews.* What did *mures* mean?

A quick check on his phone told him. The sign said, *King of the Mice.* In Latin.

He stared at the phone for a long moment before he realized why he hadn't put it away. He found Elder's number and pushed dial.

"Deke," he said, his voice hollow. "You need to come down to the church right now."

Before he could answer Elder's follow-up questions, a police car parked behind his truck, and Bernard Jones got out. "Hurry," Anthony said, and ended the call.

Bernard strode over, hands on the butts of his gun and flashlight, taking in the crucified mice as if it was something he saw every morning. "Interesting decorations," he said. "What holiday is that again?"

"Found them when I got here," Anthony said.

"When was that?"

"About five minutes ago."

"Yeah, there's a bunch of 'em down in front of the high school as well. Remind you of anything?"

Anthony said nothing.

"Seem to recall that Bolerjack girl doing something similar to a cat right before she burned up Grove Prosser," Bernard continued. His tone was casual, but his eyes were hard and humorless.

"Carlyss didn't do this," Anthony said.

"How do you know?"

"I just do."

"Well, considering that people who crucify small animals ain't exactly thick on the ground around Somerton, you can understand why I thought of her."

"Yeah," he sadly agreed.

"I need to talk to her, Anthony. Is she here?"

"I haven't seen her."

"You willing to let me go inside and verify that for myself?"

"If you want."

He nodded, satisfied. "Then maybe I better drive over to her house."

"No," Anthony said quickly. "I understand why you think she might've done this, but it's not in her nature anymore. Someone else did this, probably someone trying to get her into trouble."

"That could be," Bernard said. "But I still have to go through the numbers. And if I don't, somebody else will. I won't talk to the press about it or post pictures online."

"Can you give me today to at least talk to her first?"

"That ain't how it works, Anthony."

"I know, but I'm asking you as a friend, not a cop."

Before Bernard could reply, Elder's car squealed to a halt behind the patrol car, stopping just shy of the bumper. Elder hopped out and rushed over to join them. "What's going on?" he said. "What happened?"

Bernard gestured at the mice. "Somebody left y'all some yard ornaments."

Elder glanced, then stopped dead. He knelt, just as Anthony had done, and squinted at the tiny signs. "'King of the Mice'? In *Latin?*"

"Remind you of anything?" Bernard asked.

"Obviously," Elder said as he got to his feet.

"He knows about it," Anthony said to Bernard.

"You know that Bolerjack girl crucified a cat?"

Elder nodded sadly. "Anthony showed me the photo."

"But she didn't do this," Anthony repeated.

"So, you keep saying," Bernard said. "And *I* keep saying I got to talk to her, either way. If it's not her, it's somebody that knows her. Now, the next time she shows up here, I expect a phone call or a text. If I don't hear from you by noon, I'll have to go out and talk to her at home. I don't want to hurt a kid if she ain't done nothing wrong, but this is some weird shit, and if it ain't stopped, it's likely to be just the beginning. Y'all both know I'm right about that."

He gave them each a hard look, returned to his car, and drove away. When he was out of sight, Elder said, "Is Carlyss here?"

"No, she's not."

"Is that unusual?"

"Not really. She's not on a schedule. She'll probably show up at some point."

"She didn't do this," Elder said.

"No, of course not. Somebody's trying to make it look like she did." He looked down at the mice. "That's just creepy, Deke. I mean, who does that?"

"Somebody who's got an indwelling spirit."

"Someone *else* who's possessed?"

"I'm betting."

"Are you going to blame it on the TLC-Mart?"

"You know damn well I'm right about that place."

"I know you're sure you are."

Elder missed the sarcasm as he thought hard for a moment. "I need to go talk to Haven. Call me if Carlyss shows up here, okay?"

"Okay. But be careful."

"I'm always careful."

17

Carlyss brushed her wet hair straight as she stood in her underwear. The voice was, as usual when she was partially or totally undressed, keeping up a running monologue.

...and he'd run his tongue down your belly, toward your--

"That's enough," Carlyss said out loud.

I just want you to know what you're missing. Fat boys are great at going down.

"I'm not listening to you when you talk about this."

That's a good one. You can't help it.

"Maybe I'll go back to the TLC-Mart and see if I can find your friend Dandelion. That seemed to shut you up."

You don't know what you're talking about.

"Maybe. But lay off Jason or we'll find out."

The voice didn't shut up, but it did switch to mocking her upcoming appointment with Dr. Fields. That was much easier to tune out.

Carlyss had talked to Jason on the phone for an hour last night. He'd been funny, and charming, and sweet; they discussed TV shows, music, famous people, and many other inconsequential things. Jason did not mention his bullies, so Carlyss hoped she'd done enough to scare them away for good.

On that point, the voice had almost crowed in triumph. *You didn't do anything. They didn't scare off at all until I told you their secrets.*

But by now, Carlyss had learned to tune the voice out for big chunks of time and was able to concentrate on Jason. He wasn't the handsomest boy, or in the best shape, but there was a sweetness to him that made her want to cuddle with him, and kiss him, and protect him. If that was love, then she could accept it.

Love, the voice snorted. *No one can love you but me, you know that. Once they find out what lives in the dark places inside you--*

"You mean the things that *you* put there?" Carlyss almost snarled.

Hey, if the ground wasn't fertile, nothing would grow. You would've put them there eventually; I just saved you time.

"Don't do me any favors," she said drily.

She pulled on another long-sleeved blouse, this one dark blue instead of black, and a pair of worn blue jeans. She could smell her grandfather's coffee, brewed so strong it could strip paint, and knew he'd expect to drive her to her appointment.

LINDA LOOKED up at the Baptist Church ceiling. She'd attended services here all her life and had spent untold hours gazing in boredom at the pattern of the rafters. But now, for some reason, they seemed oppressive, as if they might come crashing down on her at any moment. She had to really make an effort to step into the empty sanctuary. But she felt as if this might be her last chance.

Jesse Garon was silent, and for the moment, she didn't feel his presence. Without it, her conscience reasserted itself, and she felt horror and shame at everything she'd done. But there was no one she could go to for help, no one except, maybe, her family's minister.

She walked down the carpeted aisle to the door at the rear, past the podium where the minister assured everyone they were all bound for hell. That had been his basic sermon since she was a tiny girl, and it no longer registered. *Yes, of course, we're all going to hell, we've got that now. Can we move on?*

The hallway behind the door was also carpeted and smelled of lemon-scented wood cleaner. She heard gospel music coming from the preacher's office. She knocked on the slightly-ajar door. She knew he was here: his car was the only one in the parking lot. "Pastor Walker?"

"Come in," a male voice said.

She opened the door, but just as with the sanctuary, it took all her effort to cross the threshold. She stood just inside the office as Pastor Walker, a middle-aged man with the same haircut he'd had since his stint in the army, looked up at her and frowned. "Linda?"

"Yes, sir, Linda Scote."

"I haven't seen you in ages. You stopped coming to Sunday morning services."

"I'm there every Sunday night."

"Those are mostly social occasions," he scolded. "The Lord expects you there on Sunday morning too."

"Yes, sir. I'm sorry."

"Well, don't apologize to me." He nodded toward a large, plain cross on the wall.

Linda looked at it and then quickly glanced away. An echo of the same pain that struck her when she saw the glow from the revival tent shot through her head. She kept her gaze on the carpet.

"What's wrong, Linda?" Walker gestured that she should take a seat in one of the guest chairs. Then he perched on the edge of the desk. He wore a pale blue dress shirt and pressed gray slacks. With his salt-and-pepper crew cut, it made him almost seem to be made of metal.

A blush of shame crawled up her neck and cheeks. "Pastor Walker, I'm having bad dreams. Evil thoughts. I don't normally think this way, and it's starting to scare me. I'm afraid I've already done things that can't be taken back or forgiven."

"I see. How old are you now, Linda?"

"Sixteen."

"Sixteen. On the cusp of womanhood, then." He slid off the desk and knelt beside her chair. He put one big arm across her shoulders. "It's a time when everything's changing for you. It's like Paul says in Corinthians, 'When I was a child, I talked like a child, I thought like a child, I reasoned like a child. When I became a man, or a woman, I put the ways of childhood behind me.'"

His fingers twirled a piece of her hair. She immediately stiffened.

"No, not like that, Pastor," she said. "It's like there's a voice in my head that's not mine, telling me to do things I'd never normally do. I did something terrible last night."

His hand cupped her shoulder. "Now, Linda, everyone goes through these times, when they have...urges. It's nothing to be ashamed of."

"It's not that. It's..." She took a deep breath, then blurted. "I hear things. Things that aren't there. Things that *can't* be there."

He laughed the way an adult laughs at a small child who trips over her own feet. "What you're feeling is normal, Linda. Your body is changing, and with it, your thoughts. You're a very beautiful girl, you know."

His voice had grown low, almost a purr. His hand slid down to the small of her back.

"I'm scared, Pastor," she said, her voice soft.

"You don't have to be," he said, his own voice now low, his lips close to her cheek. "The Lord will send someone to care for you. To teach you how to control these urges."

She jumped up and ran from the office. She didn't see Pastor Walker fall back and sit awkwardly on the floor, and while she knew he called after her, she couldn't make out the words over the roaring in her own ears.

As soon as she left the church, the pain struck again, and she almost fell to the ground. She managed to reach her car, climb in and lock the doors. She put her hands to her head and screamed in agony.

You wanted to get rid of me, Jesse Garon said.

"No! No, I didn't, I promise!"

You went to see that slug of a minister. You thought he could help you, but he's no different than anyone. All he wants is to fuck you.

172

"Please, stop!"

If you ever try something like that again ...

And this time, the pain felt like it would split her skull in half. She vomited in her lap.

Then it faded, leaving her crying and weak in the church parking lot. She managed to start the car and drive toward home, thighs clamped together to keep the vomit from dripping through to the upholstery.

———

CARLYSS SETTLED into the chair opposite Haven. Haven immediately noticed a change in her, a slight but definite uptick in the way she carried herself, a tiny lifting of the perpetual darkness.

"So, Carlyss," Haven said with a smile. "What's new since last time?"

"You might be glad to know that it's official: I'm not a lesbian. I kissed a boy."

"Well," Haven said.

"That's all. Just a kiss."

"I'm glad for you. Do you plan to see him again?"

"Maybe." She sounded so adorably coy Haven wanted to laugh.

The desk phone buzzed. Haven frowned; Marguerite, the receptionist, knew not to interrupt a session unless it was an emergency. "Hello?" she answered.

At the message, she jumped to her feet. "What? All right, I'm on my way." She slammed down the phone and said, "I'm sorry, Carlyss, you'll have to excuse me for a moment. I'll be right back."

Haven froze when she reached the waiting room and saw Brother Knode and two of his big, beefy assistants standing before Marguerite's desk. They seemed to take up all the space in the lobby, their presence making those seated press back against the walls. All three were tall, broad-shouldered, big-bellied, and wide-faced. She wondered if they might all be related.

They looked more out of place than Ted Nugent at a Pride parade.

She was reminded of three great, flabby pachyderms taken from the swamp, hosed off, and then dressed in clothes both too small and too neat for their slovenly bodies. One of the henchmen was already drenched in sweat from simply walking into the office, while the other had the dim, lifeless eyes of a stranded fish. Brother Knode, away from his tent and sycophants, practically dripped unctuous hypocrisy all over the beige carpeting. He wore a garish suit that had clearly been cut to fit his physique, and his pompadour could've been made of plastic.

He extended a hand and said, "Dr. Fields. Pleasure to see you again."

"Brother Knode," Haven said. "Didn't you get my message?"

"What message was that?"

"I told one of your assistants that this was called off."

"I never got any message," Knode said. "Did you call?"

"I stopped by your tent. I'm sorry you came all this way."

He turned to the boys. "I'll be right back, gentleman. Use the time to pray and prepare." He put one big hand on Haven's shoulder and gently but firmly pushed her down the hall toward her office.

"Now, look—" Haven began.

"I understand your second thoughts," Knode said in his most insinuating voice. "It's an unpleasant thing to contemplate. But I assure you, it's so much more unpleasant for the young lady in question, living with the horror of an indwelling spirit. Is this your office?" Without waiting for an invitation, he opened the door and entered.

CARLYSS LOOKED UP. A man with slicked hair and a loud suit practically shoved Haven ahead of him as he entered the room. "Who are you?" she blurted.

The big man said, in a voice unctuous with faux kindness, "I'm Brother Knode. I want to speak with you about your soul, young lady." Before she could respond, he closed the door behind them.

The voice in her head was laughing, almost in hysterics. "Dr. Fields?" Carlyss almost shouted.

"Brother Knode, you can't—" Haven began.

Knode closed his eyes and said loudly, "Lord, grant me the power to save this child and bring her peace. In your name, I pray! Amen!"

Even if the voice hadn't been laughing like a hyena in her head, Carlyss would've known this man for what he truly was. The genuine presence of God in someone sent demons like Merihem into paroxysms of fury. She turned to Haven and said, "Dr. Fields, please, this isn't—"

The door opened again, and the two boys from the waiting room entered. It seemed impossible that the office could hold them all, but they quickly knelt on either side of Carlyss's chair, ready to restrain her if the need arose. She looked around wildly.

Brother Knode extended one big hand toward her. "Young lady, you are a child of God, but you are afflicted. *Afflicted,* I say, with the presence of a demon! It lurks within you, whispering things, urging you to unclean and unholy acts. Well, today, I intend to deliver you from it."

"Amen," one of the boys said.

"Stop this!" Haven said. "Right now."

"Doctor, you requested this, now you have to step aside and let the Lord do his work through me."

Carlyss gasped. To Haven, she said, "This was *your* idea?"

Haven, trying desperately to regain control, said, "I can explain, Carlyss. Brother Knode, I really mean it—"

"*This* is the sword of the spirit!" Knode roared, holding up his Bible. "Do you want the sword? I take the sword of the spirit, and I pierce you right now with it!"

He touched a corner of the Bible to the center of Carlyss's chest.

Carlyss opened her mouth to yell a warning. But there was no time. This false man of God, in mimicking the actions of the true deliverance that Reverend Prosser had attempted, opened the path for Merihem to return. Not even Carlyss's fervent unspoken prayers were strong enough to block it, and she felt the familiar awful swelling inside her mind, the irresistible force as her own personality, her own *self*, was pushed aside by the rancid, petty little spirit. Her face contorted as it stretched and shifted to express this new presence.

Carlyss began to moan. The sound ached of sorrow, and pain, and misery. There seemed to be more than one voice in it, too, a chorus of agony and despair that filled the room past the capacity of human voices.

Haven grabbed Knode and forced him to look at her. "Either you leave right now, or I call the police and—"

Knode pushed her away as he held the Bible against Carlyss. "Do you want pain, spirit?" he yelled over the girl's moans. "I'll give you pain!" Then he began to speak in tongues, a gibberish he'd learned to fake so long ago that he was able to slip in whole sentences of real words and not have anyone notice. He pressed the corner of the Bible harder into the girl's chest.

The moan abruptly stopped. Knode did as well. An odor like rotten eggs suddenly filled the room, and everyone but Carlyss reacted to it. One of the henchmen began to retch.

The corner of the Bible touching Carlyss began to smoke.

And in the sudden silence, the demon Merihem said in a distortion of Carlyss's voice, through a smile of venom and mockery, *"Ouch."*

ELDER ENTERED the psychiatry waiting room. The whole building smelled of antiseptic and industrial cleaner, it was a good ten degrees cooler than it needed to be, and the sweat on his back and neck chilled him.

The woman at the receptionist's desk stared down the short hall toward a closed office door. Muffled yelling and loud thumps came from it. He knew psychiatry could be emotional, so he said nothing.

She finally noticed him. "Yes? Do you have an appointment?"

"I'm here to see Dr. Haven Fields," he said politely. "It's rather urgent. Is she available?"

"She's with a client right now and can't be interrupted, but if you'll have a seat, I'll make sure she knows you're here, Mr—?"

Elder was about to give his name when he suddenly caught a familiar, sulfurous odor.

HAVEN AND THE MEN FROZE. They forgot everything else, even the smell. The voice emerging from Carlyss was clearly not her. Her smile, so wide and tight, was also all wrong. She no longer looked like a teenager but instead like something ancient, and poisonous, and deadly. The weight of iniquity filled the room, along with the rank smell of primeval mud.

"Sweet Jesus Christ," one of the boys blurted.

From her seat, Carlyss turned and looked at him. She licked her lips, a mocking lasciviousness that made him jump back against the nearest wall. The other boy backed away as well, all the way to the office door.

Carlyss turned to Knode. "Jesus I know, and Paul I know, but who are *you?* And what is that fucking gibberish you're speaking?"

Knode choked on his own spit. Haven saw the real terror on his face, and for the first time, considered that perhaps Elder's world of spirits and demons might have some substance after all. When it was clear the minister was vapor-locked, she stepped in front of him and said, "Carlyss, that's enough. This is all my fault, and we're stopping it now."

The girl's eyes fixed on Haven. They were glassy, shiny, like the eyes of a doll, and Haven could've sworn the pupils were slitted like a cat's. The girl's smile spread wider, to almost the physical limits of her skin.

"My name is *not* 'Carlyss,'" she said in that other voice. "Don't call me by that name, whore."

"Carlyss!" Haven said.

The girl's mouth stretched, growing round, and she leaned forward. She began to retch, her whole body shuddering as something

177

ALEX BLEDSOE

tried to force itself up her throat and out. She made loud gagging noises.

Pale, pink, wet objects splattered to the carpeted floor. At first, Haven couldn't make out what they were: Each was about the size of a quarter, with some sort of string at one end. There were dozens of them, falling and splattering, covered with mucous and stomach juices.

"What is *that?*" one of the strongarm boys asked in a terrified whisper.

By the time she finished, a pile of the lumps lay at her feet. Haven saw that they were moving, feeble and pathetic.

"Oh, my God," she gasped.

They were mice. *Unborn* mice. Mice *fetuses.*

Haven stared at Carlyss. "How did you do that?"

"A gift," the voice said. "From Dandelion."

Haven turned and reached for the phone on her desk.

"Not so fast, Haven," the voice said. Carlyss had never called her by her first name. "Who would you call? The police? A real preacher?"

Haven stopped in mid-motion. Who *was* she going to call?

Saliva trickled down the sides of the girl's mouth. "Do you still watch your son sleep, Haven? When you get drunk and horny, do you watch him and think about how much he looks like your ex-husband? And then do you go and touch yourself?"

Haven dropped the phone and backed away. "What are you?" she gasped. "How can you do all this?"

"That's nothing," the voice said. "Is it, Brother Knode? You can show someone how to fake throwing up nails, screws, even razor blades, can't you?"

Knode had, if possible, turned even more pale.

"Carlyss," Haven said, trying to sound reasonable despite the terror coursing through her. "It's time for this to stop."

Carlyss's eyes narrowed, and she looked around until her gaze fixed on a particular spot low on one wall. "You're right, head-shrinker," the guttural voice said.

An incredibly loud click made them all look. The strong-arm boy

178

who'd retreated to the door now clutched a short-barreled revolver in both shaking hands, pointed at Carlyss. The hammer was back, and it would take only a slight squeeze of the trigger to fire.

"Fucking bitch," he said, barely able to choke out the words.

The grating voice said, "Bad call, Metcalf Holling. Maybe I should come into you. Would you like to be turned into a willing faggot, Metcalf? I can do that."

"No!" Metcalf screamed in horror. He fired the gun at point-blank range, right at Carlyss's head, but it looked for all the world as if her neck grew longer and prehensile in the same instant. She dodged the bullet, and it struck the opposite wall, bursting through the plaster and striking the gas line behind it.

The explosion threw them all off their feet. The windows blew out as well. Only Carlyss in her chair remained upright and conscious. She laughed at those sprawled bleeding on the floor as more gas hissed into the room.

LINDA SCOTE WAS MASTURBATING in the shower when she heard the explosion. Of course, she didn't *literally* hear it; but she, or rather, Jesse Garon, was as aware of it as if she had. She turned off the water and slid the frosted door aside, listening. There was no follow-up.

The air conditioning vent, covered with one of those plastic arches that changed the air flow, blew in the direction of the mirror over the sink and kept it from fogging up. She saw herself in it, naked and glistening with water, and blinked in surprise.

The mosquito and chigger bites were all red, swollen, and scabbed. Her back and belly, in fact, looked like the beginning of leprosy. She ran her fingertips lightly over the scabs she could reach and wondered why they didn't itch or burn.

You look beautiful, Jesse Garon said.

Linda looked at her face in the mirror. The skin drew tight as if her skull somehow pushed against it from the inside. She didn't recognize herself.

"What are you doing to me, Jesse Garon?" she whispered, then scrunched her eyes shut in case the awful headache returned.

But he only repeated, *You're beautiful. Now, get dressed. We have work to do.*

THE EXPLOSION SHOOK the whole building, and dust from a ceiling crack rained down on the receptionist. "What was that?" Marguerite cried, jumping up and then crouching, unsure which position meant safety.

"A gas main must've burst," Elder said. "Everyone, out! Now!"

Since he was big and sounded certain, no one argued with him. He grabbed the woman, dragged her out from behind the desk, and shoved her toward the office door. The waiting patients, other workers, and therapists quickly followed.

Down the hall, he stopped outside the door to Haven's office. The distinctive demonic smell was much stronger and he recognized the laughter as well. His heart sank at the thought of what the girl must be feeling, but he also felt a surge of pure rage.

He tried the door. A huge crack ran down the center, and the jammed knob did not turn.

He drew back and kicked. The door opened but then slammed shut again. Elder put his shoulder to it and shoved. Something on the other side shoved back.

At last, he was able to get it open enough to see inside the room. Everything was broken: pictures on the walls, furniture, and worst of all, people. Haven lay bent backward over the remains of her desk, and two young men he recognized from the tent revival were slammed into the corners. He looked down and saw Brother Knode on the floor in front of the door, his bulk an effective block.

And in the center, in the only intact chair, sat Carlyss. Except when she turned and looked over her shoulder at him, it wasn't Carlyss who waggled her eyebrows in mirth.

ACROSS TOWN, at the same convenience store where he met Carlyss, Jason Stein flipped through the magazine, but he didn't really see the girls on the pages. Instead, he saw Carlyss as she'd been that night at the bowling alley, in her black blouse and jeans, dark hair falling in her eyes. He felt her fingers threaded through his, then gently on his face, then her hand on the back of his neck, holding him as she kissed him. He had made the first tentative move, but then she had taken control, or at least it seemed like that to him. Her lips had been soft and warm, and he'd felt the kiss throughout his body, not in a disturbing way, but as something simple and beautiful.

When they'd separated, she'd continued to look in his eyes, her gaze steady and filled with wonder. He couldn't imagine what he looked like to her: he was fat, sweaty from his earlier encounter with Danny, and he knew his own hands trembled when he touched her. But she seemed to see past all that.

He blinked back to the moment. The girl in the magazine, clad only in bra and panties, reclined suggestively. It now seemed so fake it was ludicrous. Jason almost laughed as he put the magazine away.

Then someone slapped him hard on the back of the head. "Hey, fatso. You and me got some business."

He knew the voice, of course. His stomach plummeted.

He tried to look past Danny Blazer, to the counter where the clerk should be, but no one was there. Only Sam, Danny's chief toady, idly picking through the candy. He wondered if Troy, the other sidekick, was somewhere near as well.

As usual, there would be no help for him, and all he could do was try to endure it until Danny got tired of tormenting him again. He lowered his eyes and let himself go limp, the better to absorb the blows that Danny would claim were just "taps."

This time, though, Danny grabbed him by the hair, twisted one arm behind him, and pushed him toward the back of the store. He shoved him roughly into the tiny men's room. Sam, following, closed the door.

There was barely room for all three of them. Jason wheezed with terror; there was a look in Danny's eyes he'd never seen before, a malicious gleam of triumph.

Danny picked up a plunger from beside the toilet. "This'll teach you to show your chubby little dick to people, fat-ass," he said.

Later, Danny and Sam emerged from the store. Danny was laughing, while Sam looked pale and sweaty. Troy waited for them outside, holding the bag of ice he'd bought to distract the clerk, who had to come outside and unlock the cooler.

"How'd it go?" Troy asked.

"He ain't gonna be showing his dick to nobody for a while," Danny chortled.

"What did you do?"

"Can we just go?" Sam said. "Somebody's gonna call the cops."

"He ain't gonna say a word," Danny said with certainty. "He knows he'll get worse if he does."

Danny and Sam walked on. Troy stood with the ice in his cold-numbed hands, looking back at the door to the convenience store. A semi rumbled by on the street, and the noise seemed to echo the uncertainty in his head.

"You coming?" Danny called back. "Or you just gonna stand there playing with your ice?" He laughed at his own joke as he continued to walk away.

Troy stood there undecided.

INSIDE THE STORE, the clerk straightened the magazines. The fat kid liked to look at them but never bought one, although he did at least always buy a soda. But this time, he left the can on the shelf, which the clerk had told him repeatedly not to do. No doubt the boy's friends had distracted him, probably with drugs. All the kids these days did drugs.

The air conditioner clicked off, its thermostat making a loud clunk sound, and in the silence, the clerk heard what sounded like someone crying. He looked around, but the store was empty.

He followed the sound to the men's room and pushed on the door. It opened partially, but something blocked it. The crying grew louder; whoever it was, was inside. He was about to push harder when he noticed red liquid slowly making a trail toward the drain in the floor just outside the door.

He felt someone behind him and realized one of the teenagers had returned. He felt a rush of panic and pushed past the boy, running for the front counter to call 911. He didn't hear Troy's choked cry of horror as he saw what was on the bathroom floor.

18

Elder closed the door behind him and stepped over Knode's body. The big man grunted and moaned but did not awaken. Elder didn't know if the others were dead or merely unconscious, and he didn't dare look at Haven to see if she was breathing. His priorities were clear: he had to take this demon down fast, so he kept his eyes locked on what used to be Carlyss.

The demon inside her smiled at him.

"Merihem," Elder said. He picked up Knode's charred Bible, half-expecting to find that it was a porn novel inside the cover. "I don't know how you did it, but here you are. Now I have to kick you out again, for good this time."

"Your friend Grove Prosser couldn't do it."

"Yeah, but I'm not old and weak."

"Doesn't matter, not this time. I'm too strong. I'm in for good."

Elder looked around at the destruction. The gas continued to flow, but luckily the blown-out window let it dissipate to a bearable level. "Maybe you are. But this time, you attracted too much attention."

"How could a poor little goth girl have done all this? That dumb redneck shot the wall." She looked down at Metcalf, his eyes fluttering behind closed lids.

"So, you say. I'll say *you* shot it. And you'll be carted off to a mental hospital for good this time."

Merihem frowned at this. "I'll deny it."

"Sure you will. But everyone knows Carlyss is crazy. They'll believe me over you. You won't have a chance."

The demon laughed. "Believe you? You once gutted an Afghani who had done nothing wrong but be in your way. You tied up a whole Muslim family and burned down their house with them in it for just looking at you sideways. And what about all those married women you fucked? You're already halfway to hell; why not make the rest of the trip?" She leaned forward. "Give yourself to me in her place. Trust me, you'll love it. We have so much in common."

"I have nothing in common with you," Elder said, fighting the rush of shame. His past was filled with atrocities both literal and emotional, and every demon he confronted seemed to have unfiltered access to it. He'd learned to ignore it for the most part, but this situation was so unique that his usual defenses threatened to desert him. "And as far as the authorities are concerned, I'm a war hero. Who are you? A teenage girl they already think got away with murder."

"You think your authorities are powerful? Wait 'til you meet mine."

"I've met yours, remember? And sent them running plenty of times." He held up the burnt Bible. "You couldn't even destroy the *words* of my authority, let alone resist it."

"Just wait until he makes himself known, and then—" She stopped, biting back the rest of the words.

Something clicked for Elder. *"Who* makes himself known?"

"You'll see."

"Dandelion?"

"Just wait, smartass."

Elder chuckled. "So, your 'powerful authority' is named after a weed?"

"He'll show you power. You just wait. Quote your words at *him*, see what happens."

"Well, when he shows up, I'll deal with him just as easily as I'm dealing with you."

"'Shows up'?" Merihem said, then laughed. "Shows up? And you think you're strong enough to battle *him*."

Elder thought hard. This was like no deliverance he'd ever prayed before; he already knew the demon's name, so there was nothing to force it to reveal. What he needed to do was break its grip on Carlyss, either by force or distraction. But how?

Carlyss stood awkwardly as Merihem re-learned to move the girl's body. "I'm done here. I'm walking out that door."

"Carlyss," Elder said quietly but firmly, "if you want him out, you have to help me. Show him once and for all that you won't accept him."

Carlyss's head jerked once, so hard Elder feared she might snap her neck. Her eyes rolled back and then, in a shivering voice that echoed as if it came from a great distance, Carlyss said, "Let...me... go!"

She shook her head hard, shuddered, and said in Merihem's voice, "You're wasting your time, little girl."

But Elder knew better; for a moment, Merihem had lost control. He needed to shake him loose even more. He couldn't surprise him, and he couldn't shock him. But he could ...

"Merihem," he said suddenly.

"What now?"

"You know about the Last Supper, I assume?"

"Yeah. So?"

"It's not in the Bible, but you want to know a secret about it?"

"What's that?"

"It was really difficult to get it scheduled."

Merihem, through Carlyss's face, looked confused. "What?"

"Do you know why?"

"Why?" the demon asked suspiciously.

"Jesus was really hard to nail down."

For a moment, there was nothing. Then Merihem burst into laughter. Not just amusement, but verging on the insane, twisting Carlyss's face into a mask of unhinged delight, her mouth open so wide Elder worried the skin might split.

Elder stepped forward and pressed the Bible against the girl's cheek. He called out over it, "Now, Carlyss! Push him out, send him away! In the name of Jesus Christ our Lord, Merihem, I order you to leave this child!"

As he held the Bible against her, the back of her head swelled as if something inside her skull was trying to burst its way out. She emitted noises as if an ark full of different animals was being simultaneously tortured, and the smell grew so rank that even Elder's hardened senses threatened to rebel. The swelling continued until a fist-sized lump had pushed so hard that the bone, strained to the breaking point, creaked in protest. Still, Elder held the book in place and continued to pray.

HAVEN STIRRED and opened her eyes. Her office was destroyed, and in the middle of the rubble stood Elder, holding a Bible against Carlyss's face.

Except it wasn't Carlyss. It was the same girl physically, but the expression revealed a personality that had nothing to do with the Carlyss she knew. It reeked of debauchery, of ancient humiliations gleefully experienced, of the kind of evil she'd never believed really existed. She accepted evil as a manifestation of personality, but this— this was evil incarnate. Awake, aware, and alive.

The lips had grown thick and crude. Her head seemed misshapen. Her hands, clutching at the arms of the chair, looked gnarled, like an old woman's. And the sounds she made...

Haven's vision blurred then, and her head began to spin. Before she had time to form another thought, she was again unconscious.

SHAKEN by his own response to the joke, shoved from both within and without, Merihem was caught off-guard. His renewed but tenuous grip on Carlyss began to slip.

Then, over the fire alarms and sirens, past the voices of people elsewhere in the building, came a new noise. It sounded at first like a crowd of people gathering nearby, all shouting and yelling in anger, but soon it was apparent the sound originated in the demolished room itself, although Elder could not identify a direction. It came from all sides at once. It started as demonic laughter, but as it increased, it took on a different identity: it was the sound of total, unyielding sorrow, as felt by thousands of souls at once. They seemed to all be in agony, expressing through their cries the regret and anger that fueled their unending torment. Soon it drowned out all other noise.

And whatever made it, it wasn't Merihem.

Elder stepped back, but still held the Bible out toward Carlyss. She stood perfectly still, eyes rolled back, face turned up. Elder realized he'd begun to crouch as if something huge loomed overhead. But except for the damaged ceiling, there was nothing.

"No, no, *no!*" Merihem whined. "I'm doing my best here! Let me stay!"

As Elder watched, the distortion slipped from Carlyss's face, an invisible mask that had distended her features into the face of Merihem dissolving into nothingness. Something that had lurked in her eyes drained away.

The noise faded as well until the only sound was one last, ululating cry, the voice of Merihem that receded into silence.

Carlyss fell back into the chair.

Elder knelt beside her. She was breathing, and he inhaled deeply. He smelled sweat and urine but no trace of the demonic. Merihem really was gone this time.

But what had chased him away, Elder or the source of that ghastly noise?

Carlyss opened her eyes and looked at him. "My head hurts," she said, her voice raw.

"I bet it does," Elder said, and tried not to laugh.

"I don't feel him," she whispered. "I don't hear him."

"He's gone." The sirens were outside by now, and he heard voices ordering people on the other floors out of the building. "Listen,

Carlyss, this is important. The rescue folks are about to get here, and there's no way to explain what really happened. So, we both need to pretend to be unconscious. You don't remember anything except a blow to your head."

"Why?"

"Because the questions you'll get asked are things you can't answer without ending up back in a mental hospital. Do you understand me?"

She nodded.

"Hopefully, we'll get out of this without being arrested. If I can't find you in the hospital, we'll meet back at Anthony's church. Agreed?"

She nodded again.

He kissed her on the forehead. "God loves you, honey. He really does."

He turned to Haven, still bent backward over her desk. He checked her pulse; she was still alive.

He risked a quick kiss on her lips. Then he picked a spot on the floor and stretched out, eyes closed. Just then, the first fireman opened the door and said, "Holy shit, there's three—no, *six* people in here!"

19

"Deke. Deke. *Deacon*."

Elder opened his eyes. Anthony Acred leaned over him, so close it made him jump. That made Anthony jump as well. Both let out a yelp.

Elder put a hand over his suddenly-pounding heart. "Son, you shouldn't sneak up on somebody asleep like that."

"Sorry. Didn't know how badly you were hurt."

Elder rose on his elbows. The other bed in his hospital room was empty, and beyond it, the door open to the hallway. He had a saline IV in his arm. He motioned Anthony closer. "I'm not hurt at all. I had to pretend I was if I wanted to avoid answering a bunch of really inconvenient questions."

Anthony's eyebrows rose. "You didn't blow the place up, did you?"

"Good lord, no. Why would you even think that?"

"Well, I remember that gas station thing."

"I did *not* blow up that gas station. Cell phones don't cause explosions. Even Mythbusters says so. It was that three-headed crow demon, Naberius. I saw him in a tree, laughing."

"Right. So, who blew up the office?"

"Merihem. Well, to be fair, one of Brother Knode's muscle-heads. He panicked, shot the wall, hit the gas line."

Anthony's eyes opened wide. "No shit?"

"No shit, my friend."

"And Carlyss?"

"She's fine. Merihem's gone for good."

Anthony looked back toward the door. "There's a lot of questions floating around here. I imagine you'll be hearing from the cops."

"Then I'd better make myself scarce." He began removing the tape that held the IV needle in his arm. "Look in that wardrobe and see if you can find my pants."

After he dressed, he spent several minutes restoring his hair to its perfect coif and shaking out the wrinkles in his snakeskin jacket. Anthony kept an eye out for the police, who he'd seen in the hospital, but not yet on this floor.

"Let's go," Elder said. "I need to see Haven and Carlyss."

"Somebody's going to notice you're not in your hospital room. You should officially check yourself out."

Elder smiled. "Then they'll know where to send the bill. Do I look like I have insurance?"

HAVEN'S HEAD THROBBED. She'd had plenty of regular headaches, even migraines, and of course hangovers when she was younger, but this was the first blow to the head she'd ever gotten. *Some people go their whole lives without being knocked out,* she thought bitterly. *Lucky me.*

But worse than the headache was the guilt. It was all her fault: she'd sought out Brother Knode, let him overpower her in her own office, and essentially betrayed her client. Whatever had happened, they were all in that room because of her.

Then she thought, *What exactly* did *happen?*

The events were scattered through her recollections, pieces only slowly finding their place. She remembered Carlyss coming in and Knode's assistants lurking beside her chair. And that *smell.* Then things got hazy. No doubt it was due to getting knocked out, but the moments leading up to the actual explosion were fuzzy and indistinct. She hoped they'd come back to her.

"Are you awake?" Carla Norman asked.

"I'm awake," Haven assured her without opening her eyes.

"Think of anything else you need from home?"

"Nah, just what I already told you. Thanks."

"Next time I tell you to proceed with caution, what are you going to do?"

Haven opened one eye and looked at her friend with mock disdain. "Make sure you're right there with me."

There was a knock at the door, and Troy poked his head in. "Mom?" he said in a small voice. "Are you awake?"

"Yeah, come on in," she said. She pushed the button to raise the bed so she could sit up.

"I'll let you two visit," Carla said. "I'll bring your stuff by later tonight."

"Thanks again," Haven said.

Carla left. Haven noticed immediately that Troy had been crying, something she hadn't seen him do in a couple of years. Her heart swelled with love for him, and she said, "Oh, son, I'm all right. I just got tapped a little too hard when the gas line blew. No concussion, no fractured skull. I'll be out of here tomorrow."

Troy nodded, seemed to hesitate, then rushed to her and began to sob. She put her arms around him as much as she could from the bed, heedless of the IV tube in her arm. "Troy, sweetie, I promise you, I'm fine," she said as she patted his back. It wrenched her own heart to feel his big, almost adult-sized form shudder with emotion.

"It's not that, Mom," he choked out. "It's not that."

"It's not?" Haven said. She felt both puzzled and, she hated to admit it, a little disappointed. "What is it, then?"

"I can't tell you."

"Well, you better. If you're this upset—"

"I'll get ..." He didn't finish the sentence.

"You won't get in trouble," Haven assured him.

"No, I'll get my ass kicked!"

She pushed him back enough to take his face in both hands. His checks were tight with emotion, and his eyes red-rimmed and running with tears. "Troy, take a deep breath. Come on..." It was the kind of encouragement she'd given him as a child. "In and out, come on. Count to five."

Troy grew calmer. She grabbed tissues from the bedside table and wiped his eyes. He blew his nose for her, just as he'd done as a small boy. Then she said, "Now tell me, what's wrong?"

He took a deep breath. "Somebody did something terrible to this other kid. This boy he likes to pick on. He...he..." Troy seemed to be unable to get out the words.

"Shh, it's all right, just take your time," she said, stroking his hair like she'd done when he was small enough to sit in her lap.

"He...he shoved a plunger handle up the boy's ass, mom. The kid was bleeding, he was crying...he stuffed his underwear in his mouth so no one could hear him...Jesus, mom..."

Haven's heart turned to ice. *"Who* did this?"

"I can't tell you."

"Then how do you know about it?"

Troy's face wrenched even more. "I was there. I was the lookout." He began to sob again.

Haven hugged him, but she was trying to catch up with all the curve balls the universe had thrown at her today. Her son, her *little boy,* had helped someone do something that horrible Where had she failed?

At last, when he'd calmed down a bit, she said, "Get my phone from my purse," Haven said.

Troy sat back. "What are you going to d-do?"

"I'm calling the police. You're going to tell them what—"

"No! Mom, you can't; he'll *kill* me!"

"Who, Troy?"

"I can't *tell* you!"

This was a situation she was, at least by training and experience, equipped to handle. "Troy, what's the right thing to do here?"

193

Troy couldn't get any words out. Haven had never seen him this terrified. It both broke her heart and enraged her on his behalf. Nobody treated her son like this.

"If you don't know," she said through clenched teeth, "then I've done a terrible job raising you."

He turned, picked up her purse from the chair, and handed it to her. He said numbly, "We'll have to move."

She found her phone. "We'll see about that. Nobody should ever get away with that sort of thing." Then she looked at her phone. "Shit. No signal."

As she reached for the room phone, there was a soft knock on the door, and a voice said, "May I come in?"

Haven's eyes opened wide as she recognized the voice. "Deke?"

He entered, followed by Anthony. Elder looked incredibly handsome in his disheveled clothes, his snakeskin jacket shimmering in the fluorescent light. "Haven. How are you?"

There were so many things she wanted to say, they all logjammed in her throat. At last, she fell back on the Southern standard, politeness, and managed to choke out, "Deke, this is my son, Troy. Troy, this is Reverend Elder and Reverend Acred."

Elder offered a hand. "Hello, son. Nice to meet you."

Troy shook his hand but said nothing.

"How are you?" he asked Haven again.

"I'm fine. They want to keep me overnight for observation. It lets them bill you for thousands instead of hundreds."

"I hear you. That's why I checked myself out before they got my mailing address."

"Why were *you* in my office?"

With a discretionary glance at Troy, Elder said, "Finishing what Brother Knode had no business starting."

Haven started to reply, then thought better of it. Elder was right; with everything else going on, Troy didn't need to hear about demons and possession. "What will you do now?"

"Talk to Carlyss. I took care of her immediate problem, but I'm worried there's more on the way."

Despite everything, hearing that her patient was in trouble made Haven sit up straighter. *"What's* on the way?"

"Hopefully, nothing."

She took his hand. "I *saw* her," she said softly. "I saw what she was."

Elder sighed sadly. "I'm sorry. I thought you were knocked out."

"You were right about her, then. Weren't you?"

"Yes."

"What do we do?"

"Like I said, hopefully nothing. But I'll let you know."

CARLYSS LOOKED up as the door opened without the usual preliminary knock. She expected her grandparents, but the girl who entered took her totally by surprise.

"Hello," Linda Scote said. "I'm glad you're awake."

"Yeah," Carlyss said.

Merihem's absence in her head actually left her feeling incomplete and unmoored. She'd gotten used to it after all this time, and even though she hated it and what it said to her, the presence had become a defining thing in her life. Now, like a splinter or a bad tooth, it was gone and left a space sore and sensitive around the edges. Her own thoughts seemed impossibly loud and distracting, and she caught herself mentally asking questions that, before, Merihem would've answered with his typical sarcasm.

And now Linda was here—Linda, whose presence had silenced Merihem after he'd reveled about "Dandelion." Carlyss felt weak, and small, and scared.

Linda closed the door. "You're my second friend to be hurt this week. I could take that personally."

Carlyss remembered what Bethany had told her, about how Linda had set her up to be hurt. "Well, I can't speak for Beth, but I didn't do it just to inconvenience you."

Linda smiled; Carlyss didn't. In fact, Linda just stood there looking her over, inspecting her with a thoroughness she found unsettling.

"What do you want, Linda?" Carlyss asked at last.

"I saw your little art project. At school and down at that black church you go to."

Carlyss frowned. "What?"

"Row after row of crucified mice. Pretty neat. Must have taken hours. Were they alive when you tied them to the crosses?"

"I don't know what you're talking about." But inside, Carlyss went ice cold. She remembered the cat that she—well, Merihem—had killed and crucified the previous year. "I think you better go."

Linda stepped closer. "Listen, you white trash little bitch," she said with a smile, "you shamed the greatest thing in the universe. He doesn't take that shit lying down. When you get out of here, you'll suffer like you never thought possible, and there won't be a thing you can do about it."

Carlyss stared into Linda's eyes, not believing what she saw there. It was the same thing she'd once seen in her *own* eyes, back when Merihem had full possession of her before Grove Prosser had reduced it to a mere voice. "Oh, my God," she whispered.

"Shut up!" Linda screamed. Her voice echoed around the room. She grabbed Carlyss by the throat.

Carlyss tried to wrench the hand away, but it was too strong, inhumanly strong. "I want you to know what's coming, whore," Linda hissed. Her breath stank of sulfur and bile. "Humiliation, pain, suffering, and best of all, watching everyone close to you feel it first. Starting with that fat boy you got all wet for." Linda released her with a contemptuous shove, turned, and strode out the door without looking back.

OUTSIDE IN THE HALL, Linda nearly ran into Elder. She stopped, stepped back, and looked up at him. "Excuse me."

Elder stared at her. She had the *smell.*

Linda frowned at him. "What?"

"I'm sorry, it's...are you one of Carlyss's friends?"

"Are you?" she shot back.

Elder cocked his head as if he couldn't believe what he saw. Linda said, "You're weirding me out, old man. I have other friends to go see. Excuse me."

Elder watched her walk away. Anthony cleared his throat and said, "You're staring at a teenage girl's ass in public, Deke."

"Not her ass." When she turned the corner, he continued. "Didn't you sense it?"

"Sense what?"

"There's something awful inside that girl. I could smell it."

"She's possessed by a demon too?" Anthony said skeptically. But Elder had already gone into Carlyss's room.

Before Carlyss could say anything, Elder demanded, "Who was that girl that just came out of here? One of your friends?"

"What? No! She's...I don't know why she was here."

"Yes, you do. You saw it in her, too, didn't you?"

Carlyss started to protest more but realized that if anyone in the world would believe her, it was Elder. "Yes."

"Wait, wait, what are you both talking about?" Anthony demanded. "That girl we just saw in the hall?"

"Yes," Elder said. "She has an indwelling spirit."

"Really?"

"Yes," Elder and Carlyss said together.

Anthony closed his eyes and sighed. "Of course, she does."

"How are you?" Elder asked her.

"It's weird not hearing the voice. I keep waiting for it to say something. And I'm tired, but I still can't sleep."

"That'll come," Elder assured her.

Anthony asked, "Have the police talked to you about the mice, Carlyss?"

"No, but Linda did. Somebody left crucified mice at the church?"

"And at the high school. They think it was you because of the whole cat thing."

"It wasn't me. It was her."

"The girl who just left?"

Carlyss nodded slowly as all the pieces fell together. "She wanted it to look like I did it. She said I embarrassed someone by not accepting Merihem and that there would be all kinds of hell to pay."

"Good choice of words," Elder said. "Did she mention anything called Dandelion?"

Carlyss's eyes opened wider. "No, but I was at the TLC-Mart with my grandpa, and I saw Linda and some other guy. Merihem was in the middle of talking to me, and when we saw them, he shut up, but not like he stopped talking, like he was silenced. Out of respect, like someone more important was around. And then he started chanting something like, 'dandelion.'"

"There's a demon named Dandelion?" Anthony asked, slightly mocking.

Elder turned to him. "Anthony, I thought you'd seen enough over the years to know this sort of thing is not a damn joke."

"I don't think it's a *joke*, Deke. I just think maybe you're seeing demons because you *want* to. Like they say, a man with a hammer sees every problem as a nail."

"I understand why you'd think that, Reverend Acred," Carlyss said. "But I promise I'm telling the truth. And Linda Scote and I barely know each other. She has no reason to hate me."

"Teenagers don't always need reasons," Anthony said. "I just don't want us—*any* of us—going off and doing something stupid."

Elder's fists clenched in frustration. Anthony was being entirely reasonable, but this was not the time for reason. He had just seen a demon walk out of the hospital in the form of a teenage girl, and it had to be stopped before it did more damage. "All right," he said at last, "maybe so. It's been a busy day, and maybe we should all try to rest before we make any decisions."

"Okay," Carlyss said.

"And..." He paused as he searched for the words. "I want you to know how brave I think you are. To have that voice in your head for so long and yet to not let it warp you into something awful. You're the strongest person I know."

"Thank you," Carlyss said in a small voice.

"Come on, Anthony. Let's get out of here. I need a beer and a cigarette."

In the hall outside, a voice called, "Reverend Elder!"

Assuming it was the police, Elder looked around for a quick exit, but Anthony put a hand on his arm.

Two of Brother Knode's apparently infinite supply of big, meaty young men in white dress shirts came down the hall toward him. One wore butterfly bandages over a gash on his forehead and had dried blood on his collar.

Anthony stepped in front of Elder. "Now, boys," he said calmly, "we don't need to make a scene here."

"We're not out to cause trouble," the uninjured one said. "Brother Knode would like to have a word with you."

"Really?" Elder said. "What about?"

"What do you figure, snakeskin?" the bloody one said sarcastically. "The weather?"

"Delphi," the other one warned. To Elder, he said, "If you'd come with us?"

Anthony looked questioningly at Elder, who shrugged. "Now I'm curious."

"So was Eve," Anthony muttered.

20

A half-dozen people crowded into Knode's private room, including three women, who Elder took to be Knode's wife and daughters. A man in a suit was just closing a briefcase on the rolling lap table.

Knode sat in the hospital bed with his elaborate pompadour askew. When he saw Elder, he said, "I'm conferring with my lawyer. I won't be a moment."

"I don't have all day," Elder said.

"We should be able to sue the state and force a settlement," the lawyer said. "And possibly the therapist personally. Negligence in both cases should be fairly easy to prove."

"Wonderful," Knode said. "And the press?"

"I'll have them waiting for your statement when you're ready."

"Praise Jesus. Thank you." As the lawyer closed his briefcase, Knode said, "Would y'all mind waiting outside? I need to speak with Reverend Elder in private."

The others did as he asked, and at least one of the women gave Elder a blatant once-over while batting her enormous false eyelashes.

"Does that include me?" Anthony asked Elder.

"Yeah. But stay close."

"'He who walks with the wise grows wise, but a companion of fools suffers harms,'" Anthony said as he followed the others out.

When they were alone, Elder asked Knode, "So, what's up?"

Knode had a gun leveled at him.

"For a preacher, you're sure quick to reach for a firearm," Elder observed.

"I learned a lot about people before I became a preacher. I figure you did as well, you thievin' son of a bitch. Where's my money?"

"It's my money now. Let's not get sidetracked."

"I found out a lot about you, boy. You got arrested down in Corinth just last week for abusing a child."

Elder said nothing.

"And what about the time you handcuffed a twelve-year-old boy to a chair for three days?"

"Bet you wish someone had handcuffed that girl this morning, don't you? If you really knew anything about deliverance, you wouldn't be asking these questions."

"You keep saying I don't know anything about it."

Elder snatched the gun from Knode before the big man could react. Expertly, Elder ejected the magazine, moved the slide to check the chamber, and put the empty gun back in Knode's hand. "You know as much about real deliverance as you do weapons. Which means you should start listening to people who know a lot more than you do about both."

"Like you?"

"Like me. You faced off against a real demon this morning. Its name was Merihem. He's nothing much, but he's more than you've ever run across before, and now he's gone back to where he came from. And you know what he's going to do first thing? He's going to tell all his pals about you. So, you're likely to start seeing real, genuine indwellings at your tent shows instead of those deluded idiots you fleece right now."

Knode sat there holding the empty gun. "You're crazy," he said at last, his voice ragged.

"Maybe. But I'm the one who drove Merihem out of that girl, not you." He paused. "But I think you already know all that, don't you? Why did you really want to see me?"

Knode looked out the window, and when he spoke again, his voice was small and hollow. "Reverend, what exactly happened in that office?"

"From what I could tell, one of your boys shot at a teenage girl, missed, and hit the gas line."

"No, I don't mean that. I mean..." He looked back at Elder, and all the arrogance was gone. "What *happened?*"

"You saw the devil," Elder said quietly. "For real. And you blinked. And now you know that they're for real. But that's not the part that should truly worry you."

"What, then?"

"Now they know that you're *not.*"

Knode said nothing for a long moment. The fear in his face was real, and primal, the terror of someone who just got their first glimpse of how the universe really worked. All the things Knode had used to scam and bamboozle the marks who came to his revivals had been revealed as true. The bamboozler had become the bamboozlee.

Elder considered making the man beg, stripping him of his last bit of pride as revenge. But he chose compassion instead. "Look, if anything happens, let me know. I'll come help you when you need it. And you will."

Knode managed a weak smile. "I can't afford your help. Your rates are too high."

"You can afford a dozen like me, big man, and you know it. But I don't charge for what I do."

Knode looked genuinely surprised, as if he really couldn't fathom it. "Why not?"

"I don't expect you to understand this, but I've already been paid. With my soul, which I was real close to losing. But there is a way you *can* pay me."

"How?"

"Call off your lawyer and drop the lawsuits. Because if they call me to testify, it'll get real interesting for everyone."

Knode chewed his considerable lower lip as he weighed the potential windfall against the threat of the unseen realms. "All right."

"Then we're even." Elder turned to go.

"Listen, would you—" Knode started, then stopped.

"What?" Elder prompted.

"Would you...pray with me? I haven't done it sincerely in a very long time, and I think I could use the help."

"Of course," Elder said. He took the empty gun from the preacher's hand, grasped the meaty fingers in his own, and closed his eyes. After a moment, Knode said, "Who should start?"

"I've already started," Elder said. "You don't need words out loud."

Knode nodded, closed his own eyes, and tried not to see the smile on the girl's face in the moments before he lost consciousness. He failed and suspected he'd fail every time his eyes closed from now on.

"WHAT DID HE SAY?" Anthony asked Elder when he emerged from the room. The big bodyguards watched the two of them with undisguised belligerence.

"A lot of self-serving bullshit. But at least he's a believer now."

"Excuse me," a woman called. They looked up to see the unmistakable form of a hospital administrator approach. Her heels clacked on the tiled floor as she approached. "Mr. Elder, you haven't filled out your paperwork."

"Let's go," Elder said, and rushed for the nearest stairwell.

Anthony shook his head and followed. *A companion of fools, indeed.*

21

It was late afternoon when Anthony dropped Elder off at Haven's clinic to pick up his car. Yellow tape and particle board covered her shattered office window. A firetruck still sat outside the building, but its lights weren't on. The lot was mostly empty: the clinic had been closed down until the source of the supposed gas leak could be found. Elder did not envy the frustration that would be associated with that.

He drove aimlessly around Somerton, not wanting to just sit at Anthony's house or the church, thinking alternately about the possessed girl he'd seen and Haven Fields. He wanted to simply concentrate on work, but the memory of the woman's touch, her smile, her eyes, and everything else he'd learned about her wouldn't leave him alone.

Elder had been married once, fresh out of high school. He hadn't gotten her pregnant, although everyone thought that was the reason; he simply saw in her a lightness and sweetness that he desperately wanted to touch. Unfortunately, he soured the very things that drew him to her, and she divorced him while he served his first tour in the army. That led him to choose the military as a career, something that did not improve the worst aspects of his personality.

He tried to remember the same things about her that he now recalled so vividly about Haven. What had her smile looked like as she sat across from him in homeroom? What had her touch felt like in the dark? Hell, what color were her eyes?

He hated to admit it, but she was no longer real to him; she never actually had been. She'd been an image, an ideal, something to possess and then tarnish. Which he had done. He truly hoped she was happy now, wherever she was, whoever she was with.

When he saw the neon Budweiser sign glowing in the window, he pulled into the parking lot of the bowling alley. A sign advertised the Ten-Pin Lounge. Only a few cars were parked there; it was a Monday evening and early. He took a last drag off his cigarette and tossed it down the chimney of the receptacle by the door.

Inside, there were a couple of men playing pool, four more seated at a table, and one tall, stringy guy on a stool at the bar. Elder took a seat at the other end.

The bartender came over. "Got Heineken Dark?" Elder asked.

"Only Light."

"That'll do. No glass."

"Wasn't gonna offer one," the bartender said.

TRAVIS SCOTE LOOKED up as the newcomer entered the bar and almost did a double-take. He was big, broad-shouldered, and looked like that old movie star his mother simply wouldn't accept had died from AIDS, Rock Hudson.

This guy also wore a shimmering snakeskin-textured jacket, something Travis had never seen before. He'd seen boots and belts, even hatbands, but never a whole coat. He watched the guy take it off, drape it carefully on the back of his stool, and sit down.

Travis had been drinking for a couple of hours, after spending the morning masturbating. The memory of sliding his hand down inside his niece's shorts, feeling that soft hair and the wetness beyond, made his dick hard again minutes after he'd last ejaculated. The sheer forbidden nature of the touch, as well as the obvious relish with which she received it made it the most erotic thing he could ever imagine, even if it had lasted for a three count at most instead of the promised ten. His porn stash now looked hopelessly staid and boring.

Putting out the dead mice on their little crosses had not taken long, but it felt so weird, he'd had to get seriously stoned first to do it. At least he'd had sense enough to wear a dark jacket, stuff his long hair into a cap and hide his face behind a respirator in case there were any security cameras watching.

When it was over, he'd gone back home, smoked some more weed, and jerked off until he fell asleep. His dreams had been a troubling, hazy mishmash he could not quite remember, except for the image of a mouse moaning like a porn actress as it writhed on its little cross.

He shook his head. The fresh beer, on top of the fading dope buzz, was making it hard not to think of that stuff. To break that train of thought, he said to the newcomer, "That's a fancy jacket."

The big man looked over at him and nodded. "Thanks."

"What's it made of?"

"Snakeskin."

"What kind?"

"What kind of snake?"

"Yeah."

"I don't really know. Rattlesnake or boa constrictor, I suppose. Have to be something fairly big."

"Where'd you get it?"

His eyes narrowed slightly. Travis knew that look: the man was wondering why Travis was being so friendly to a stranger. "It was a present."

Travis moved down a couple of stools, not directly beside the man but close enough to talk more easily. "I ain't seen you in here before."

"New in town. Staying with some friends."

"Looking for work?"

The big man shrugged.

Travis snorted. "Ain't no work in Somerton unless you get on out at the TLC-Mart. And they don't pay enough for you to live on."

"Travis, what the hell do you know about work?" the bartender said.

Travis laughed. "Now, Vinton, you know I'm waiting to take over your job."

"You'd just drink up all the stock and blame it on the mice."

Travis laughed again, but the reference to mice made it catch in his throat. He took a quick drink before he choked.

ELDER COULDN'T PUT his finger on it, but every instinct he had, both the natural ones and the ones honed by years of combat, told him this skinny, long-haired guy with the mustache was bad news. He sensed nothing demonic about him, but that didn't mean the guy wasn't trouble. Plenty of people in the world were just evil on their own initiative, with nothing supernatural involved. He knew because once he'd been one of them.

But there was a whiff, fainter even than Carlyss, about him, almost like a contact high. Had he been around someone with an indweller?

"You're out of work too?" he asked to keep the conversation going.

"Can't be out of what you ain't never had," the bartender muttered.

"Why you giving me such a hard time, Vinton?" Travis said, an adolescent whine creeping into his voice.

"Because I've known you your whole life, and you ain't worth a shit, Travis. I let you drink here because I have to, but the first time you try to stiff me on a tab, your ass is out for good." He put both hands on the bar, revealing muscular, tattooed forearms. "Now, you want to make an issue of it? I'll be glad to toss your skinny ass out with the trash right now."

"Whoa, now," Elder said. "Travis, my friend, sit down, have another beer on me." He smiled at Vinton.

Muttering, the bartender retrieved another Miller and put it in front of Travis. Then he went out and began wiping down tables.

"Thanks, man," Travis said and raised the bottle in salute.

Deacon was an expert at drawing people out, and with Travis, he needed very little effort. In short order, he learned that Travis had been a star track athlete in high school and had dumped his prom date because she wanted him to hire a limousine instead of picking her up in his old Z28. He'd once made out with the social studies teacher his senior year.

Deacon didn't believe half of this, but he listened anyway. It kept him from dwelling on his own worries about the girl from the hospital. How was he going to find this Linda Scote and then convince her she needed deliverance?

"Hey, we ain't been introduced," Travis said suddenly. "I don't even know your name."

"Deacon Elder," he said, and offered his hand.

Travis shook it. "Travis Scote. Pleased to meet you. Pleased to meet anybody who buys the drinks."

Elder kept the surprise off his face. There might be many Scotes in Somerton, but coincidence like this was a sure sign of the Lord's hand at work. Travis wasn't old enough to be her father, but he could be a cousin or even an older brother.

He decided to risk a straight shot. "Oh, so you're related to Linda, then?"

Travis jumped so hard he knocked over his beer; luckily, the bottle was mostly empty, and he didn't spill much. "Whoops, sorry about that, bumped my elbow. Why do they call it the 'funny bone' when it ain't funny at all?"

Elder handed him some more napkins and waited for the blather to cease.

"I tell you what, sometimes I get so drunk, I go to look at my watch, and I just turn my hand with the beer in it and spill it right there on the floor," Travis said.

"I bet. So do you know Linda?"

"She's my niece," he blurted. He was sweating now, too. "How do *you* know her?"

"Ran into her at the hospital. We were both visiting the same friend."

Travis drained the rest of his beer and said quickly, "Aw, fuck, man, look at the time. I have to get home for dinner. Pleasure talking to you, Deacon. Have a good evening. Oh, and thanks for the beer!" Before Elder could respond, Travis was gone out the door.

Vinton came over and cleaned up the rest of the mess. "If you're going to be in town long and drinking at my bar, I do wish you wouldn't encourage him."

"Is he that bad?"

"Oh, hell, yeah. I know him and his brother Blanton. Blanton's all right; he's got a job at the Hungerman plant and stays out of trouble. He's a gun nut, but hell, so are half the people in Somerton. But Travis ain't worth the dog shit you'd scrape off your shoe."

Elder tried to sound as casual as possible. "Met Travis's niece at the hospital today. That's Blanton's girl, right?"

"Linda? Yeah."

"You know her?"

"See her at church when I wake up to go. That's all."

"Which church?"

"First Baptist."

Elder nodded. Then he struck up a conversation about football, which led to one about politics and hopefully kept Vinton from remembering that Elder had ever asked about the Scote girl.

22

Carlyss was bored with being in the hospital. Her grandparents visited and offered to stay, but she convinced them that there was no need. She'd be released in the morning, and they could come pick her up. They agreed, no doubt grateful to get home in time to catch the late reruns of *NCIS* and *Law and Order.*

They brought her phone, and she texted Jason several times but received no reply. She even risked calling once, but it went into voicemail. Now she lay in the hospital bed staring at the ceiling, wondering why, with Merihem gone, she could still not sleep. She wasn't even tired.

Then the door opened, and in walked the demon.

He looked like a joke, or a bad Halloween costume. All the distorted pieces she'd seen before were now brought together, and she noticed new details, like the way his knees seemed to be at different heights on his legs. He wore no clothes, but his genitalia was so negligible that, like the rest of him, it was almost ridiculous. But there was nothing ridiculous about the hate blazing in his eyes.

Still, he smiled and said casually, "Hey."

"Merihem," she said, her voice trembling.

"Oh, don't freak out; I'm gone. I'm just visiting while you're sleeping to tell you goodbye."

"I'm sleeping?"

"Of course, you are. Like a baby. Between the year of no sleep and the pills they gave you, you're sleeping so hard you might piss yourself. But if you do, this time it's not my fault."

"What do you want?" She looked around for some clue that he was right, that she was in fact asleep and dreaming, but everything looked normal and solid.

"Like I said, I want to say goodbye. We've gotten to know each other pretty well, and believe it or not, I'll miss you."

"I won't miss you. You did awful things to me."

"Hey, you liked some of them."

"No. And even if I did, I also knew they were wrong. Weakness isn't the same thing as complicity."

"Listen to you and those big words. No wonder the boys are afraid of you." Then he sighed. "Then again, I'm in no position to criticize anymore."

Only then did she notice that he was covered with cuts, scrapes, and other small injuries, most of them scabbed over but some still bleeding. None of them looked serious, but it must have taken hours to inflict them all.

"What happened to you?"

"This? Oh. The boss wasn't happy."

"Satan did that?"

He snorted. "I'm not quite at that level. No, this was my immediate superior, not the big boss."

"Dandelion?"

Merihem scowled and thought about what to say next. "Look, here's the thing, Carlyss. You've won, but you haven't, if you know what I mean. Yeah, you got shed of me, but my boss had to come and take a hand in things, and he's in a much better position to do some damage."

"Inside Linda Scote."

He shrugged. "She's cute, popular, and really and truly doesn't care about anyone but herself. Man, if only you'd been that way, I could've done all sorts of things. But, hey, live and learn."

"What are you telling me?"

"Don't fight it. Let them arrest you and put you back in that hospital. Ride it out. You'll get out when you turn twenty-one and you can start over. By then, my boss will have gotten bored with this and moved on."

"Why would anyone arrest me? The crucified mice?"

Merihem smiled. "Yeah, that was a good one, wasn't it? Leave it to the boss to take my idea and do it even better. You and I did one cat, in private. He made a fucking public statement."

"But I didn't do it."

"You think anyone will believe you? And do you think you can make them believe Linda Scote did it? She's one of the cool kids, and you? You're a freak." He smiled sadly. "But a freak I'll miss."

"Your boss won't win. No matter how perverted he gets."

"You think that weirdo preacher is up to the challenge? You're a fool, Carlyss Bolerjack. Deacon Elder, or should I say Avo Gleason, isn't nearly as tough as he thinks he is. Ask him why he changed his name if you want to see what he's really like."

"I don't care. He drove you out. He's doing God's work."

"He did drive me out. Or..." Again, he smiled, mischievously this time. "Did I leave because my boss made me?" He went back to the door. "Have a good nap, Carlyss. See you in Hell."

Carlyss snapped awake. The room was dark, except for the ambient night lighting and the harsh hallway illumination around the closed door. She *had* been asleep.

She dug in the nightstand for the notepad and little pencil. She scrawled down *Avo Gleason,* even as the words faded from her consciousness. She looked at them and wondered if it was true or if her sleep-deprived brain was just going a little mad and making up for lost time.

ACROSS TOWN, Linda Scote couldn't sleep, either. She'd masturbated and sipped from a bottle of whiskey she'd sneaked into her room, and now sprawled naked on her bed, wondering when Jesse Garon was going to appear to her. She craved that more than anything, wanted to hear his approval and follow his instructions and feel that sweet, vaguely disgusting sense of release he could bring about.

Finally, when the clock read 3 A.M., she got out of bed, went into the bathroom, and got a drink of water. She turned on the light and was momentarily frightened by her own reflection. She was pale, and the infected bites on her body were now radiating red lines to each other, like a crimson net. She touched one, and it oozed a clear liquid that she then licked from her finger. It tasted harsh and acidic; was she now leaking bitterness?

She knew, deep down, that something awful had happened to her and was growing worse. Yet most of its manifestations felt so *good*. Certainly the power she'd gained over Danny, and her uncle Travis, filled her with a sense of her own importance greater than any she'd ever known. And when Jesse Garon spoke to her in that Mississippi purr, she felt it inside, intimately, and responded with an intensity she hadn't thought possible. He could make her come by just saying her name.

But what did he *want*?

He could never be with her, not really. He could never be more than the voice in her head, whispering and cajoling, occasionally dictating what she should say, as he had when she visited Bethany and Carlyss in the hospital. But he could never be her boyfriend the way Danny might. Yet really, she didn't like Danny that much; he had a cruel streak that she'd manipulated, but only to accomplish something she couldn't personally do: hurt that fat boy, and therefore Carlyss, at Jesse Garon's command. Otherwise, he was just a hard dick attached to a good-looking face.

And her uncle Travis...well, he was just pathetic. Letting a teenage girl yank him around like a dog on a leash. Please.

She went back into her bedroom, pulled out her Ouija board, and set it up on her desk. She closed her eyes and whispered, "Jesse Garon? Are you there?"

The planchette did not move.

"Jesse Garon?" she repeated, just as softly. One of the sores on her belly began to itch.

The planchette twitched under her hand and slid to the word, NO.

She stared. Was Jesse Garon playing a trick? She asked, "Then who is this?"

The planchette rushed to the letters so fast she could barely keep up. L-I-T-T-L-E-H-O- R-N.

"Little Horn?" she repeated. The planchette slid to YES.

"Do you know Jesse Garon?"

The planchette slid away, then returned to YES.

Suddenly the board flew across the room like it had been slapped off her desk. It slammed into the wall by the door. She gasped; in the silence, the noise was incredibly loud. She turned and saw the shadowy form of Jesse Garon in the corner.

What are you doing? he said angrily. She'd never heard him angry at her before.

"I-I-I was l-looking for you—"

I come to you when I wish. You will wait. I thought you understood that. Was I wrong?

She began to cry. "No, I was just lonely, and—"

An unseen hand struck her across the face, hard enough to knock her from the chair. Then the same hand grabbed her by the hair and pushed her face-down on the floor.

You have no will but mine. You only do what I wish.

Linda was terrified. She'd never been treated this way. "Please," she whimpered, "don't hurt me."

She heard something wet hitting the carpet and realized she was urinating with fear.

The hand released her. *Now, on to our next task. We will bring the girl Carlyss back to us. Do you understand what that means?*

"No," she whimpered.

The girl once harbored an indwelling spirit, as you do. She will host another, one more powerful than before.

Linda's mind raced as fast as her heart. What the fuck was an "indwelling spirit"?

Tomorrow, you will take that boy Danny to visit the fat one in his hospital bed.

"D-Danny won't go there, he might get arrested."

Danny will do anything you tell him if you give him the right incentive.

Linda felt a rush of revulsion as she remembered Danny's mouth on her, coating her breasts with his saliva. How had she allowed that? It was disgusting. And then suddenly, like a light going on, she understood the truth: *she* had not allowed it; Jesse Garon had. He had been inside her, moving her body, speaking through her lips. The words "indwelling spirit" suddenly made sense.

Now. Let's go to bed.

Hands, too many hands for one person, began touching her all over, only it wasn't erotic, it was filthy and terrifying. Yet she did respond physically and crawled back to her bed, where she gave herself over to them, crying silently as they had their way with her.

23

When her grandfather pulled his old but immaculate Chevy into his driveway, a police car was already there.

Two officers, one Black, one white, both in uniform, spoke to her grandmother on the porch. Carlyss recognized the Black one as Anthony's friend Bernard. When she got out, the white one said, "Miss Bolerjack, we'd like to speak with you."

"She just got out of the hospital," her grandfather said. "Can't you give her a day or two? It's not like she blew up that doctor's office."

"They think she killed some more animals," her grandmother said. She looked distraught and clung to the porch rail as if she might fall without it.

"Oh, fuck this," the white officer said wearily. "Carlyss Bolerjack, you're under arrest for trespassing, vandalism, and animal cruelty." He grabbed her arm and roughly turned her. "Put your hands behind you, please."

"Granddaddy!" she cried as she was handcuffed. "I didn't do anything, I swear!"

"Is this really necessary?" her grandfather demanded.

"Ask me that when you see what she did," the white officer said, then began reciting her Miranda rights.

"You want to meet us at the station," Bernard said gently, "you can be there when we question her."

Her grandmother moaned and almost collapsed. Her grandfather and Bernard ran to catch her and help her back into the house.

"Get inside, you fuckin' weirdo," the white officer muttered as he pushed Carlyss into the police car's back seat.

HAVEN PICKED up her ringing cell phone. She didn't recognize the number and started to ignore it, then her conscience got the better of her. What if it was patient-related?

They'd let her out of the hospital that morning. Since she'd gotten home, Troy had been silent and morose, spending most of his time playing Minecraft, a game he'd ignored ever since she'd allowed him very limited access to first-person shooters. Those went against every instinct she had as a parent, but she desperately didn't want Troy to be "that kid," the one whose mother refused to let him participate in whatever the current fad happened to be. She saw those kids in her practice, heard their pitiful desires to just be normal like everyone else, and couldn't put her own son through that.

But now, Troy had no interest in whatever edition of Halo was currently popular. He also, if the state of the house was any indication, had no interest in eating or sleeping.

They had not spoken again about what Troy said he witnessed. There had been nothing on the news or in this morning's paper. But using her work credentials, Haven had confirmed that Jason Stein, age 15, had been admitted to the hospital and was in serious condition after some sort of assault.

She knew what Troy was supposed to do: man up, go to the police, and tell them what he saw. Then, when the perpetrator was on trial, testify against him. It's what she would advise any client to do and might do herself if the client balked.

But she saw his terror, his utter fear of this other boy, and just couldn't make him do it. And so she said nothing. And neither did he.

She'd already called the school and gotten him excused for the day. The clerk had seemed preoccupied as if something strange was going on just outside of Haven's hearing, but she hadn't asked about it.

Now she pushed the button on the phone, grateful for any distraction. "Haven Fields," she said.

"I hope so," responded the masculine voice.

"Deke," she said. She hoped it didn't come out like the girly, wimpy sigh she heard in her head.

"I hope it's okay to call. Are you out of the hospital?"

"I got home about an hour ago. How are you?"

"Me? I'm fine. How are you? How's the head?"

She bit back the giggles as she started to reply, *Well, you didn't complain the other night.* Just hearing his voice made her want to smile. "It's fine. No headaches, luckily, so no concussion."

"If you feel up to it, I'd like to see you."

"I'd like to see you, too." *Don't make it too easy for him,* a voice she recognized as her twenty-year-old self protested. But that voice was from a different era when she had a lot more time for games. "Do you want to come over?"

"To your house? Will we have privacy?"

His words drove home what she was asking. Did she really want to introduce him to Troy now, when he was so depressed and withdrawn? Did she want to make casual conversation while watching Troy try to decide if he liked Elder or not? And, of course, there was no way they could simply adjourn to her bedroom once the social niceties were completed.

"Let's meet where we met before," she said.

"The motel?"

"Yes. My treat this time."

"Hopefully, it's a mutual treat," he said, and she could hear the smile in his voice.

CARLYSS and her grandfather sat at the table in the little interrogation room. Since the police conducted few actual interrogations, it was also used to store old paperwork waiting to be digitized, so the room had a heavy, musty smell that immediately aggravated her grandfather's allergies. The obligatory one-way glass in the wall displayed their reflections.

Bernard sat opposite them while Officer Jernigan stood against the wall and stifled yawns.

"Carlyss, do you and your grandfather understand your rights?" Bernard asked.

"Yes, of course," her grandfather said, wiping his nose.

"You can stop and request a lawyer at any time."

"Just get on with it."

Bernard nodded. "Carlyss, where were you early Monday morning? Between midnight and three a.m.?"

"Wait," her grandfather said. "Shouldn't you be recording this? They always record it on TV."

"This ain't TV, old man," Jernigan said. "This is the real world, where we don't put up with shit like your granddaughter did."

"Officer Jernigan," Bernard said patiently. "Carlyss, could you answer my question?"

"At home."

Bernard turned to her grandfather. "Can you verify this?"

"She was there when I got up," he said and sneezed.

"Bless you," Bernard said and waited while her grandfather blew his nose.

"Show 'em the pictures," Jernigan said impatiently.

Bernard glared over his shoulder at the other officer, then took out his phone. "We found these at the high school and at Reverend Acred's church."

Carlyss just stared. The rows of crucified mice sent a chill through her.

Bernard continued, "Carlyss, I'll get right to the point here. You have a troubled past. You also, by your own admission, once did something very similar to this. You can see why we'd think of you."

"I didn't do this," she said numbly. *So, this is what Linda was talking about.* It was both sadistic and brilliant.

"I know you wander around town at night," Bernard said. "There is a curfew, you know, even though it doesn't get enforced that often. But I need you to tell me the truth." He lowered his voice. "I don't want to send you to jail, Carlyss. If you're still sick, you need help."

"I'm not sick," she said vehemently.

"Yeah, right," Jernigan snorted.

"Does she need to get a lawyer?" her grandfather said, then snorted up congestion. "Do you have any evidence that isn't circumstantial? Just because some other kid did something similar—"

"That's not all. We also have this." He produced another picture, this one from the high school security system. It showed a black-clad figure placing one of the mice. The face was hidden by a baseball cap and a respirator.

"Well, *that's* not her," her grandfather said at once. "That's a boy. You can tell."

"Yes, we agree," Bernard said. "We believe this person placed them at the high school while Carlyss did so at the church. Who is this, Carlyss?"

"I honestly have no idea. I had nothing to do with any of this, I swear."

"Do you have a boyfriend?"

"No," she said.

"It won't be hard for us to find out if you're lying," Jernigan said.

"I'm not. Why would I?"

"Because you're a freak. We'll get a warrant to search your house, and we'll find the shit you used to make those. Then we'll haul your weirdo ass before a judge and get you put away."

"Jernigan!" Bernard said sharply. "Go get some coffee."

With a final glare, Jernigan left the room.

"I apologize, he works third shift and usually he's asleep by now," Bernard said. "But he's right. If we have to, we'll get a search warrant."

"You won't find anything," Carlyss said, "because I didn't do this." But even as she spoke, she had a momentary fear that someone broke in while she was in the hospital and planted incriminating evidence, as might happen in a TV show or cheap thriller movie. Was the spirit inside Linda that devious?

"I hope not," Bernard said sincerely. "But I'd consider getting a lawyer anyway." He stood. "If you'll excuse me, I need to see about some paperwork. I'll be right back."

When they were alone, her grandfather said, "They're watching through that one-way mirror. Just like they do on TV. They want to see if we'll incriminate ourselves when they're not around."

"I can't," Carlyss said, "because I didn't do this."

"Carlyss, if you did, then—"

"Granddaddy, I swear to you, I didn't."

"Who did, then?"

"I don't know." She hated lying to him, but how could she possibly explain the truth without sounding as nuts as they thought she was?

———

IN THE OBSERVATION ROOM, Bernard accosted Jernigan. "What is *wrong* with you?"

"What?" he said defensively.

"Intimidating a girl and an old man is your idea of a good interrogation?"

"For fuck's sake, we know she did it. Why are we pussyfooting around?"

"Because we have no proof. I was hoping to get a confession out of her but not now."

"She's got no alibi!"

"And we've got no witnesses, and the one person we have on video is very clearly *not* her. I know you're worn out, Bennie, but if you ever want to get off third shift, you need to start *thinking* before you speak, especially to suspects."

"Yeah, and you need to stop coddling pretty white girls just because—" He caught himself and stopped.

For a moment, there was dead silence in the observation room.

"I'm going home," Jernigan muttered.

"Good idea," Bernard said coldly.

When he was alone, Bernard watched Carlyss through the glass. She sat hunched over, arms on the table, sad and defeated. It was not the defiance of a delinquent or the knowing performance of a guilty suspect. Unless, he thought bitterly, she was a better actor than he thought.

HAVEN AND ELDER lay sweaty and gasping on the bed. The midday sun peeked in around the closed curtains, making visible shafts in the dusty air. The covers had been kicked to the floor, and their exertions had dislodged the fitted sheet, so they now lay directly on the stained and sagging mattress. Somehow that made the encounter that much more erotic. And it had been pretty erotic to begin with.

She crawled on top of him and kissed him. She wore his snakeskin jacket—her idea—and enjoyed the way his hands slid beneath the fabric to touch her. "If I say I was afraid we'd never do this again," she breathed, "will you take advantage of me?"

"I need about fifteen minutes," he said with a smile.

She laughed. "I meant emotionally. But I'll take you up on the other when you're ready."

"And I'll let you."

She crossed her arms on his chest, rested her chin on them, and looked down at his face. This close, he looked older than he appeared, and his eyes more haunted. In their previous encounter, she hadn't cared to look too closely, but now she did, and what she saw made her like him even more. He might have been big and strong enough to wrestle a bear, but there was something soft and kind and weak in him, too. "Are you really a minister?" she asked, mock-seriously.

"I am," he said. "Why do you ask that?"

"Well, you have to admit, this is not the kind of ministry they probably teach in seminary."

He smiled. "That's true enough. I'm self-taught. But I do take it seriously."

"Where's your church?"

"I don't have a church. I'm more of a free-range consultant."

"You help other ministers in trouble?"

He nodded. "Not all of them are comfortable with deliverance."

She moved her body against his, luxuriating in the touch of skin on skin. "What happened to make you believe in demons?"

He raised his head to look at her. "If I tell you, it might make you sorry we did this."

She said sincerely, "If you don't, I know I will be."

"All right. I served in the army, in Afghanistan. We—me and several guys from my unit—started going rogue pretty early in the game. Our sergeant convinced us that every Afghan we saw was in Al Qaeda, so anything we did was cool. He covered up for us too. We did...pretty terrible things. To people who may not have deserved it. We didn't care."

His eyes grew wet, and tears trickled down the side of his face, although his voice didn't change.

"We killed a *lot* of people. I didn't think about it much. I wasn't raised to have much empathy, especially for people with dark skin. They weren't really human to me. Which made me the perfect soldier for that war. But our sergeant..."

She wiped one tear from his cheek. "I'm sorry, Deke. I didn't realize it would be so painful for you."

"No, you're right, I want you to know. Secrets are never good." He cleared his throat. "So, the sergeant walked into what turned out to be a daycare center and killed everyone. All the kids, the women watching them, everyone. Then he took the kids' bodies and..." His voice trembled. "He put them in positions like they were having sex. So that's how their parents found them."

"Jesus, Deke."

"I saw the look in his eye, Haven, but for the first time, I could *smell* something, a distinctive kind of odor around him. Something lived in him, something more vile than anything mankind has ever produced. I'm not saying he wasn't evil on his own—plenty of people are, *most* people are—but the spirit that lived in him urged him to commit worse and worse crimes. And he loved it. He absolutely loved it. It wasn't a situation like Carlyss, where she was fighting to get it out. He wouldn't have given it up willingly if Christ himself had commanded him to do it."

"So, what did *you* do?"

"I fragged him. Do you know what that means?"

She nodded.

"I claimed it was a sniper. The others knew, but they also understood. We were bound to get caught if we kept going. And I couldn't get that look in his eye out of my head. The truth of what I'd seen there, and that godawful smell that no one else seemed to notice..."

"Can you tell me what it smelled like?"

"It wasn't like you'd think. It wasn't rot, or garbage, or shit. It was...you know that kind of purple-yellow color a bruise turns after a few days? If that color had a smell, that's what it would be." He shivered a little at the memory. "So, when I got out, I went to see a minister. Who turned out to be Grove Prosser."

"The minister who tried to help Carlyss?"

"Yes. He told me about the reality of demons and about the way they worked. When I told him about the smell, he said I had the gift of discernment. And one night in his church, the Holy Spirit spoke to me and told me this was my new path. That I was forgiven for all the awful things I did and started clean, doing God's work."

Haven put her cheek against his chest. His heart was strong and regular, and she rose slightly with each inhalation. How could she feel such tenderness, such compassion, for a man so clearly deluded? She didn't doubt his belief; she just knew that it couldn't be possible. Sure, she'd glimpsed Carlyss's supposedly possessed face, but that had been in a moment of crisis and trauma; now that her head was clear, she knew that it had just been mental illness and that the words and sounds she'd heard came from an unbalanced mind, not a possessing spirit. Right?

She slid her leg along his. "So, tell me: how do demons get in?"

"They look for a crack. A chink. A bit of damage. If a woman craves things she can't afford, it might open her to a demon of avarice. If a boy finds his father's *Playboys,* a demon of lust can get in. If we constantly say 'yes' when we know we should say 'no,' we open the way to the demonic."

"Nice stereotypes."

"Just common examples."

"And nobody stashes *Playboys* anymore. They look at porn online."

"And that's why it's so much easier for the demons."

"You don't think it could have anything to do with the hyper-sexualization of our culture, or the pervasiveness of advertising, or anything like that?"

"Those aren't causes, Haven. Those are effects."

She said nothing.

"You don't believe me, do you?"

"I've successfully treated plenty of people with those problems. I didn't need an exorcist to do it."

"I can only tell you what I know to be true from first-hand experience."

"And so you just...became an exorcist?"

"Only Catholics are exorcists. I pray deliverance."

"So noted."

"I was very arrogant when I started out. It was the same arrogance I had as a soldier: that belief that everything I did was right, and if I was wrong, well, it was everybody else's fault for not getting out of my way."

"I have a hard time seeing you like that."

"Believe me, I was. One of the first deliverances I was called to preach was for this young man, seventeen years old, who'd been a star athlete before he got into meth. His parents weren't very bright or sophisticated, and instead of seeing a doctor or a therapist, they went to their preacher. He wasn't bright or sophisticated, either, so he tried praying deliverance over the boy and got a broken nose for his trouble. That's when he heard about me and called me in."

Elder's expression grew sad and distant as he spoke. "By the time I got there, they kept the boy out in a shed. He had a dog collar locked around his neck, and he was chained to a couple of cinder blocks. He was out of his mind by then, the demon had gotten almost total control."

"So, he was mentally disturbed?" Haven said, unable to keep the skepticism from her voice.

"Haven, he was *possessed*. The demon had fried his brain with its lies and promises, and all the things demons do. The meth had just made it easier, knocking down the normal barriers we all have between good and evil thoughts."

Haven nodded and bit back any subsequent comments.

"Now, what I *should* have done was to immediately tell the demon inside him that it could no longer act out on its desires. It's called a binding, a prayer that I've used many times since. But because I was new and thought I was tough, I went in there with guns blazing. In a spiritual sense, that is."

"What happened?"

He half-smiled. "The little bastard threw his shit at me."

"Oh, my God. What did you do?"

"I threw it right back."

She giggled, then caught herself.

"No, it *is* funny," he said. "It shows how unprepared I was. The Lord does all the hard work of deliverance, but I learned pretty quickly that I also had to bring my A-game. Demons don't mind fucking around with a preacher. They don't mind that at all."

"How do you keep from becoming possessed yourself, then? You've hinted that you've certainly had your share of cracks and chinks in your armor."

"I plead the blood of Jesus."

"What is that?"

"I claim the power of Jesus over any vulnerability."

"So, it's like that radioactive spider that bit Peter Parker?" He looked blank. "Never mind." She paused, watching the way his eyes caught the light. "Is that how you can do what we're doing and not become possessed? I mean, aren't we breaking at least one commandment? The one against adultery"

"The commandments were written before Christ."

"I didn't know he revised them."

"'These three remain: faith, hope, and love. But the greatest of these is love.'"

The mention of the word made her own heart speed up. She tried to stay casual. "This is love? We barely know each other."

"We don't have to know each other to be kind. You've certainly been kind to me, and I've tried to be to you. I wouldn't say either of us has been selfish."

She looked into his eyes and saw the truth of his words. She ran a fingertip over his lips. "No," she said tenderly. "You're right about that. We could have been, but we weren't."

"So, I don't think God will begrudge us this."

She smiled wryly. "Can we stop talking about God? I didn't sign up for a threesome."

He returned her smile. "You know how to shut me up."

"Yes, I do." And she crawled atop him until his mouth closed around her nearest dangling nipple.

"AT LEAST THEY LET YOU GO," Carlyss's grandfather said as they drove home.

"That's because I didn't do it," Carlyss said. "I keep telling you that."

"And I'd sure like to believe that."

After a moment, in a small voice, she asked, "So you think I'm a freak too?"

"Troubled. I think you're troubled. I think this is why the judge made you promise to see that doctor last year." He shook his head. "One doctor drops dead on you the other one gets blown up. Might not be able to find a third one to take you."

Carlyss said nothing. She watched the streets pass, the sun bleaching all the colors into a wan yellow-white light that scorched everything it touched.

24

Troy's cell phone rang. He looked at it and saw Danny Blazer's name and number. He did not answer it. It went into voicemail with all the others.

He knew Danny would eventually come looking for him. He hadn't seen or spoken to his friend since that day, and Danny wouldn't let that go. He needed loyalty like a South American despot, something Troy had once studied for a report.

Troy felt that same old knot in his stomach. He still couldn't quite believe Danny had done that to Jason. Sure, he expected the fat kid to get beaten up, maybe even get a broken nose or something, but this...it was a level of cruelty he'd never imagined someone he knew, someone he'd known since they were six, was capable of. What sort of world let someone like that live in it?

And he had to do *something*. But what? His mom wanted him to go to the police and he knew that was the right thing, but he also knew Danny would get out on bail; the juvenile judge attended the same Baptist Church and was well-known for being lenient toward other Baptists. And then Danny and Sam would come looking for him.

His own worries kept him from being very sympathetic to his mother. He'd gone to see her in the hospital, but the knowledge that

Jason was also there creeped him out to the point he couldn't stay very long. She thought he was just upset at seeing her that way, and he let her think that.

In the hospital hallway, he'd spotted Linda Scote coming out of a room. He ducked aside before she saw him. Linda was distractingly hot and had always known it and made use of it. She was the only person, male or female, who could get Danny to do anything she wanted. But something about her had changed; she now vaguely disgusted Troy. He wondered if that was Danny's doing too.

He was curious who she'd been visiting, so he slipped over and looked at the name written on the door. **Carlyss Bolerjack.** He had no idea she and Linda were friends.

He did remember vividly, though, when Carlyss had chased them away from the fat boy at the bowling alley. It was like she knew something secret about each of them, something there was *no way* she could've known.

And if she knew about him, about the deepest secret he had...

He curled up on the couch, clutching one of the pillows. His mother had gone to run errands and had warned she might be away for a while. The house was silent, and he could practically hear his heart racing in his chest. He'd never been so scared in his life, and he had no idea where to turn. He began to cry again, something he'd done an awful lot of in the last few days. He'd never felt so alone, but he knew it was his own fault. His mother would help him if he just told her the truth. Wouldn't she?

Or would she simply turn away in disgust?

He held the pillow tight over his head.

HAVEN LOOKED down the length of her body and saw Elder rising from between her legs, his face damp with sweat and her body's juices. He smiled. "Liked that?"

"Couldn't you tell?" she gasped, her voice still trembling.

"I think they could tell in the next county," he said, crawling over

ALEX BLEDSOE

her. She wrapped her legs around him and kissed him deeply, their mutual tastes mingling in their mouths.

"So," she said at last, "is this a vacation romance or something else?"

"What are the other choices?"

She looked into his eyes. "I think you know."

"Haven, we've done this exactly twice now. That's not—"

"It's not the sex. It's the stuff in between when we talk."

"Really?"

"Oh, don't get me wrong, the sex is great." They both giggled a little. "But I can take that for what it is. It's the rest that has me thinking maybe..."

He slid off her, leaving one leg draped over her, and ran his hand over her cheek. "I'm here on business. There are things I have to take care of, and as a rule, it's usually better for me to leave town afterward. I mean, I've already been there when your office blew up. That's the sort of thing that happens around me. Besides, I don't have a job, a place to live—"

"Blah blah blah," she said with a little smile. "Those are details. What's happening in here?" She touched his chest over his heart.

He took her hand and kissed her fingertip. "We hardly know each other."

"And that'll never change if you run off. I'm not giving you an ultimatum, Deke. If you leave, I'll kiss you goodbye and wave with a smile. You'll be a great memory. But there's something here. I think it's what I've waited my whole life to feel."

"You don't believe in demons."

"Or angels. Or UFOs, or Bigfoot. Is that really that important?"

"What would you say if I said I didn't believe in mental illness?"

"You think it's *all* the work of the devil?"

"Not at all. But you think it *never* is."

"Convince me, then. Show me. I'm not dogmatic."

"You were about a half-hour ago," he said, remembering when she'd been on her hands and knees while he took her from behind.

She laughed. "Seriously, though. You had to be convinced. Convince *me*."

"Haven, once you're convinced, you can't be un-convinced. That's like un-seeing something awful. It can't be done. It'll be in your head forever."

"I've already got plenty of awful things in my head, Deke. I can handle one more."

He got off the bed and went to the window. He opened the curtain just enough to send a slice of sunlight through the room. She rose on her elbows and looked at him, naked and unselfconscious, as he thought over what she'd said.

"All right, then," he said at last and turned back to face her. "There's another girl in town who's harboring a demon."

"Really?" she said, trying to stifle her own sarcasm.

"Yes, really. I ran into her at the hospital. I know her name. I need to find her and try to help her. When I do, you can be there. If what you see doesn't convince you... " He left the rest unspoken.

She reached out to him, and he let the curtain fall closed. He sat on the bed beside her. She took his hand and put it on her hip, covering the bare skin where the waistband of her panties would normally go. She sighed at her body's response. "We've had enough seriousness. I have to get home soon. I told Troy I was only running some errands. Do you think you have one more in you?"

"Even if I don't, I bet I can get one more out of you."

"You better not stop at one, Reverend," she said as she kissed him. And the moment their lips touched, she knew she'd bring him home.

CARLYSS SAT at the dinner table with her grandparents, picking at her food. She had no appetite and could hardly hold her eyes open. Now that she *could* sleep, it was all she wanted to do. And except for that one time in the hospital where Merihem showed up, she hadn't dreamed a thing. Hours passed in what seemed to her the space between blinks.

"Hmph," her grandfather said, looking up from his iPad. "A boy got attacked at a convenience store."

"Who?" her grandmother asked.

"Stein, Jason Stein. Do you know him, Carlyss?"

"What happened?" she asked in a whisper.

"Just says here he was attacked in a convenience store bathroom. He didn't see who did it. Police are asking for help."

Her heart began to pound. "Is he okay?"

"Serious but stable condition."

She stood up before she even realized it. "I have to go to the hospital and see him. Can someone drive me?"

"Oh, sit down and finish your dinner," her grandmother said in the same sing-song way she'd spoken to Carlyss her whole life. "It can wait."

"No!" Carlyss almost shouted. "I'll walk, then. I'll be back later."

"You won't walk," her grandfather said grumpily. "Let me find my glasses and get my shoes on."

She clenched her fists in frustration while the old man wrangled his shoes, tying them with such deliberation it made her want to scream. By the time he was ready to go, she felt as if she could run there faster than he could drive.

It felt strange to be back in the hospital corridors so soon after leaving, and she found herself looking around for Linda Scote as if the girl was stalking her. She reached the room with Jason's name on the dry-erase board, knocked lightly, and said, "Jason? It's me, Carlyss."

After a moment, a woman opened the door. She was dark-haired, and her skin was splotchy from crying. The resemblance to Jason was there in the eyes and chin. "Jason's sleeping right now," she said quietly. "He's on a lot of pain medication. Can you come back later?"

"Yes, of course. Please tell him Carlyss came by."

"You're Carlyss?"

"Yes, ma'am."

She pondered for a moment, then said, "Come in."

It was a private room, and evidently, the windows faced west because the afternoon sun through the thin curtains tinted everything orange. Jason's father sat in the guest recliner, watching CNN on the TV in the corner of the ceiling. He stood up as Carlyss entered.

"This is Carlyss, the girl Jason told us about," Mrs. Stein said.

Carlyss's heart wrenched when she saw Jason. He lay on his side, one eye blackened and swollen shut. His other eye opened and looked at her with all the pain and despair she imagined anyone could hold. Tears burned in her own eyes.

"Hey," Jason said weakly.

"Hey," Carlyss replied. She stepped close and took his hand where it lay on the bed.

"Sorry you have to see this," he said. He didn't change positions.

"What happened?" she choked out as she felt tears down her cheeks.

"Mom," he said more loudly, "could you let me talk to Carlyss in private?"

"You're going to tell *her* who did this to you and not the police?" Mr. Stein said bitterly.

"I'd just like to talk to her alone, Papa. Please."

"Come on," Mrs. Stein said, and the two adults slipped out into the hall.

When they were alone, Jason said, "Danny Blazer did this. He shoved a plunger handle up my ass. It tore up..." Now he started to cry. "It hurt me a lot."

"Oh, my God," Carlyss whispered. "And they haven't arrested him?"

"No. I said I didn't see who did it."

"What? Why?"

"He sent his girlfriend to see me, Carlyss. Here, in the hospital. Linda Scote. She showed up, acting like she was my best friend in the world. She said if I tell, then when Danny gets out of jail, he'll come back and do worse. You know how he is."

Carlyss remembered what Bethany had said about Linda, and then her own conversation with the girl.

"Look, I can't do anything to protect myself," he said bitterly. "I can't even lie on my back. I can't even shit on my own." He began to sob. "I just want to die, Carlyss. These people ... it's their world, not ours. The bullies, the rednecks, the cops, the soldiers, the...the *assholes*. They own this world. The rest of us are just here for their fucking amusement."

Carlyss wiped furiously at her tears. "That's not true, Jason. That's *not true.*"

The door opened, and his parents came back in. When they saw he'd been crying, Mrs. Stein said, "Carlyss, I'm sorry, but you better leave. I don't want Jason getting too upset."

"Did he tell you who did this to him?" Mr. Stein demanded.

"No," Carlyss said and saw the relief in Jason's eyes.

Mr. Stein clearly didn't believe him. "When I find out which one of these backwards rednecks did this, I'll make him wish he'd never left the TLC-Mart."

"Thank you for coming, Carlyss," Mrs. Stein said. "Jason will be in touch when he's feeling up to a longer visit."

She was numb as she rode the elevator down to the lobby, where her grandfather sat flipping through a fashion magazine. Her anger simmered just below her consciousness, waiting to flare into life. But all she felt at the moment was sympathy for that sweet boy who deserved so much better from life.

"How is he?" her grandfather asked.

"He's pretty bad," she said absently.

On the ride home, she fought to control the rage. It would come out at the right time; this was not it.

25

Troy was still on the couch when he heard his mother come in from the garage. "Troy?"

"In here," he said, his voice ragged. He cleared his throat and said again, "In the living room."

Her hair was wet and neatly combed, the way it looked when she was fresh from a shower. "Troy, I need to tell you something. Have you got a minute?"

"Sure," he said. He sat up and scooted to one end to make room, and she sat beside him. She took his hand and looked at him seriously.

"Troy, I've met somebody. A man. I really like him."

Troy blinked. His own problems had so consumed him that he hadn't even thought about what his mother might be doing. "Really? That good-looking guy from the eye doctor's office at the TLC-Mart?"

"What? No. That was four years ago. How do you even remember that? And just because I say someone's handsome doesn't mean I want to go out with them. No, this was...unexpected."

"So, who is he?"

"His name's Deke. And he's waiting on the porch. I'd like you to meet him."

"So, it's that serious?"

"I don't know, son," she said honestly. "There's a lot of obstacles in the way. But I do like him a lot."

Troy couldn't help but grin. "I assume he's good-looking?"

"He's *very* good-looking. But he's also kind, and thoughtful, and intelligent."

"Well, then, you should let him in off the porch, shouldn't you?"

Haven opened the door, and Elder entered. As always, he seemed to fill the space with both his size and his presence. His snakeskin jacket shimmered as he took it off and hung it on a hook by the door. He shook Troy's hand firmly. "Pleased to meet you, Troy."

"Likewise, sir," Troy said.

"Why don't we all sit down and have some iced tea?" Haven said.

Just then Elder's phone buzzed. "Excuse me," he said as he took it from his pocket and looked at the screen. "I really need to take this. If you'll pardon me?" He stepped back out onto the porch.

"He's a big guy," Troy observed.

"But what about him as a person?"

"Mom, I've talked to him for, like, a minute and a half. That's not much time to form an opinion. How did you meet him?"

"Through work," she said without missing a beat. It wasn't a lie, and the details could always be filled in later.

"So, he's a counselor too?"

"More or less." Before she had to do more verbal tapdancing, Elder returned. His expression was serious. To Haven, he said, "That was Carlyss. She's on her way over."

"Over *here*?" Haven said. "Deke, I'm her therapist, I can't have her just showing up—"

"I need you to hear what she has to say, so you can ask her all the questions I know you're going to want to. We could meet somewhere else and do it, but this seems like the long way around.

"Wait, Carlyss Bolerjack?" Troy said.

"You know her?" Elder asked.

"Yeah. I mean, I see her around and stuff."

"Good. You might make her feel more at home."

Troy turned pale. "Mom, can I talk to you in private for a moment?"

"Of course. And then, Deke, I'd like to speak with *you* in private." Haven led her son to the kitchen, leaving Elder in the living room.

"Mom, I don't want Carlyss Bolerjack coming over here," Troy said.

"Neither do I, son, but my reasons are professional. What are yours?"

"She gives me the creeps. The *serious* creeps."

"Why?"

Troy thought about how to phrase it. "She knows things she shouldn't know. Things I don't see how she *can* know."

"Like what?" When Troy didn't answer, she said, "Does this have anything to do with what you wouldn't tell me before? About that boy who got attacked?"

"No!"

"I haven't forgotten about that, Troy. I'm giving you time to decide to do the right thing. If you don't, I will."

The implied threat Troy heard in those words made him angry. "Yeah, well, at least I'm not bringing strange guys home. When did you start seeing this guy, Mom?"

"Just this week."

"And you think it's already okay to bring him to our house?"

"Sometimes, you just know about people."

"Like you knew about Dad?"

She finally realized how upset he was. "Actually, I did know about your Dad. I just thought what women have always thought: that if I loved him enough, he'd change. I stuck with it for as long as I could." She fought to keep her own temper under control. "But that has nothing to do with this. We have two separate issues here: your reaction to Deke and your problem with Carlyss. Since she's on her way, I think we should concentrate on that. What do you mean, she 'knows things?'"

"Nothing," he said, unable to meet her eyes. "I'll be in my room." Before she could respond, he ran out of the kitchen and up the stairs.

She returned to the living room. Deke immediately stood, the kind of deeply ingrained manners she somehow expected from him. "Is Troy all right?"

"He's got a lot on his mind," she said. "Now: what do you mean, inviting one of my clients to my home without asking me? That's arrogant and presumptuous, and I won't stand for it."

"And I wouldn't do it if it wasn't an emergency. But she told me she knew who was behind the crucified mice. And it was the same person I told you I was certain was possessed. Linda Scote."

"So, the two of you are ganging up on this poor girl?"

She expected anger, but instead, he smiled. "That's exactly why I want you to talk to Carlyss. I need you to believe in this stuff, Haven. Or at least in the possibility of it. I want *you* to question her. Ask her anything. I'll even leave the room if you want. But I want you to convince yourself that she and I have not colluded on anything."

"Deke—"

He stepped close. There was something so gentle, so boyish in his face that she almost gasped. She'd never imagined he could look at her that way. He said, "You know why this is important. You almost said it back at the motel. This may not be the time to say it, either, but we both feel it. And if it's going to go any farther, then you have to believe I'm not crazy. Because the only other option is to believe that I *am*."

She looked into his eyes. She saw no guile there, none of the secrecy of her ex-husband. If he *was* lying, he was the best she'd ever seen.

"All right. I'll talk to her. But I promise I'm not going to come away believing in demons and Satan and possession. I'm just not."

He kissed her quickly, gently on the lips. "Whatever happens, your willingness to try is all I can ask. Thank you."

———

"WHY ARE WE HERE?" Danny Blazer asked as he pulled into the parking spot.

"Yeah," Sam repeated from the back seat. "Why?"

"I need something," Linda said, and opened the passenger door. The TLC-Mart shimmered in the heat rising from the parking lot's asphalt.

"What?" Danny said, annoyed.

"Tampons," she said. "You two just wait here and keep the air conditioner running."

As she walked away down the row of parked cars, Sam asked, "Dude, what's all over her? She looks like she's been swarmed by fleas or something."

"I dunno," Danny muttered. In truth, there was now a layer of disgust beneath his feelings of arousal, and he was beginning to hate himself for finding her so damn hot. But he was temperamentally and emotionally incapable of looking at himself with any honesty, so he just tried to ignore it.

He turned up the radio. Kid Rock blasted from the speakers, as always making Danny feel even cockier and more indestructible.

"You heard from Troy yet?" Sam asked over the music.

"No. He better not talk to anyone about what happened."

"You think he will?"

"If he does, I'll shove something even bigger up *his* ass."

Sam nodded. He'd had nightmares ever since that day, and only his utter weakness of character kept him from hiding as well. A vengeful Danny Blazer was the scariest thing he could imagine. "Yeah," he agreed.

"Tampons," Danny mumbled and shook his head. "Guess I won't be getting any tonight."

———

THE TLC-MART'S cool air immediately dried the sweat on Linda's skin. She dodged an elderly couple picking their way slowly toward the pharmacy and headed to the long, open aisle between the grocery section and the rest of the store. What she saw, thanks to Jesse Garon, made her almost laugh with delight.

Near the ceiling, thirty feet above, drifted the image of a knight on a horse with reptilian dragon legs. The knight's face was that of a lion, with burning red eyes. *Allocer,* Jesse Garon told her.

Perched atop the freezer that held rows of pizza was a man with the face of a great cat and the feathered wings of some enormous bird. *Sitri.*

Scurrying along the floor between the produce bins was a wolf-like creature with the scaled and plated tail of an alligator. *Nahum.*

The creatures were everywhere, and Linda couldn't keep up with the names Jesse Garon used to introduce them. The human shoppers wandered, oblivious to them; occasionally, one would leap onto a person, perch for a moment, then fall away, unable to break through. But they never quit trying, and with each effort, they tore loose a tiny bit of the human's soul, just enough to make sure they were inexplicably drawn back to the place.

And then over the loudspeaker came the maddening jingle:

You always find Tender Loving Care
  And the best prices anywhere
  at TLC-Mart!

Every diaphanous creature threw back its head, or heads, and howled along with this as if it signaled for them a battle cry of triumph. Linda couldn't hear them, but she didn't need to.

I will find homes for all my brethren, Jesse Garon told her. *We will spread into the world and remake it to suit ourselves, just as I've remade you.*

"Yes," she agreed. At this point, she could do nothing else.

Attention, he called, and the plethora of demons all stopped moving and turned to face her. Their scrutiny made Linda feel filthy and worthless, but the voice in her head ignored her. *Prepare for the great exodus,* it announced. *Soon, very soon, you will all be free.*

Once again, Linda couldn't hear the replies, but the mouths opened as if the demons cheered along.

IT TOOK Carlyss an hour to walk from her grandparents to the address Deke gave her. The sky grew overcast, and she couldn't remember if her grandfather said it was supposed to rain. He followed the weather the way some of his friends did the state lottery.

The strangest part of the walk was the silence. Without Merihem's constant monologuing, the trip seemed to take forever. The air was filled with summer noises: lawn mowers, bass-thumping music, traffic, and even the occasional distant train rumble, but none of these were interesting or commanded her attention. Without that omnipresent voice to ignore, her brain went off on tangents, and twice, she had to back up and take a turn she missed.

Two carloads of young men, one black and one white, catcalled at her. She just stared at them, wondering if they did that to every girl walking alone. Then she realized that there were no other girls walking alone; there was no one walking, period. Despite the clouds, it was nearly a hundred degrees, and she was drenched with sweat.

The address was in one of the few remaining nice neighborhoods in town, and as she approached, she wondered if she was being set up for something, perhaps another surprise deliverance. But when the door opened, and her therapist smiled uncomfortably at her, she found herself speechless.

"Hello, Carlyss," Haven said. "I guess Deke didn't tell you this was my house."

"No," she managed. "He just gave me the address. Is he here?"

"He is. And if you want to leave, you're free to go. I'm not totally in favor of this, either."

She didn't know what "this" Haven referred to, but Carlyss wasn't going to leave without seeing Elder, who Haven called "Deke." Did they *know* each other? "No, I'll stay."

"Come in, then. You look exhausted. Would you like some iced tea?"

"Yes, ma'am."

Inside, Carlyss tried not to stare. Despite her year-long association with Haven, Carlyss had never really thought about how the woman lived away from the office. The house was nice and reasonably neat,

ALEX BLEDSOE

but there were piles of things and dust in the corners. She spotted a strand of cobwebs stretched between two bulbs on the chandelier. Her grandmother worked diligently every day despite her illness keeping their house clean; evidently, Haven did not have the time, the inclination, or the money to hire someone to do it for her.

This took Carlyss by surprise, and she suddenly realized the woman was, in fact, a human being. It was like that time she saw her first-grade teacher at the TLC-Mart and realized Mrs. Jones, too, needed to buy stuff.

Elder came out of the kitchen. "Hello, Carlyss. Thanks for coming. Let's sit down."

They took three of the four chairs at the kitchen table. Carlyss gratefully drained the first glass of tea, and Haven fetched her another. "What are we doing here?" Carlyss asked.

"We have to find Linda Scote," Elder said. "We have to pray deliverance over her to drive out the demon inside her."

"She doesn't want it to be cast out," Carlyss said.

"That may be. But I need to hear her say it."

"Deke," Haven said carefully, "listen to yourself. You don't even know this girl. You have no authority over her."

Carlyss looked from Elder to Haven and back. "Okay, maybe I'm being dense, but...how do you two know each other?"

The discreet silence that followed, complete with glances between the two, told her all she needed to know. She almost giggled aloud. "Well. Didn't see *this* coming."

"It's not really germane to the problem," Elder said.

"We don't even know what the problem *is,* Deke," Haven said.

"She doesn't believe it's possible," Carlyss said to Elder. "Even after what she saw in her office. This is why I could never talk to you, Ms. Fields. If I'd said, 'a demon keeps talking to me,' you would have had me committed."

"No, but I would've given you a different treatment."

"Where can I find her, Carlyss?" Elder asked.

"I don't know. She's one of the popular kids, so she and I don't exactly move in the same circles."

242

"Can you find out?"

"I can try."

"And what will you do?" Haven demanded. "Kidnap her and take her off somewhere? Deke, not only is this not legal, it's not sensible. You haven't even remotely convinced me."

An impossibly loud crack of thunder rattled the whole house. Immediately afterward, rain and hail peppered the windows like repeated rounds of buckshot.

"That was sudden," Haven observed. "Hope the power doesn't—"

The lights flickered and went dark.

"Go out," she finished.

Above the noise of the storm, something heavy creaked in the room directly above them. Elder asked, "Who's up there?"

"That's Troy's room," Haven said.

Elder stood, just as a heavy brass apple flew across the room, through the spot his head occupied a moment before, and smashed into the wall, punching a hole in the plaster before dropping to the carpeted floor.

Continuing to stare at the ceiling, Elder asked, "Haven, do you have a Bible?"

Haven, staring at the hole, said blankly, "What?"

"A Bible."

"Deke, that apple almost hit you!"

"Yeah."

"What *was* that?"

"A warning shot. A Bible, Haven. Do you have one?"

"I—no, I don't think so."

He nodded. "I'll have to do this the hard way." He headed up the carpeted stairs. Haven rushed to follow, looking back at the hole in the wall and the apple on the floor beneath it. Carlyss was directly behind her.

On the second floor, a cacophony of noise came from behind Troy's closed door. In addition to the storm's roar, there were animalistic growls, shrieks of either extreme pain or insanity, and the scratching of what sounded like enormous claws. Elder stopped and listened, but Haven tried to push past him.

He grabbed her and said, "Wait, Haven."

"That's my son," she snapped and wrenched free.

When she threw open the door, all the noise except the storm ceased. Troy sat on the edge of his bed and looked up startled as his mother entered. "Mom," he said in surprise.

Haven looked around. In the near darkness, nothing seemed out of place. "Are you all right?"

"I'm fine. Why?"

"What was all that noise?"

"What noise?"

Haven stared at him, speechless. She looked back at Elder. "What *was* that?" she repeated.

"What was what?" Troy asked.

Elder stepped into the room as if he expected a booby trap from every side. "Troy," he asked calmly, "what were you thinking about before we came in?"

"I don't know," Troy mumbled.

"Were you thinking about how much you hate someone and how much you'd like to hurt them?"

Troy said nothing.

"That's what it's waiting for," Elder said knowingly.

"What who's waiting for?" Haven demanded.

Elder took out his phone and turned on the flashlight app. He prowled the room, looking at everything on the shelf. There were souvenirs of past family trips, toys he'd outgrown but never discarded, and a few shelves of books, most of them standard teen fare. No paperback *Necronomicon* or *Satanic Bible*, no Ouija board or tarot cards. No Bible either, he noted sadly.

A flash of lightning lit up the room, and Haven jumped; she thought she saw a shape kneeling on the bed behind Troy, looking over his shoulder. She got a sense of something unkempt and leering, and it made her gasp.

"Troy!" she cried. "Come here now!"

She used her no-nonsense mom voice, and the boy instantly obeyed.

"What did you see?" Elder asked.

Haven stood between Troy and the bed. "I don't know. Probably a shadow. On the bed behind him."

Elder shone his phone light on the empty bed, then turned it off. "I'm talking to you, unclean spirit," he said loudly. Thunder crashed again, and items fell from shelves. "There's no place for you here. Show yourself, in the name of Jesus."

Lightning flashed, thunder boomed, and in the gloom that followed, a shadowy shape seemed to sit on the same spot Troy had occupied. They could see no details, but its presence was undeniable.

Haven whispered, "Turn on your flashlight."

"No," Elder said. "It gets no spotlight, no acknowledgment. Whatever it is, I order it to leave now."

Past the wind and rain, a low animalistic growl came from the shape. Haven backed up, pushing Carlyss and Troy out the door into the hall. She closed the door, leaving her and Elder alone with the *thing*.

"Deke," she said, amazed her voice didn't crack with terror, "is that... ?"

"That," Elder said, "is the manifestation of a demon."

"Why is it here?"

"I'm not sure. I don't know if it followed Carlyss, or me, or just found an opening in your son's troubles."

Haven took a step toward the bed. As frightened as she was, she was still Troy's mother and would not stand for anything or anyone hurting him. "Listen, you son of a bitch—"

"Don't engage with it!" Elder ordered. "And don't get any closer."

She wished she could see it more clearly. As it was, the lack of definition only added to her terror, and the noise of the storm made it difficult for her to think. Elder, though, showed no such hesitation. He pointed at the shape and said, "In the name of Jesus and by the power of his blood, I banish you from this place and these people. Tell me your name, demon!"

The shape shifted on the bed and growled something.

"In human words! Who are you?"

"Leonard," it rumbled as if speaking was difficult. "Master Leonard."

"Leonard?" Haven said in disbelief. "His name is *Leonard?"*

"Quiet," Elder ordered. "Master Leonard, there's no home for you here. No opening for you. Return whence you came, in Jesus's name."

"I want no one here," Leonard said. "I bring a message. Dandelion is afoot. He is summoning others. Soon we will all have dwellings."

"Who is 'Dandelion'?" Elder demanded.

"You will see," Leonard said. "You will know."

Another flash of lightning illuminated the room, and Haven got a momentary glimpse of the bulbous, deformed thing seated on her son's bed, with three long, goat-like horns. Then when the light faded, so did the shape. The room was empty.

She jumped as the electricity came back on.

Elder ran a hand through his hair. He looked over at her but didn't have to ask the question out loud.

She nodded. Now she believed.

Elder opened the door, where Carlyss and Troy waited. Troy asked, "Mom, are you all right?"

"I'm fine," Haven said numbly. "I'd just like to sit down for a while if that's okay." Without waiting for a response, she went downstairs.

Carlyss turned to Elder. "Did you get rid of it?"

"Yes, I'm pretty sure. I don't think it was here to find an indwelling. It was just a messenger."

"From who?"

"Dandelion."

"Reverend Elder, who is Dandelion?"

"I wish I knew."

They followed Troy downstairs. Haven got a beer and sat at the table, staring blankly at the wooden surface. The storm was already ending, and although the wind continued, the sun peeked out through the clouds.

"Was that storm from... ?" Troy asked, not daring to finish the sentence."

"Maybe," Elder said. "Or they might've just used it to their advantage. They're very theatrical."

"And they're real," Haven said without looking up.

"Yes," Elder said. He put a hand on her shoulder, and she covered it with her own.

Haven looked at Carlyss, who stood by the window. "I'm so sorry. I had no idea. It goes against everything I've been taught. Everything I believed."

"It's okay," Carlyss said quietly. "You didn't know."

"What do we do now?" Troy asked.

"'We' don't do anything," Haven said sharply. "I'm going to call my parents in Nashville and send you to stay with them."

"Haven," Elder said gently. "That won't help. If they want him, they'll find him."

Her eyes welled with tears. "Then tell me what to do to protect him."

"We need," Elder said, "to stop them. To find this Linda Scote and drive out the demon inside her. And to figure out what Dandelion is and what it wants."

"How do we do that?"

He turned to Troy and Carlyss. "Tell me, you two: does Linda Scote have a boyfriend?"

"Yes," Carlyss said. "His name is Danny Blazer. He's the one who hurt Jason."

"Who's Jason?"

"Jason Stein. A friend of mine."

"How did he hurt him?"

"He raped him with a plunger handle."

Haven felt the blood drain from her face. She looked up at her son. "Is that true?"

Troy again seemed about to cry. He nodded.

"Danny Blazer is a friend of Troy's," Haven said. "Do you think a demon's behind that too?"

"It's possible," Elder said. "It's much more likely he's just an entitled jerk. Or that his girlfriend, who we know is possessed, put him up to it. That's one of the points of possession, to make those around the possessed person do and feel horrible things."

"You're right," Troy said. "Danny's always been an asshole. The only thing Linda did was sic him on Jason. Told him Jason had been texting her pictures of his dic—I mean, his private parts." He blushed and looked away from his mother.

"Jason would never do that," Carlyss said.

"Troy, do you know how to reach Danny?" Elder asked.

"He keeps calling me and threatening me. He's worried that I'm going to tell someone what he did."

Haven took Troy's hand. She felt so angry and helpless.

"Call him back," Elder said. "Tell him you want to talk to him. Tell him to come here. Tell him you *are* going to the police."

Troy looked terrified. "What? Why would I do that? You can't scare him off. You don't live here. As soon as you're gone, he'll come after me. And maybe do worse than what he did to Jason."

Elder leaned close and put one big hand on Troy's shoulder. "Troy, I understand why you feel that way. But son, I promise you: when I scare somebody, they *stay* scared."

"Can't he just call the police?" Haven said with an edge of desperation in her voice.

"We need to get to Linda Scote," Elder said. "If the police get involved, we never will."

Haven watched Troy absorb at least enough of Elder's certainty to make him slowly take out his phone, then stand up and go into the kitchen. She looked from her son to Elder and said, "Deke, seriously, this is my son. If you're playing games—"

"This is no game. This is life or death of someone's eternal soul."

She looked away. "Please be right, Deke. That's all I ask."

Troy came back in. "Boy, he's mad. He didn't say he was coming here, but he was in his car, so I imagine he will."

"Good. And if we're lucky, he'll have the Scote girl with him." Elder stood and again put a hand on Troy's shoulder. "That wasn't easy, son. I appreciate you doing it."

"I'm not your son," Troy mumbled, but he didn't pull away.

———

TROY LEANED on Danny Blazer's car at the curb outside his house. Sam was in the back seat, smoking a joint and watching him. But Danny, seated behind the wheel, held his attention.

"I'm serious, Troy. You fucking tell anyone what happened, and I'll shove a goddam flagpole up your ass. And then another one up your mama's pussy for good measure." He smiled with a bully's certainty. "You just forget that fat boy even exists, you hear me?"

"Or what?" Troy mumbled, trying to follow Elder's instructions. He didn't sound defiant, though; he sounded like a scared little boy. He was *so* scared; all he wanted to do was cry some more in the darkness of his room.

"Just because that bitch mama of yours works for the state, and she knows all the cops and state police and everything, don't mean they can protect you, shithead. If they come after me, I'm coming after you."

"Me, too," Sam said from the back seat.

"Yeah, whatever," Troy said, hoping his voice didn't shake. "But how you gonna stop Jason? It's not like he didn't see us."

"Ain't your problem. That fat-ass ain't gonna tell nobody nothing about what we did. He knows he'll get fucked up worse if he does." He looked at the person in the passenger seat. "Am I right?"

"What fat boy?" a new voice said.

Both Danny and Troy snapped their heads around. Elder stood on the sidewalk, arms crossed. His snakeskin jacket was still inside, and his formidable muscles filled his shirt. Wind from the still-hovering storm tousled his hair.

"Who the fuck is this?" Danny said.

"Somebody who knows you did something to a fat kid," Elder said.

Danny looked back at the others in the car, then opened the door. Troy barely stepped out of the way. The sky had grown darker, and the wind whipped Danny's hair back from his face. He puffed out his chest, ready to intimidate. "I don't know who you are, old man, but you're—"

Elder slapped him so hard he spun in place and fell to his knees. He jumped back up, his face red with rage.

Elder punched him right in the center of his chest. Again, he fell down, this time with the wind knocked out of him.

Elder grabbed him by the hair and lifted him to his feet. "You ain't got enough ass in your britches to go around threatening people," he told the boy, who gasped and wheezed as he tried to catch his breath. "Especially friends of mine. I know what you did to that boy, and you *will* pay for it."

"Yeah, well, your boyfriend was right there with us," Danny croaked.

"That's his problem. I'm *your* problem. You better start praying that nothing so much as a bee sting happens to Troy or his mom because if it does, I'm coming after you."

"My dad'll sue you for everything you've got!"

Elder released him, and Danny immediately took a wild swing at Elder's face. Elder leaned back and easily dodged it. Then Danny drew a pocketknife and snapped it open.

Elder smiled. The way the boy held the weapon told him he had no idea how to use it in a fight. Distant thunder rumbled as Elder locked eyes with Danny and spread his hands in a "make-your-move" gesture.

Instead, Danny backed to the car. "You keep looking over your shoulder, old man," he said as he got back inside, "because one day I'll be there." His voice shook, and his trembling fingers couldn't close the knife blade.

Elder crouched to look inside the car. In the passenger seat sat Linda Scote. Hatred radiated from her, stronger than anything Danny could ever express. A trickle of yellowish fluid ran from an infected bite just under her hairline.

"Name it," Elder said to her.

Danny looked from Elder to Linda in confusion. "How the fuck do you two—"

"Name the one inside you. Or is it too cowardly?"

"You know where to find me," Linda growled. Then to Danny, she said, "Get me the fuck out of here, you useless faggot."

Danny threw the car into gear and screeched away from the curb. Elder stood and watched them drive away, knowing where they—or at least Linda—was going. The place where the entity inside her would have the most power. "We need your mom's car," he said to Troy. "There's not room for all of us in mine."

But now Troy was crying, his face contorted, his shoulders slumped. Elder put an arm around him. "I told you I'd scare him off. Did you see how frightened he was?"

"But h-he'll always be here. Even if he goes to jail, he'll g-get out eventually."

Elder smiled coldly. That was warrior thinking: as long as your enemy remained alive, he could strike back. "We'll talk about settling up with him for good later. Right now, we have to get going."

Inside, Haven immediately hugged Troy and said to Elder, "Will they leave Troy alone now?"

"Troy can tell you about it on the way to the TLC-Mart."

"Why are we going to the TLC-Mart?"

Distant thunder again boomed. The storm was returning and seemed even more ominous. Elder said, "Have you ever seen a town after one of those moves in? It dies. Just like Somerton is dying. That's because every TLC-Mart is home to a thousand demons."

"The TLC-Mart is possessed?" Haven said, unable to keep the sarcasm from her voice. She stroked her son's hair; he hadn't clung to her like this since he'd been a toddler.

Elder did not smile. "This is how evil works in the world: by giving you what you want at the lowest price."

"You'll always find tender loving care," Carlyss said without irony.

"Exactly," Elder said.

Haven kissed Troy on the cheek, then took Elder's snakeskin

ALEX BLEDSOE

jacket down from the hook. She held it out for him. He looked at her questioningly.

There was no mockery in her voice. "If he's going into battle," she said, "a knight needs his armor."

Elder slipped on the coat.

252

26

The skies grew darker as Haven drove the four of them toward the TLC-Mart. She was numb from the overall onslaught against her view of how the universe worked. There were two options: either Elder and Carlyss were both certifiable, or else there were insubstantial spirits in the world working their malevolence behind the scenes. And she'd seen one for herself. Hadn't she?

If they *were* crazy, what did it say about her that she was in love with an insane itinerant preacher who believed he could smell evil spirits?

She glanced at Troy, in the back seat beside Elder. My God, what kind of world was she raising him in? How could she ever protect him from this? She couldn't even ensure his safety from the bullies who drove up to her very own house.

"How do you know she'll be there?" Haven finally asked.

"Because it's where she's most powerful," Elder said. "Just like, if it was up to me, we'd face her in a church."

"Do you plan to perform an exorcism in the middle of the store? With everyone watching?"

"Deliverance, not exorcism. And yes, I plan to drive that spirit out of her if I can. I can't worry about what other people think."

"She doesn't want it driven out," Carlyss said.

"I know. That's why it's going to be so hard."

"Then why do it?" Troy asked. It was the first time he'd spoken since they left the house. "She's a selfish, stuck-up bitch. Why do you care?"

"Because if I don't, no one will," Elder said simply. "And evil wins."

When they reached the enormous parking lot, the wind was incredibly strong, and just starting to drive new droplets of rain ahead of it. They parked and walked quickly to the nearest entrance.

Anthony waited there for them. The phone call from Elder had puzzled but not surprised him. And its urgency was hard to ignore. "I haven't seen anyone that matches the description you gave me," he said at once. "But it's hard to watch all the entrances by myself."

"It's okay," Elder said. "Everyone got a cell phone? Then split up and look for them. When you see them, don't draw attention to yourself, just call me. Let's go."

The five people split up, each going off in a different direction. Before they separated, Troy and Haven exchanged a long look. Neither knew what to say to the other about what they were getting into. A huge crack of thunder rattled the building, and lights flickered for a moment.

Troy said, "I love you, Mom."

"I love you, too, son. Be safe."

"You too."

CARLYSS WENT STRAIGHT FOR THE LADIES' room in the back. She opened the door just as another thundercrack struck.

A middle-aged Hispanic woman primped at a mirror. When she saw Carlyss, she finished quickly and left. Carlyss crouched to see if any feet were visible in the stalls. There were none, but she didn't feel alone.

"Linda?" she said quietly. "If you're in here, come on out. Let me help you. I know that *you* know what's happening to you and that deep down, you don't want it. No one does."

The lights flickered. She began pushing open the stall doors, growing more tense with each one.

When she reached the end, she'd found nothing. Or at least nothing else human.

Then she realized what she sensed. "Merihem," she whispered. "So, this is where you ended up. Waiting for your next host in the most degrading place imaginable, huh?"

There was no reply.

She looked around. Nothing moved; nothing changed. But the atmosphere became heavier, the air thicker. A breeze with no source moved around her.

She fought the urge to taunt him with his expulsion. And, stranger, she fought the pang of sympathy that welled up in her. That sudden sense of emptiness she felt after Elder banished Merihem for good seemed to ache now, its edges quivering with the desire to hear that voice, feel that presence. All she had to do ...

"No," she said simply. Then she turned and walked out. Just as the door shut, she thought she heard a faint, wailing cry of such despair that it seemed nothing could utter it and live. But she knew better.

TROY EDGED into the shoe department. Truthfully, he'd chosen it because it seemed like the least likely place to find Linda, Danny, or Sam. He found one of the little benches with a mirror that showed your feet and sat down with his back against a shelf. He was no hero; he just wanted all this to be over. He was still scared to death of Danny, of what they'd done to Jason, and of what might happen if the police found out. He didn't believe anyone, including Elder or his mom, could protect him.

And he was numb from everything he'd witnessed and horrified by what he'd participated in. The assault on Jason had been just the start:

now he wondered if his mother was crazy for dating a man who believed in demons and if the man himself might be dangerous. His mother was the only thing in the world that centered him; if he lost her, he'd lose himself.

He thought briefly of his father, who he hadn't seen in a year. He e-mailed on Troy's birthday, a couple of lines wishing him well that sounded like he'd cut and pasted them from a greeting card site. He was a tightly wound man who drank too much and was always on the verge of some big "deal." He would've been no protection, either.

He drew his knees up to his chin and made himself as small as he could on the bench.

You're right, a voice said in his head. *That man Elder is crazy. And he'll turn your mom crazy if he isn't stopped.*

Troy fought the tears that burned his eyes.

HAVEN TURNED a corner in the pharmacy and came face to face with Danny Blazer and his sidekick Sam.

"Oh, shit, It's Troy's mom," Sam said. "I'm outta here, dude, you're on your own." He ran off without another word.

Haven kept her eyes on Danny. He'd been in Troy's classes since kindergarten, and she'd watched him grow up. Even as a little boy, she'd sensed he was not a good person, the way you can with some people. But she trusted Troy to know good friends from bad and real-ized that she couldn't monitor all his friends every day. Now she regretted that *laissez-faire* attitude.

"Danny," she said in her best clinical tone. "I have things to say to you."

"Why are you talking to me?" he said, his voice almost in a panic. One cheek still glowed red from Elder's slap.

Haven wanted to ask him where the girl Elder sought was, but a cold knot of rage churned in her stomach as she thought of what he'd done to that other boy and what he'd forced her own son to endure. "You son of a bitch," she said tightly. "You deserve to go to jail for the rest of your miserable life, you know that? There's no excuse for you. Somebody asked me if I knew what evil was, well, now I know what it looks like."

"Fuck you, whore," Danny said, trying to sound tough but failing. The pharmacist behind the counter looked up sharply.

Haven's fists clenched, and the words spilled out. "You think because your dad has money, you can get away with this, don't you? Well, guess what: I'll make sure anybody who ever does an internet search on your name knows what you did. Doesn't matter what the cops or the courts say. Every time someone looks for Danny Blazer, they'll read about what you did."

"My dad'll sue you," he said weakly, pulling out the ace that he always used in confrontations with adults. He had backed away from her and was now flat against the allergy medicine shelves.

"No, he won't, because that'll just draw more attention. No, there's nothing you or your daddy can do, Danny Blazer. You've found the one person you can't bully or intimidate. And if you so much as blink at my son again, I'll find you, and I'll kill you. And your daddy can't stop that, either."

Haven had never even considered saying such words before, but as they left her mouth, she knew they were true. It was no idle threat. Even though she'd never physically harmed anyone in her life, even when they were physically harming *her*, she knew she could kill this smug bastard as easily as snuffing out a candle.

The knowledge should've felt awful. But instead, she experienced a rush of euphoria, of power.

She said, "Now tell me where that Scote girl is."

"I don't know, she ran off. She told me to wait here."

"Then you do just that, Danny. Do as you're told. That's all you're good for." She gave him another hard look, then strode away down the aisle. A few shoppers had overheard enough of their conversation that they stepped aside and then regarded Danny with guarded, frightened eyes.

ANTHONY TURNED a corner in sporting goods and saw Elder ahead of him. "Any luck?"

"No," Elder said. "I wonder if it was a setup, and they're not here at all."

Thunder banged again, rattling the metal rafters overhead. Lightning must have struck nearby. Then came the rushing patter of torrential rain. "Probably don't want to go out in this."

"No," Elder agreed. "We'll keep looking."

"What's your plan here, Deke? Do you really intend to pray deliverance over her right here in the store? In *this* store, of all places?"

"First, I'm going to try to talk to her. I hope I can convince her to come to your church."

"Deke, from what you've said, she's not like Carlyss. She's a popular white girl. She'd never be caught dead at my church. In fact, if she did come to my church, *I* might get caught dead, if you know what I mean."

"I'll be there."

"That's nice to hear, but it won't stop those people who burn crosses instead of praying to them."

"If you want to go—"

"No, that's not what I meant, you know that. Get back to work."

"Thanks, Anthony."

Anthony watched Elder go, then looked around and tried to decide which way to go next. There were dozens of people shopping near him, but none were teenage girls.

He picked up a pellet pistol that had been left out of the box. As a boy, he'd inherited one of these from his older brother. It had been useless for anything except knocking bottles off a fence post; it lacked even the power to shatter the glass. But it had made him feel incredibly masculine and powerful.

He was so lost in his reverie that it didn't even register that the voice screaming, "That boy's got a gun!" referred to him.

The first bullet struck him low in the back. The second ripped through his lungs. The third and fourth missed him completely because he was already falling.

The sound of the shots blended with the pounding rain on the building's roof. Anthony managed to stay on his hands and knees long enough to look at the man who'd shot him.

It was a pot-bellied, short-haired white man with a mustache and goatee, his face splotchy with fear. He still held the gun in trembling hands. Was he an off-duty cop or just one of the many people who felt the need to go armed into the world?

"It's just a pellet gun," Anthony managed to say, but his voice was weak, and the rain grew, if possible, even louder.

Just before he died, Anthony saw the teenage girl they sought standing right behind the shooter. Linda Scote had been the one who screamed. She smiled at him, malicious and satisfied.

Other people crowded into the aisle. They began to applaud the shooter. Anthony couldn't keep his eyes open.

Then his late wife appeared in a bright shaft of light, took his hand, and as always, he followed where she led.

ELDER STOPPED in the toy section and listened. Had that been gunshots? Inside the building? He looked around, but none of the other shoppers seemed to have heard it. The pounding rain was so loud, though, it might drown out the sound of Gabriel's horn.

He hated being in one of these stores. Not only did they all look the same, they all *felt* the same: cold, sterile, like a morgue. Everywhere you looked, there were piles of merchandise made cheaply overseas and sold at such low prices that American manufacturers could never keep up.

He headed down the aisle past the Barbies, then turned and doubled back through the baby department, up against one of the building's walls.

And then Linda Scote stepped out from the diaper aisle.

Every sign was there: the glassy eyes, the tight and shiny skin, and the malicious smile. She also had running sores visible on her neck and along her arms, infected and connected by red welts. Only the demon's presence made her seem attractive to the boys she manipulated.

"So, you're Dandelion," Elder said.

"What? I'm just a kid. My name's Linda." But even though her voice was girlish and vulnerable, she sported a wolf's vicious smile.

"You are. Deep down, that's your true self. I can help you, Linda. But you have to want it."

"Are you coming on to me, old man?"

There was no one else in the whole department, and Elder momentarily wondered why. But he couldn't waste his attention on that. He took a step closer, and it felt like the very air tried to push him back. The packages of diapers on the shelf beside him vibrated.

"I wouldn't touch you to scratch you, Dandelion. But you know that. And I know your name can't really be 'Dandelion,' so tell me who you are. I order you in Christ's name."

She laughed as if this was the stupidest thing she'd ever heard. "You're wasting your time. This whore welcomes me. There's nothing inside her that regrets anything I've done. Including killing your Black preacher friend."

Elder choked down any reaction. If it was a bluff, no harm done. And if it was true, there was nothing to be done for Anthony now.

And then the girl's face changed. The smile fell away, the glassiness dissolved, and the real Linda looked out at him. Softly, confused, barely audible over the storm, she said, "No. That's not true. I don't want this."

Then the smile returned. "Psych," the Dandelion voice said.

But Elder recognized the moment. Deep down, Linda did *not* want the demon's presence. That was the toehold Elder needed.

He pulled out the cross on its chain around his neck. "That's enough, Dandelion. Tell me your real name."

She laughed. It was the coldest sound he'd ever heard. A long rolling peal of thunder seemed to echo and amplify it.

He stepped closer. "By the power of Jesus, I demand you tell me your name."

"I'm a flower with puffy white seeds," she said mockingly. "Blow me and make a wish."

"By the shed blood of Jesus Christ, *tell me your true name!*"

Linda's face wrenched as the demon fought the command. She grabbed at the boxes of Pull-Ups beside her, shaking her head and making animal noises. The air grew heavy with ozone, and another thundercrack rattled the building. Again, the lights flickered, and for a full thirty seconds they only came up halfway, before surging to full brightness. In that momentary dimness, Elder saw the countenance of something inhuman and primeval where the pretty girl's face should have been.

Then Linda looked at him and spat, *"Dantalian!"*

"Dantalian," Elder repeated. He knew the name from the Lesser Key of Solomon: a duke of hell, capable of knowing all secrets and teaching all arts. And close enough to the other word that someone uneducated in their ways might hear it as "dandelion."

A little shiver of fear went through him at the thought of facing such a powerful demon here, in the TLC-Mart. *Talk about home-field advantage,* he thought bitterly.

Dantalian grinned even wider, stretching the girl's face to its physical limit. "I see ye know me, man of the pitiful God."

"It's the God that commanded you to speak," Elder said. "And you complied."

With no warning, she screamed at him, her voice blending with the sound of thunder and rain as if she summoned the storm with her rage.

Elder was now close enough to see that sweat speckled her face like condensation on a wax candle. He said, "In the name of Jesus, Dantalian. In the name of Jesus Christ, our savior. Linda, I know you're still in there, and I know you want this evil gone. Say, 'in the name of Jesus.' *Say it!*"

Linda's face twitched and squirmed. "I-in the name of...of..."

"Say it!"

"Jesus!"

Linda howled and fell to the cement floor, dragging packs of diapers off the shelves on top of her. The storm was now loud on the metal roof, making the rafters overhead tremble as if in fear. Birds trapped in the building flitted from crossbeam to crossbeam, looking for a safe place to land and hide. Elder rushed forward, the tiny cross held out before him.

"Get away from me!" Linda screamed and threw diaper boxes at him. *"Get away from me!"*

Elder bent over her and touched the cross to her forehead. She froze and cried out in agony. The cross left no mark, but she thrashed as if it burned her to the bone.

"Go back to where you came from, Dantalian!" Elder roared, the full force of his power behind the words. "In the name of God the Father and Jesus the Son and the Holy Ghost, I *send you back!*"

"I'm not going back!" Linda cried. "No! *No!*"

"Yes, you are, Dantalian! Feel the sword of the spirit as it goes right through you, demon! I'm not the one condemning you, it's the Lord himself who does it!"

Foam collected at the corners of Linda's mouth, and her eyes rolled back. Elder pressed the cross harder into her flesh, inwardly praying, *Use me, Lord, as your instrument to save this girl from the evil inhabiting her. Not my will, but thine be done.* "Do as I tell you, Dantalian! Do as you're told!"

Arms encircled him then and pulled him back off Linda. He was totally blindsided as he was thrown to the floor. He looked up at Travis Scote, wide-eyed and bouncing in place, fists balled for a fight.

"What the fuck are you doing?" Travis demanded. "That's my niece!"

Linda wiped her mouth and scurried to hide behind Travis. "He was trying to rape me, Uncle Travis," she said. "He thought he could get away with it in the storm."

Elder got to his feet. This young man was made of soft pipe cleaner muscles, and would be no problem to overpower. Shutting him up, though, would be a bigger problem. "Travis," he said calmly, "you think you're helping, but you're not."

"Don't listen to him, Uncle Travis!" Linda said. The rain, if possible, grew even louder, and the atmosphere shuddered with the charge of the storm. Even inside the building, the air pressure suddenly dropped. "Kill him, or he'll come after me again!"

Travis was uncertain what to do. Then Linda said, so quietly that only he could hear over the storm, "Kill him, and I'll do anal with you, Travis. This very night."

Travis frantically dug in his pocket for his knife.

Elder stepped forward before he got it free and grabbed Travis by the front of his t-shirt.

He felt something on his hand. He looked down to see a tiny spider, about as big as a penny, clinging to the pad of his thumb. More emerged from behind Travis, crawling over his shoulder and onto his head.

The one on his thumb sank its mandibles into his skin. The pain was like acid.

"Ow!" he cried and released Travis's shirt. Travis stumbled to one side, and then Elder saw Linda behind him, mouth open, spiders crawling out over her lips and spreading across her face. The roof high above began to vibrate, and somewhere metal screeched.

Travis realized he was covered with spiders as well and began to swipe at the ones in his hair. *"Fuck!"* he shrieked.

Elder recognized them: brown recluses. They were small, but their caustic venom caused slow-healing, rotting wounds. He'd had a cousin who lost half a foot to one of them.

Then Linda blew a cloud of them into Elder's face.

He slapped at them, but there were too many. Where they landed, they bit down hard. He gasped in pain and fear, his brain filled with the certain knowledge that each bite would leave a gaping, festering crater, turning him from a handsome man into a deformed freak. The demon Dantalion had discovered his one great, hidden sin: *vanity.*

He tore at his face, swiped at his hair, slammed into the shelf behind him, and screamed, "Get them off, *get them off me!"*

Dantalion laughed with the triumphant voice of a teenage girl.

And then the roof was torn from the TLC-Mart as a tornado passed overhead and snatched Elder and the spiders up into the sky. In a moment, he was gone from sight.

27

W hen the tornado struck, at first no one really understood what was happening. Carlyss screamed as debris rained down around her and rain began to pelt the *inside* of the store. Her ears popped as the air pressure bottomed out.

The shoppers around her panicked, knocking each other aside as they ran for the entrances, trampling anyone who fell, even children. Carlyss huddled against an endcap of seasonal nail polish, trying to stay out of the way, ears covered against the roar.

The wind tore everything loose that wasn't attached, and the air quickly filled with merchandise dancing as if to its own tune. The electricity struggled to stay on, then went out with a loud pop. Only a few of the emergency lights came on. Carlyss looked up and, instead of the roof, saw the yellowish-green tornado cloud slowly spiraling overhead.

And then, walking past her as calmly as if she was on a summer stroll, came Linda Scote. She held hands with her uncle as if they were a couple. The water, wind, and debris seemed to deliberately avoid them. And Linda *smiled,* the smug smirk of those who know they'll never pay for anything they've done.

Carlyss looked around for Elder, but he was nowhere. More and more people tried to rush past Linda and the man, but like everything else, they were knocked aside by some invisible force.

Carlyss gave no thought to her next act.

With a roar of righteous fury, she threw herself at Linda, knocking her free of her escort and carrying them both to the floor. They crashed into a greeting card display.

Carlyss landed on top and had her hands around Linda's throat before she even realized it. "Come on, Dandelion!" she taunted. "Show me how tough you are! You don't look so scary to me! You're just another fucking loser hiding in some stupid girl!"

Travis stared at the two girls, and his head cleared as if he'd been asleep and just woken up. Where were the spiders that had covered him? He looked around and saw the destruction, then was shoved aside by a fat man with a crewcut. Rain suddenly struck his face, and Travis realized he was in the middle of a disaster. He looked up and saw the sickly sky through the immense hole in the ceiling.

He shrieked and, like everyone else, ran for the exit.

Linda turned red as she tried to breathe and fought to throw Carlyss aside. But Carlyss wasn't about to be dislodged so easily. "Is that all you got? You *are* a damn dandelion, aren't you? You're not scary, you're just a damn weed, growing up in the cracks!"

Both were soaked by the storm that poured through the open roof. If anyone noticed the fighting girls, they were too busy with their own escapes to intervene.

Linda's face changed. Nothing actually moved, but the personality behind it was now completely different, completely demonic. Carlyss had never seen such rage.

Carlyss's field of vision swam, and the floor beneath Linda seemed to open up, revealing a vista of rocky crags and sharp metallic devices, all of them rusted and worn with time and use. A naked human being was attached to each device by his or her most sensitive areas, and they screamed and writhed in torment. And around them, operating the devices or simply dancing in delight, were...things. Carlyss knew them for what they were.

And the tormentors were singing.

You always find Tender Loving Care
  And the best prices anywhere
  at TLC-Mart!

The odor of urine, feces, and decay washed over her, and Carlyss fought the urge to vomit right in Linda's face. It didn't frighten her, though. If anything, it made her own rage rise to match the demon's.

"You will come back to us," Linda said, her voice clear and strong despite Carlyss's fingers around her neck.

"Yeah, you think? Show me then. Come on, you think you're so tough! Come on and take me! Merihem said you were such a badass." She drew one hand from Linda's throat and punched her in the face. "God protects me! Jesus protects me! You can't do a thing to me, Dandelion! You hear me! Not a thing!"

But Dantalion, through Linda's voice, only laughed.

HAVEN PUSHED THROUGH THE CROWD, fighting to get further into the store as everyone else fled. She had to make sure Troy was safe; her parental programming overrode everything else. Something had gashed her thigh when the tornado first hit, and she felt hot blood soaking her leg, warmer than the rain.

She suddenly saw Carlyss astride Linda, the black-haired girl punching her rival with all the ferocity she could manage. Linda writhed as she tried to escape, and suddenly her face was fully visible to Haven. And she saw it: the same pure demonic evil that she'd glimpsed earlier in Carlyss's own face.

She couldn't move. She forgot to breathe. She could only stare at the visage of Dantalian, peering out through the face of a teenage girl.

Travis saw light ahead through one of the entrances. The glass in the automatic doors had been broken, either by the storm or by people desperate to escape.

"Travis!" a voice called. "Travis, help me!"

He looked around. His parole officer, Carla Norman, lay beneath a heavy display that had once held televisions. They, too, were smashed on the floor around her. She bled from her mouth and reached one hand out to him.

"Travis, please, it's me, Carla." Rain and blood pooled around her.

Travis just stared at her, then slowly smiled. He gave her a middle finger, then ran for the entrance.

"You bastard!" Carla screamed. "You bastard!"

Danny's friend Sam knelt beside her. "Hang on," he said, lifting one of the TVs. "I'll get you out."

Carlyss's fingers were bloody, the knuckles split from pounding Linda's smug face. The rage felt so good coursing through her, all the fury she'd choked down coming out at last.

Then her eye fell on one of the greeting cards scattered around them. It showed the same picture of Jesus that was in the church basement and her grandparents' house. Across the bottom was printed the legend, "What Would Jesus Do?"

Carlyss suddenly stopped. She uncurled the fist she was about to drive into Linda's battered face. "No," she said. "No, no, no."

Linda growled but didn't move.

Carlyss wiped the rain from her face. She had never felt so certain about anything in her life. "Dandelion, you're not who I'm talking to anymore. This is for Linda."

She bent close and put her hands on either side of Linda's rippling, contorted face. Everything was clear to Carlyss now: why she had been possessed, why she had been saved, and what her life meant. Grove Prosser had not hesitated to give his life for her, to free her soul from damnation, and now, he reaped the reward of that selflessness as she suddenly understood. She could do no less.

She said calmly, "Linda, I know you never believed it, but you are loved. By God. By Jesus. You haven't been able to feel it before, but now you have no defenses left. Dandelion has torn them down, and he thinks all you can feel is his hate. But it's not. God's love is everywhere, and it's all for you. I don't hate you, Linda. I love you, too, because God does." And then she kissed Linda on the forehead, right where Elder had so recently pressed the burning cross.

At the moment they touched, a torn electrical cable dropped from the edge of the wrecked ceiling. The ragged end landed in the puddle of water that surrounded them and there was a loud pop, followed by the smell of ozone.

Linda's eyes opened in horror, and she screamed. But it was a human scream, not a demon's.

Carlyss, without a word or a sound, fell limp and rolled off.

This broke Haven out of her momentary shock. She ran over, kicked the cable away, and knelt beside Carlyss. She felt for a pulse, knowing from the way the girl fell that she wouldn't find any.

Then Linda sat up. She was confused and lost and looked at Haven the way a terrified little girl might. She began to cry, and Haven reflexively took her in her arms.

As she held onto the living girl, she saw that the dead one bore a soft, beatific smile.

She comforted Linda as the rain poured in, and the sky turned from green to normal gray as the tornado dissipated. Firemen crawled across the rubble toward her. She let them take Linda, then she got to her feet and yelled, "Troy! Troy!" until the firemen gently pulled her toward the entrance, one of them remarking on the vicious gash in her leg and saying, "Didn't I pull you out of another building just, like, two days ago?"

28

eacon Elder's body was never found. Troy had taken shelter beneath a fallen shoe display and was unhurt. Haven lost a lot of blood and spent three days in the hospital, unconscious for most of it. Carla suffered a collapsed lung, but thanks to Sam's intervention, she survived.

The damage from the F4 tornado was, miraculously, limited to the TLC-Mart. It had only touched down for an instant before retreating back into the clouds. The company assured Somerton that the building would be rebuilt as soon as possible, although it also put all the store's employees on unpaid leave. The death toll stood at 75, and included Danny Blazer, who was decapitated by the sharp edge of a plastic Viagra display flung at him by the storm's fury.

Anthony Acred made the news once it was discovered he'd died of gunshots and not from the tornado, but no shooter was ever identified. His body was sent to Smyrna and buried beside his wife.

Carlyss Bolerjack was buried beside her parents. Linda Scote attended, as did Susie and, in a wheelchair, Bethany. Haven spoke at the funeral, but of course, she couldn't tell the small group of mourners what she knew for certain: that Carlyss had willingly sacrificed herself for someone who'd never been anything but cruel to her, simply because she believed it was the right thing to do. But Haven knew, and so did Linda.

Afterward, Haven saw the Scote girl standing alone at the grave, crying. The diggers waited patiently for her to finish so they could fill it in, but as Haven and Troy drove away, Linda was still there.

———

LINDA LOOKED DOWN at the fresh burial. A worm, dislodged when the grave had been filled in, wriggled in search of a way out of the sun. She knew what that worm felt like: ever since the evil spirit had left her, she'd felt conspicuous, as if the whole world knew what had happened in her soul. She, too, wanted only to hide. But she also knew that wasn't an option.

"Hey, honey, you all right?" one of the gravediggers asked. He was black, heavyset, and smoked. "Do we need to call somebody for you?"

"No, I'm fine, thank you," Linda said.

"A friend of yours, huh?" he said, indicating the grave.

"My best friend," Linda said. "And I never even knew it."

The gravedigger gave her an odd look and returned to his backhoe, driving it back down the little road that ran through the cemetery.

"Carlyss, wherever you are," Linda said, "I swear I will use the life you gave me to do something meaningful. I hope you found the peace you deserve and that you're watching me with your blessing."

Something blew across her field of vision. Her eyes followed the little white puffs, dancing and twirling on the gentle summer wind, as the dandelion seeds rose into the sky and vanished.

———

"So: do you understand what to do?" Brother Knode asked Travis Scote. The minister shut off the video of prior deliverances.

Travis nodded. His crash course in mimicking the effects of

possession and exorcism had been going on for three days, ever since he'd approached Brother Knode about help.

After what he'd seen, he now knew he was possessed, too, and hoped Brother Knode could cast out the demons inside him. He'd gone to the revival site, where the tent was being repaired after the storm had shredded it and begged for an audience. He told Brother Knode all about the worst things he'd done and requested that the minister pray deliverance over him until the demons departed.

But Brother Knode simply laughed and said, "Travis, you're in luck. Any other time, I'd be telling you that yes, you are possessed, and for a small offering, I can help you out. But you know what? Today I'm honest. You're not possessed."

Travis couldn't believe what he was hearing. "B-but my thoughts...the way I act..."

Brother Knode placed his hand on Travis's shoulder and leaned close. "Travis, that ain't a demon. That's just *you*. You're an asshole. You got nobody to blame for that but yourself."

The weight of that final statement settled on him like a leaden shroud.

And then Knode said, "But you know what? If you're looking for a job, I need somebody who can fake being possessed in front of a crowd. If you can do that and keep it a secret, there's a fair bit of money in it."

Travis had only, numbly, nodded.

A FEW DAYS after the funeral, Haven opened her door. A black uniformed policeman stood there, a paper bag in one hand. "Yes?"

"Are you Ms. Haven Fields?"

"I am."

"I'm Bernard Jones. I wonder if I might speak to you for a moment."

"What's this about?"

"It's not official. I was a friend of Reverend Anthony Acred. And he was a friend of Deacon Elder, who I understand was a friend of yours."

"All right. Come in, please."

He stepped into the foyer and no further. She closed the door. He said, "I'm sorry for the loss of your friend. I understand you were at the TLC-Mart as well."

"And my son. We were both incredibly lucky."

"Yes, you were. I'll get right to the point. That big revival tent that was set up near the store was blown clean down across the railroad tracks. When they found it and went through it, they found this tangled up in it." He held up the bag.

She took it, opened it, and pulled out Elder's snakeskin jacket. Something caught in her throat as it unrolled.

"We still haven't found any trace of him," Bernard said. "But I thought you might like to have this."

"Thank you, officer," she said numbly.

"I'll be going," he said, and turned to leave. He paused halfway through the door and said, "You're in my prayers, ma'am."

"Thank you," Haven said. As soon as the door shut, she carefully put the coat on a hanger and smoothed out as many wrinkles as she could. It wasn't a memento or a keepsake, she told herself. Until she knew for certain, it was simply something a friend misplaced, like the car still in her driveway, and she would keep it safe until he came back to claim it.

IN A MODERATE-SIZED ARKANSAS CITY, in a generic industrial park, inside a nondescript red brick building, six incredibly powerful people met in a room so secure it could survive a direct nuclear blast. The meeting had nothing to do with the ostensible purpose of the corporation they guided; this was an inner sanctum for a very special purpose.

The six people, four men and two women, were all immaculately dressed. The youngest was in his fifties, while the eldest, a woman who needed a motorized wheelchair to get around, had just passed the century mark. None had ever truly worked; they had all inherited their wealth and had devoted their lives to creating a world in which they could keep it with the least possible effort.

And they were all related. All members of the Beleth clan.

One of the men said formally, "Mr. Chairman, I have the report from the incident in Somerton."

"Please share," another man said, gesturing with a liver-spotted hand.

The first speaker glanced down at his tablet screen. "The formerly possessed girl, the one inhabited by Merihem, is dead. That has been verified. The girl possessed by Dantalion is alive but is of no further use to us. The other survivors involved have been evaluated and pose no threat. Eliminating them would simply draw more attention."

"Who sent the tornado?" an old man with disheveled hair said. He was ignored.

"And that itinerant deliverance minister?" the chairman asked.

The first speaker said, "I'm afraid he's still alive."

"I thought he was carried away by the tornado," the younger of the two women said.

"He was. And yet...he's still alive."

"How do you know?"

"We *know*," he said, and the certainty carried its own explanation. "We've found no trace of him. But we will."

"Who sent the tornado?" the disheveled man asked again, more forcefully. Again no one paid any attention.

"That man is a danger," the old woman in the wheelchair said. "A true danger to our purpose and our goals. He knows what we are and how we operate. He must be found and eliminated before he sways others to his cause."

"He will be," the chairman said. "And as for his cause, I think we've got a better solution. We'll simply make that cause look foolish."

He pushed a button, and a screen lit up on the wall. It showed three beautiful teen girls: one Black, one Latina, and one Asian. They each had beauty pageant smiles and held up large, ornate silver crosses as if fending off vampires. One clutched a red Bible. They were dressed as any girls their age might be, as if to reassure people that deep down, they were entirely normal.

"Who are they?" one of the men asked.

"The three adopted daughters of Fighting Rob Stovall."

"The exorcist?" the younger woman snickered. "The 'Nashville Naysayer'?"

"Yes."

The other five exchanged looks. Stovall was famous, or notorious, for claiming to have performed fifteen thousand exorcisms in his long career. He was, in fact, a total fraud. Yet no matter how often he was exposed, somehow he managed to continue fleecing the unwary.

"I don't see how this will help," one of them finally said.

"Simple," the chairman said. "These daughters of a fraud cannot help but be frauds as well, and they will eventually be exposed as such. Yet because they are beautiful, desirable young women, before that happens they will be embraced by the public. We have a marketing team already working out the product launch of their books, fashion, and cosmetic lines. And later, nude photos will be leaked. They will become the face of deliverance ministry and exorcism, and their exposure will destroy all of its credibility."

He smiled with smug satisfaction.

The disheveled man slapped the table and roared, *"Who sent the tornado?"*

"You know who sent it!" the chairman impatiently shouted back. "Our...opposition."

"These teenage whores will never work," the skeptical man said. "We can't make people buy into that. No one will take them seriously."

The chairman faced the naysayer. "Really? We have grown our fortune by exploiting the lowest common denominator among the rural populations. We have destroyed everything that could possibly compete with us in any significant way. I think if any organization is qualified to know what the great unwashed, unthinking, unfeeling public will accept, it's us."

"And how do our silent partners feel about it?"

The chairman smiled. He pushed another button, and the conference table lit up from within, revealing an enormous Ouija board layout embedded in the Lucite. He retrieved an overlarge planchette from its special compartment and placed it in the center of the table.

He said, "Why don't we ask them?"

THE END

BIBLIOGRAPHY

Many books helped in the writing of this novel, but these were particularly useful.

American Exorcism: Expelling Demons in the Land of Plenty, by Michael W. Cuneo (New York: Doubleday, 2001)

Beware the Night, by Ralph Sarchie and Lisa Collier Cool (New York: St. Martin's, 2001)

Deliver Us From Evil, by Don Basham (Washington Depot, CT: Chosen Books, 1972)

Hostage to the Devil: the Possession and Exorcism of Five Living Americans, by Malachi Martin (New York: Harper and Row, 1976)

Will Storr Vs. the Supernatural, by Will Storr (New York: William Morrow Paperbacks, 2006)

ACKNOWLEDGEMENTS

ABOUT THE AUTHOR

Alex Bledsoe was raised in West Tennessee an hour north of Graceland (home of Elvis) and twenty minutes from Nutbush (birth-place of Tina Turner). He's been a reporter, photographer, legal copy editor and door to door vacuum cleaner salesman. He now lives in a Wisconsin town famous for trolls and tries to teach his kids to act like they've been to town before.

ALSO BY ALEX BLEDSOE

The Tufa series:

The Hum and the Shiver

Wisp of a Thing

Long Black Curl

Chapel of Ease

Gather Her Round

The Fairies of Sadieville

The Eddie LaCrosse series:

The Sword-Edged Blonde

Burn Me Deadly

Dark Jenny

Wake of the Bloody Angel

He Drank, and Saw the Spider

Blood Groove

The Girls with Games of Blood

Sword Sisters (co-written with Tara Cardinal)

FRIENDS OF FALSTAFF

Thank You to All our Falstaff Books Patrons, who get extra digital content each month! To be featured here and see what other great rewards we offer, go to www.patreon.com/falstaffbooks.

PATRONS

Dino Hicks

John Hooks

John Kilgallon

Larissa Lichty

Travis & Casey Schilling

Staci-Leigh Santore

Sheryl R. Hayes

Scott Norris

Samuel Montgomery-Blinn

Junkle

www.ingramcontent.com/pod-product-compliance
Lightning Source LLC
Chambersburg PA
CBHW020401110726
47899CB00006B/1802